ARCHIE COMIC PUBLICATIONS, INC.

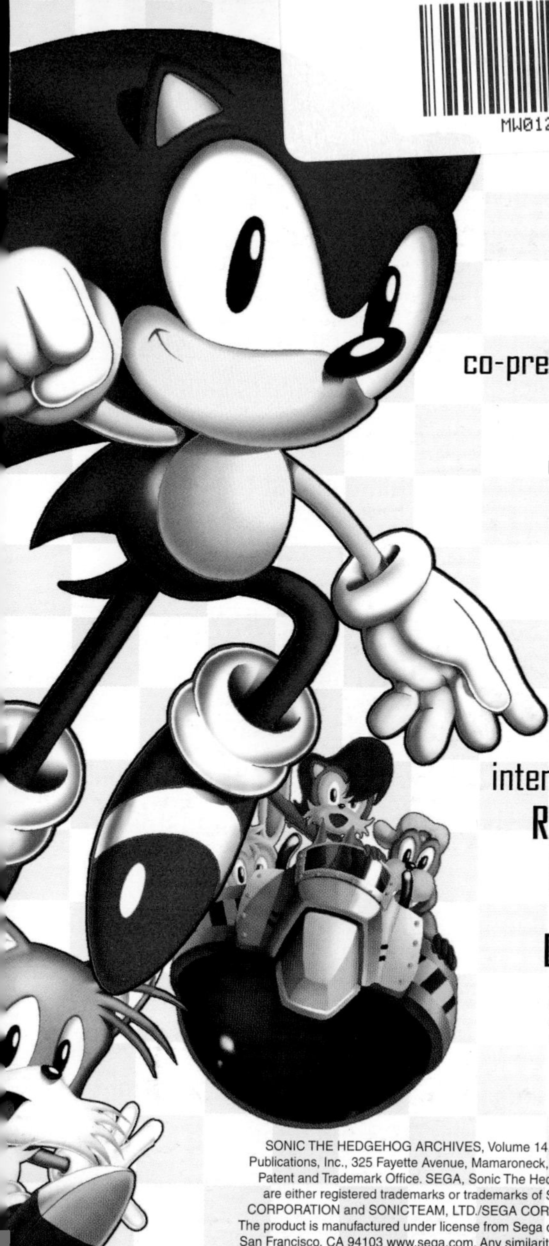

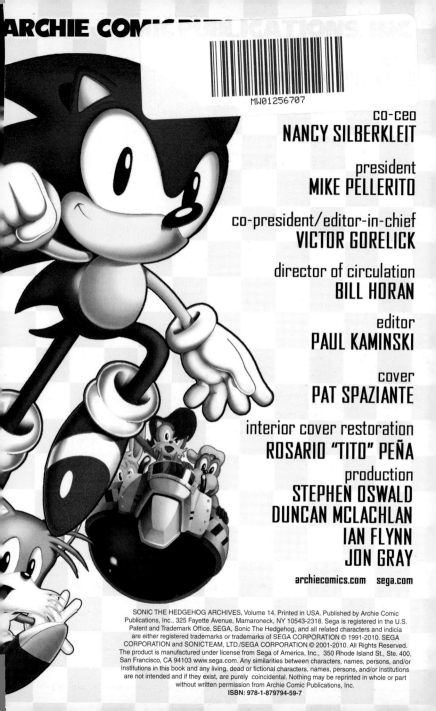

co-ceo
NANCY SILBERKLEIT

president
MIKE PELLERITO

co-president/editor-in-chief
VICTOR GORELICK

director of circulation
BILL HORAN

editor
PAUL KAMINSKI

cover
PAT SPAZIANTE

interior cover restoration
ROSARIO "TITO" PEÑA

production
STEPHEN OSWALD
DUNCAN MCLACHLAN
IAN FLYNN
JON GRAY

archiecomics.com   sega.com

SONIC THE HEDGEHOG ARCHIVES, Volume 14. Printed in USA. Published by Archie Comic Publications, Inc., 325 Fayette Avenue, Mamaroneck, NY 10543-2318.
ISBN: 978-1-879794-59-7

TABLE OF CONTENTS

Sonic the Hedgehog #53
"UNFINISHED BUSINESS"

Sonic & Knuckles find themselves face to face with their past, present & future! As Sonic makes peace with his long-lost parents, Knuckles swings by to introduce the gang to a very special new friend!

"SOUNDS OF SILENCE"

It's a VILLAIN INVASION! When a probe is sent in to learn the secrets of the mysterious ZONE OF SILENCE, our heroes discover a trio of the most evil villains to walk Mobius! Featuring the very first appearances of **IXIS NAUGUS** and **UMA ARACHNIS**!

Sonic the Hedgehog #54
"RUNNING TO STAND STILL"

What's Sonic rebelling against? Whadaya got?! As our hero struggles to find his place in a post-Robotnik world, everyone else better get out of his way! Meanwhile, trouble is brewing in the **DEVIL'S GULAG** prison when it is revealed that Robotnik's nephew, Snively, is up to his old villainous tricks! Will the restored Kingdom of Acorn be able to withstand ANOTHER villainous Robotnik?! Read on, if you dare!

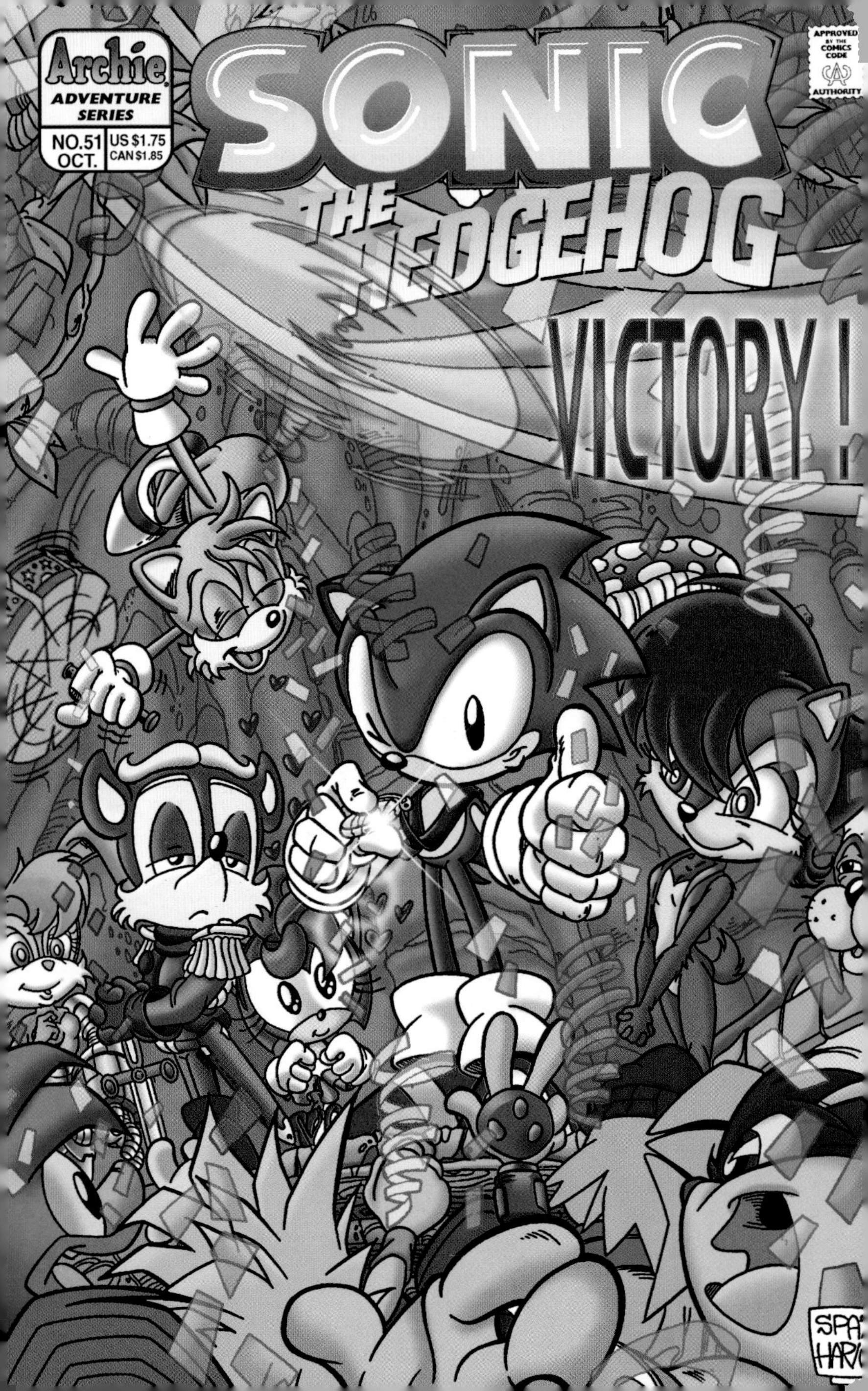
Archie
ADVENTURE SERIES
NO.51 OCT.
US $1.75
CAN $1.85
APPROVED BY THE COMICS CODE AUTHORITY
SONIC THE HEDGEHOG
VICTORY!

The planet Mobius was like a paradise... until the evil Doctor Robotnik and his mechanical legions conquered the land and its people, using his knowledge of technology and pollution. But many young, courageous citizens banded together as a brave group of "freedom fighters!" They struggle to overthrow the dictator and, one day, regain what was once theirs. Among them, the greatest of the freedom fighters is the fastest and way-coolest dude on two feet... SONIC The HEDGEHOG!

But now, with Robotnik's seeming demise, the freedom-fighting band of 'bot-kicking rebels who brought an end to his tyrannical reign of techno-terror can finally enjoy a long-awaited peace... or can they? Read closely, speed freaks 'cause only Sonic The Hedgehog can answer that question for you!

The celebration is already underway! Let's join the freedom fighters as they corner Sonic away from the other villagers...

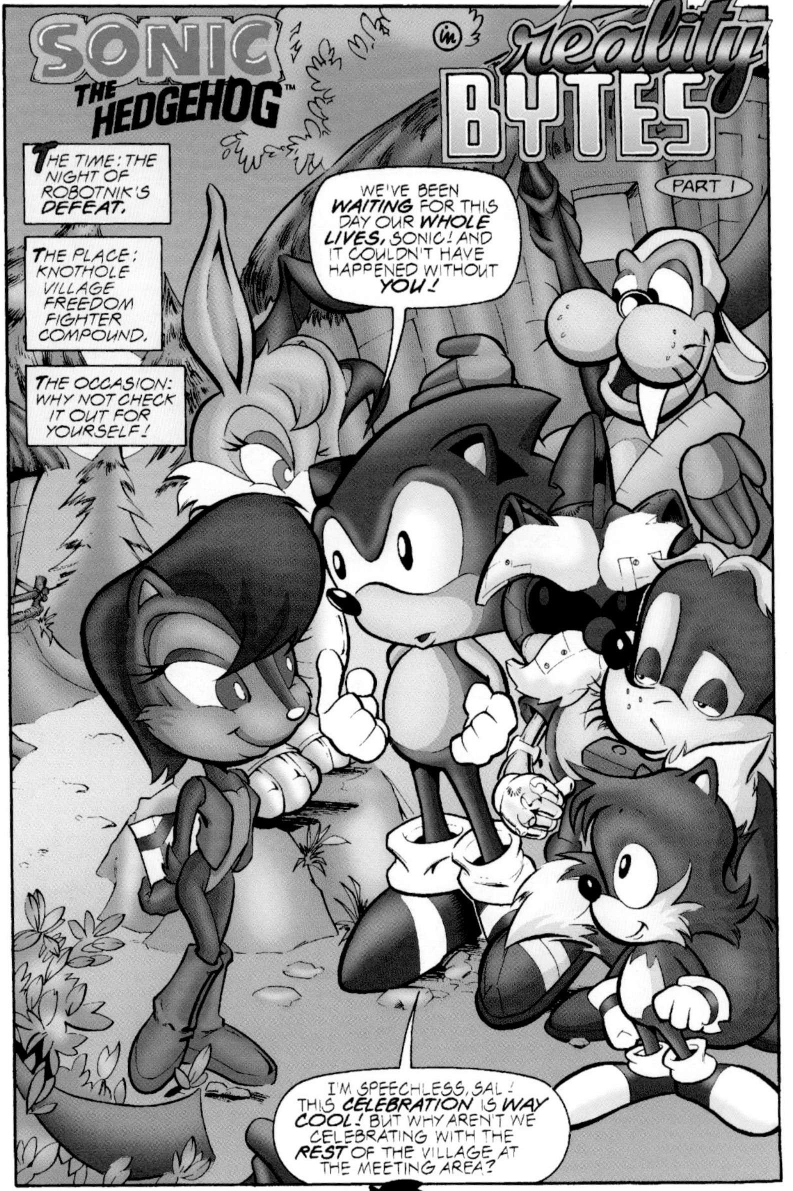
SONIC THE HEDGEHOG™
in
reality BYTES
PART 1
THE TIME: THE NIGHT OF ROBOTNIK'S DEFEAT.
THE PLACE: KNOTHOLE VILLAGE FREEDOM FIGHTER COMPOUND.
THE OCCASION: WHY NOT CHECK IT OUT FOR YOURSELF!
WE'VE BEEN WAITING FOR THIS DAY OUR WHOLE LIVES, SONIC! AND IT COULDN'T HAVE HAPPENED WITHOUT YOU!
I'M SPEECHLESS, SAL! THIS CELEBRATION IS WAY COOL! BUT WHY AREN'T WE CELEBRATING WITH THE REST OF THE VILLAGE AT THE MEETING AREA?

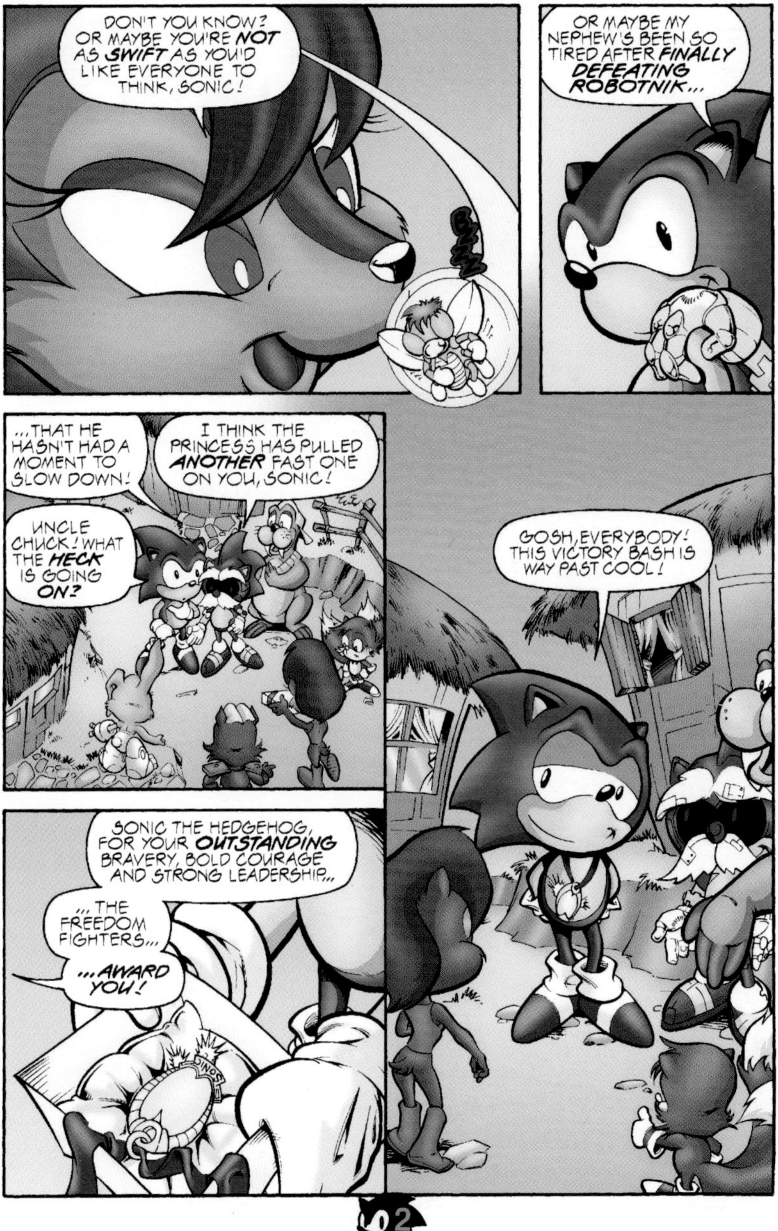
DON'T YOU KNOW? OR MAYBE YOU'RE NOT AS SWIFT AS YOU'D LIKE EVERYONE TO THINK, SONIC!
OR MAYBE MY NEPHEW'S BEEN SO TIRED AFTER FINALLY DEFEATING ROBOTNIK...
...THAT HE HASN'T HAD A MOMENT TO SLOW DOWN!
I THINK THE PRINCESS HAS PULLED ANOTHER FAST ONE ON YOU, SONIC!
UNCLE CHUCK! WHAT THE HECK IS GOING ON?
GOSH, EVERYBODY! THIS VICTORY BASH IS WAY PAST COOL!
SONIC THE HEDGEHOG, FOR YOUR OUTSTANDING BRAVERY, BOLD COURAGE AND STRONG LEADERSHIP...
...THE FREEDOM FIGHTERS...
...AWARD YOU!

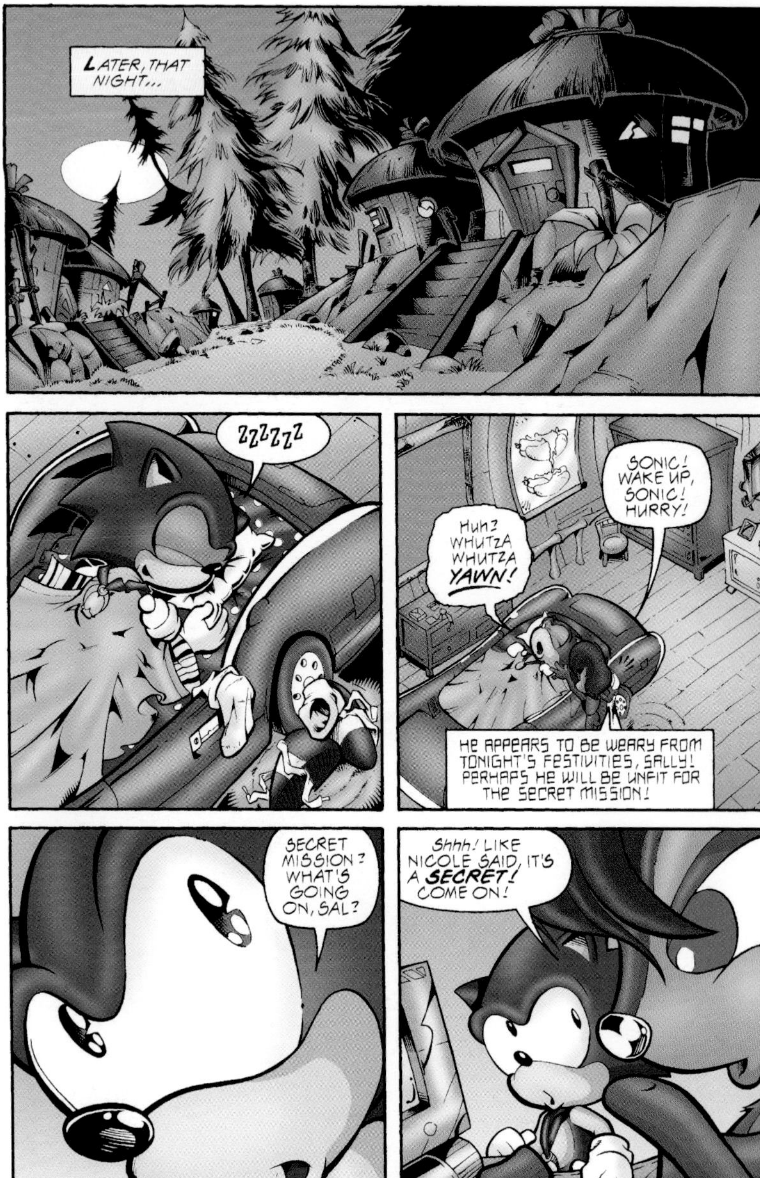
LATER, THAT NIGHT...
ZZZZZZ
Huh? WHUTZA WHUTZA YAWN!
SONIC! WAKE UP, SONIC! HURRY!
HE APPEARS TO BE WEARY FROM TONIGHT'S FESTIVITIES, SALLY! PERHAPS HE WILL BE UNFIT FOR THE SECRET MISSION!
SECRET MISSION? WHAT'S GOING ON, SAL?
Shhh! LIKE NICOLE SAID, IT'S A SECRET! COME ON!

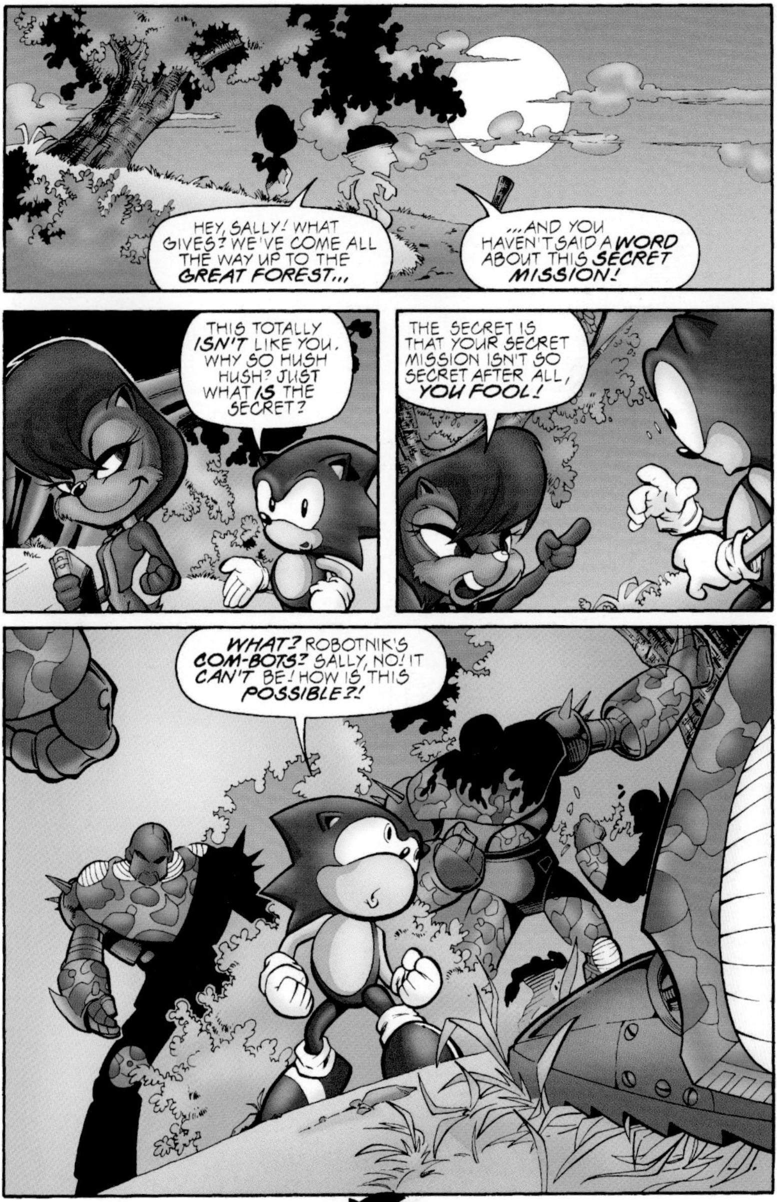
HEY, SALLY! WHAT GIVES? WE'VE COME ALL THE WAY UP TO THE GREAT FOREST...
...AND YOU HAVEN'T SAID A WORD ABOUT THIS SECRET MISSION!
THIS TOTALLY ISN'T LIKE YOU. WHY SO HUSH HUSH? JUST WHAT IS THE SECRET?
THE SECRET IS THAT YOUR SECRET MISSION ISN'T SO SECRET AFTER ALL, YOU FOOL!
WHAT? ROBOTNIK'S COM-BOTS? SALLY, NO! IT CAN'T BE! HOW IS THIS POSSIBLE?!

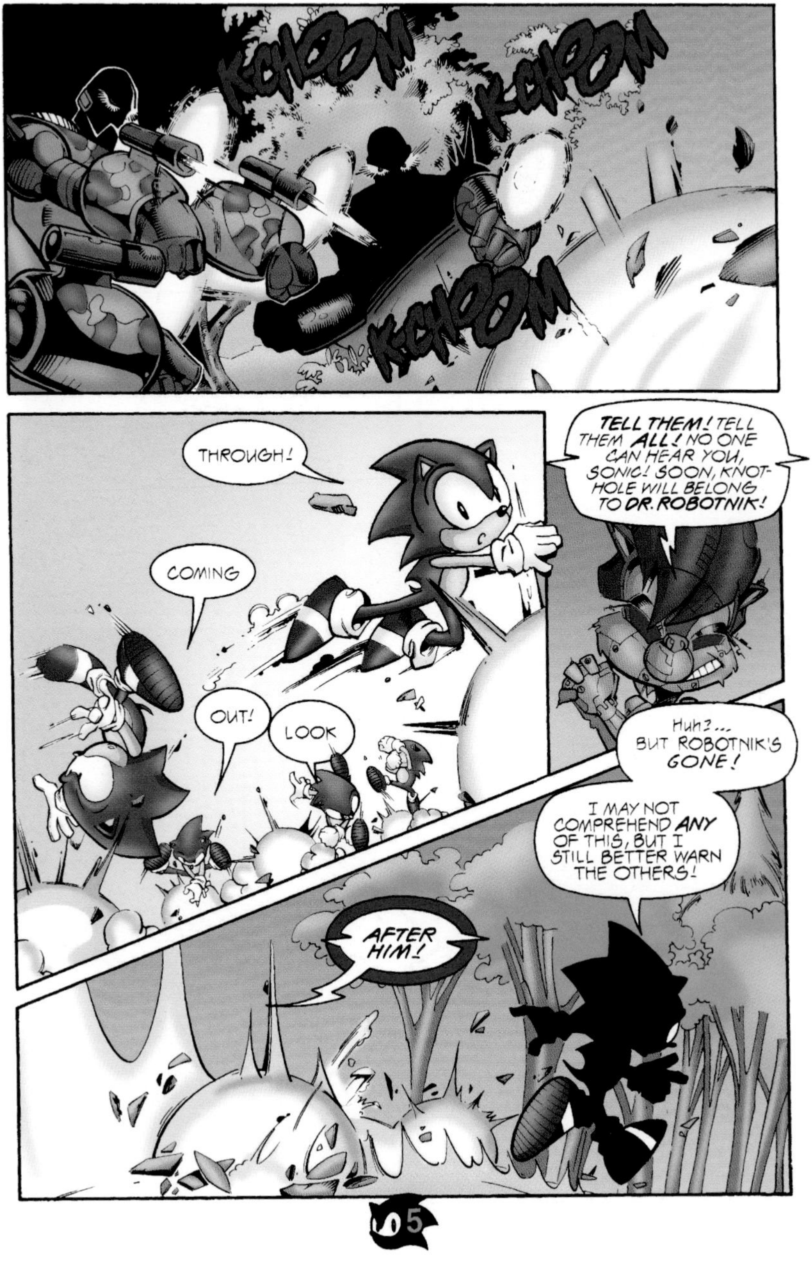
KCHOOM
KCHOOM
KCHOOM
THROUGH!
COMING
OUT!
LOOK
TELL THEM! TELL THEM **ALL!** NO ONE CAN HEAR YOU, SONIC! SOON, KNOTHOLE WILL BELONG TO **DR. ROBOTNIK!**
Huh?... BUT ROBOTNIK'S *GONE!*
I MAY NOT COMPREHEND **ANY** OF THIS, BUT I STILL BETTER WARN THE OTHERS!
AFTER HIM!

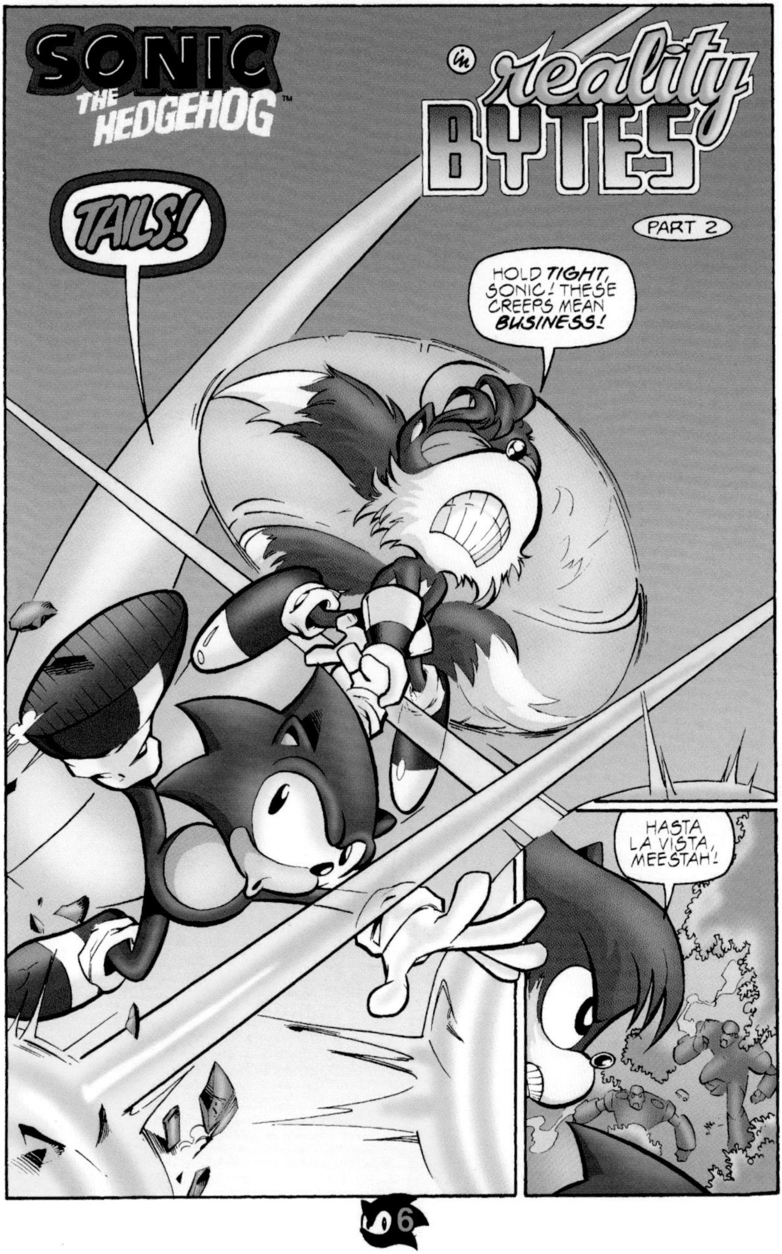
SONIC THE HEDGEHOG™
in reality BYTES
PART 2
TAILS!
HOLD TIGHT, SONIC! THESE CREEPS MEAN BUSINESS!
HASTA LA VISTA, MEESTAH!

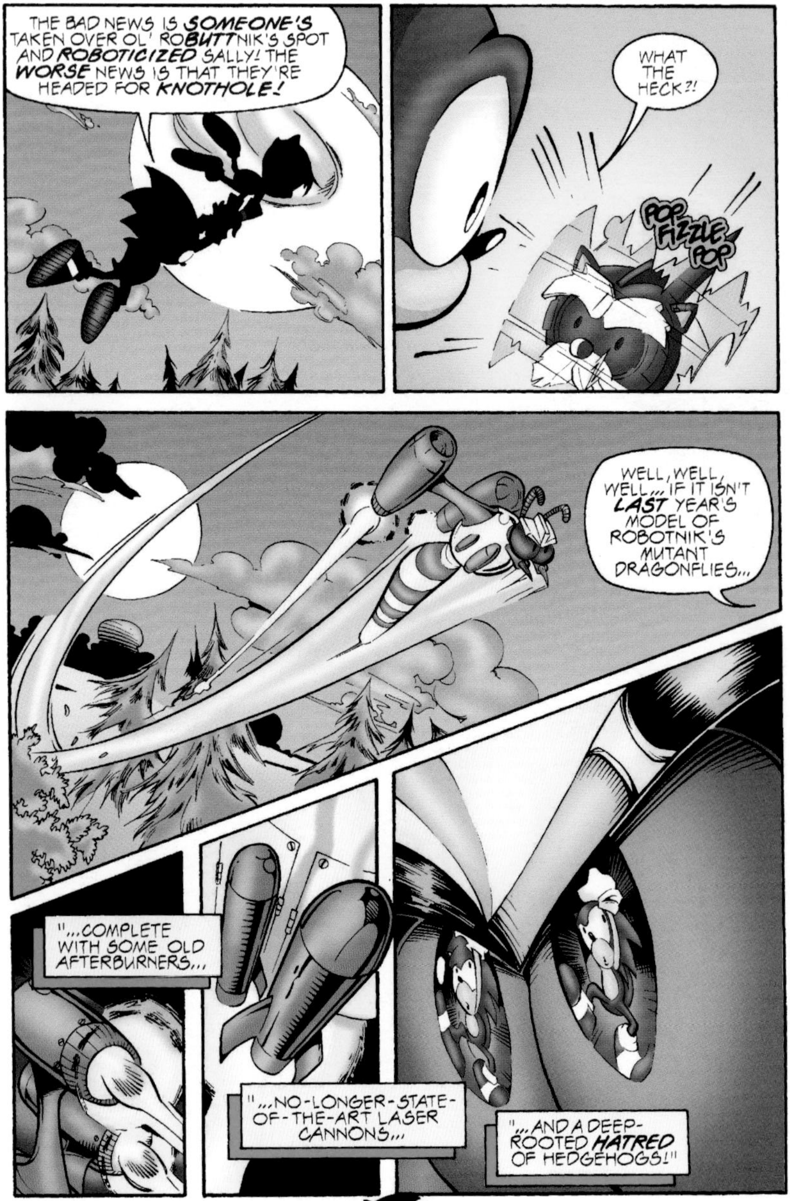
THE BAD NEWS IS SOMEONE'S TAKEN OVER OL' ROBUTTNIK'S SPOT AND ROBOTICIZED SALLY! THE WORSE NEWS IS THAT THEY'RE HEADED FOR KNOTHOLE!
WHAT THE HECK?!
POP FIZZLE POP
WELL, WELL, WELL... IF IT ISN'T LAST YEAR'S MODEL OF ROBOTNIK'S MUTANT DRAGONFLIES...
"...COMPLETE WITH SOME OLD AFTERBURNERS...
"...NO-LONGER-STATE-OF-THE-ART LASER CANNONS...
"...AND A DEEP-ROOTED HATRED OF HEDGEHOGS!"

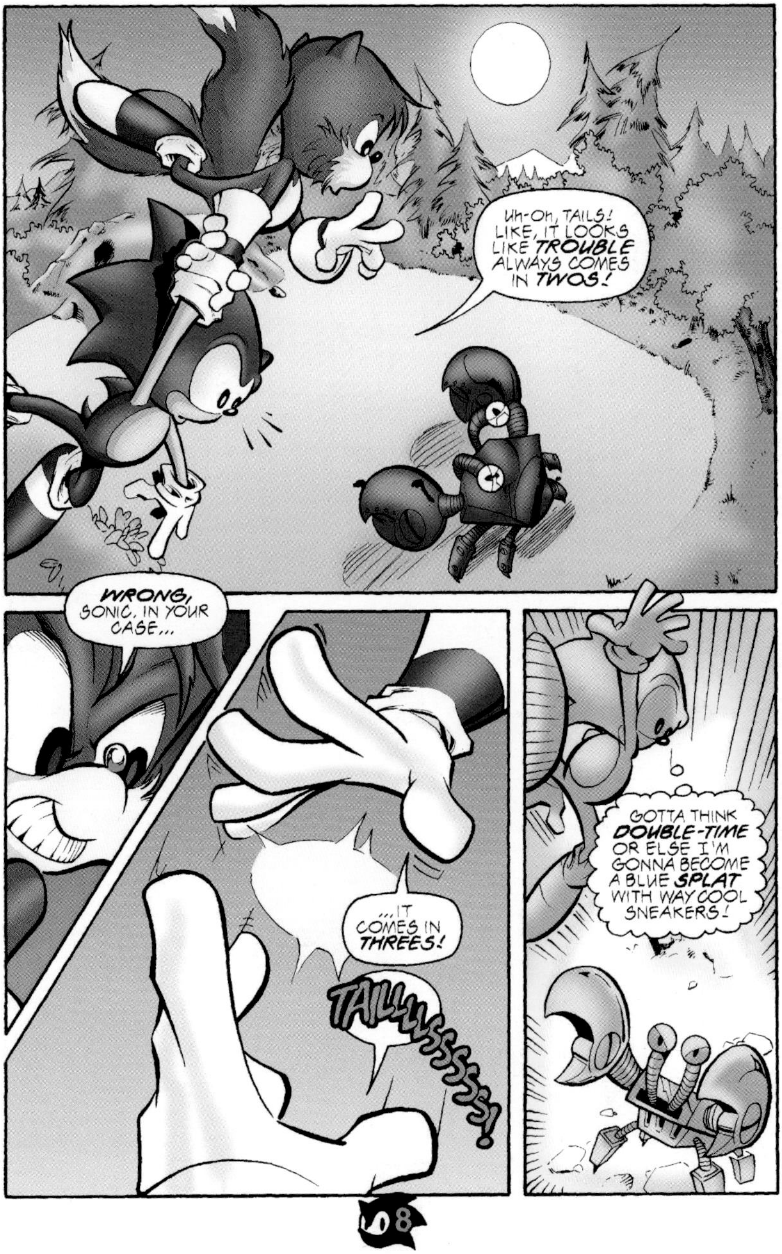
UH-OH, TAILS! LIKE, IT LOOKS LIKE TROUBLE ALWAYS COMES IN TWOS!
WRONG, SONIC. IN YOUR CASE...
...IT COMES IN THREES!
TAILLLSSSSSS!
GOTTA THINK DOUBLE-TIME OR ELSE I'M GONNA BECOME A BLUE SPLAT WITH WAY COOL SNEAKERS!

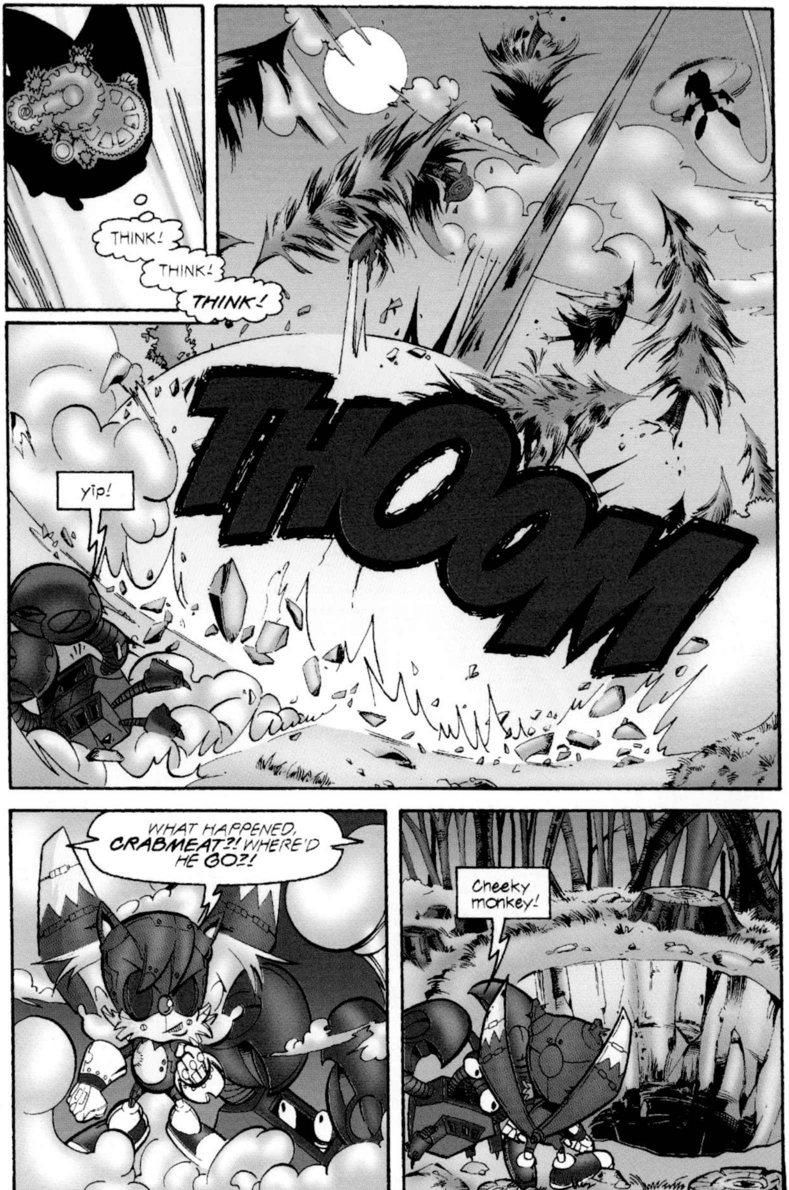
THINK!
THINK!
THINK!
THOOM
yip!
WHAT HAPPENED, CRABMEAT?! WHERE'D HE GO?!
Cheeky monkey!

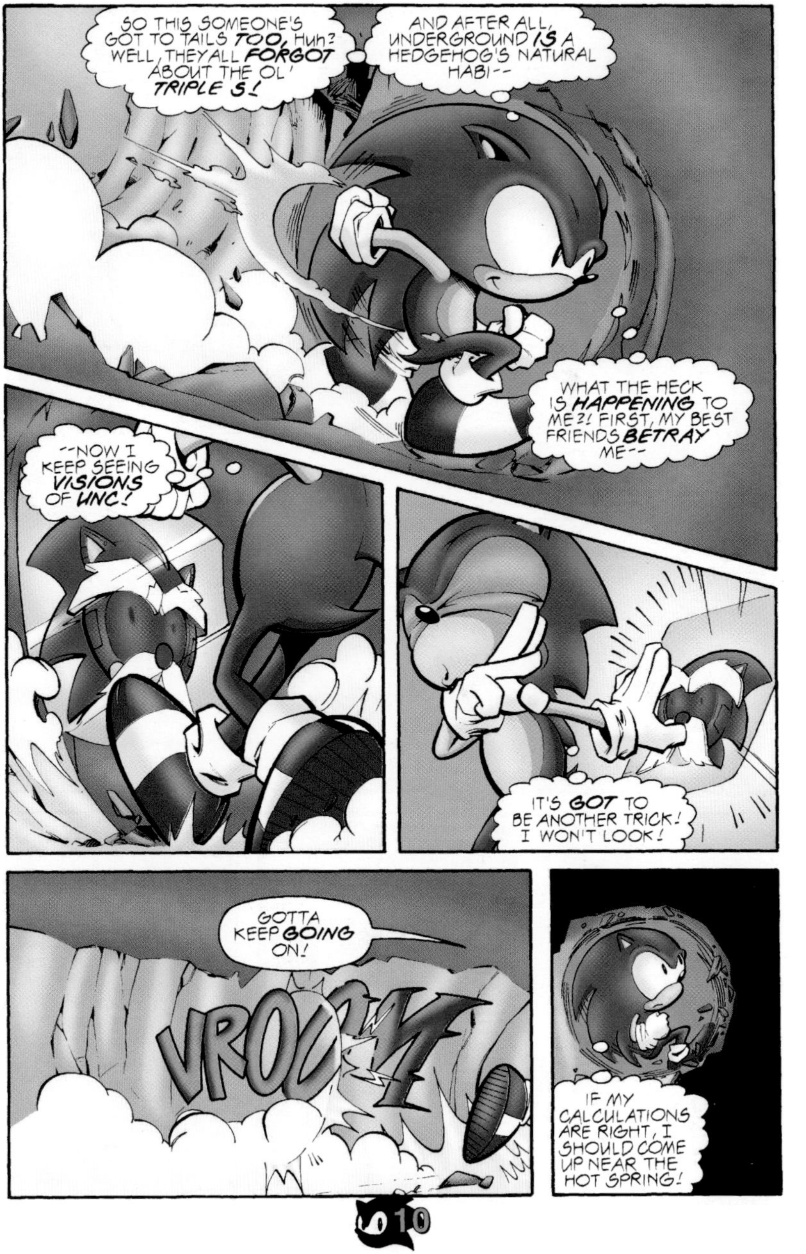
SO THIS SOMEONE'S GOT TO TAILS TOO, Huh? WELL, THEY ALL FORGOT ABOUT THE OL' TRIPLE S!
AND AFTER ALL, UNDERGROUND IS A HEDGEHOG'S NATURAL HABI--
WHAT THE HECK IS HAPPENING TO ME?! FIRST, MY BEST FRIENDS BETRAY ME--
--NOW I KEEP SEEING VISIONS OF UNC!
IT'S GOT TO BE ANOTHER TRICK! I WON'T LOOK!
GOTTA KEEP GOING ON!
VROOOM
IF MY CALCULATIONS ARE RIGHT, I SHOULD COME UP NEAR THE HOT SPRING!

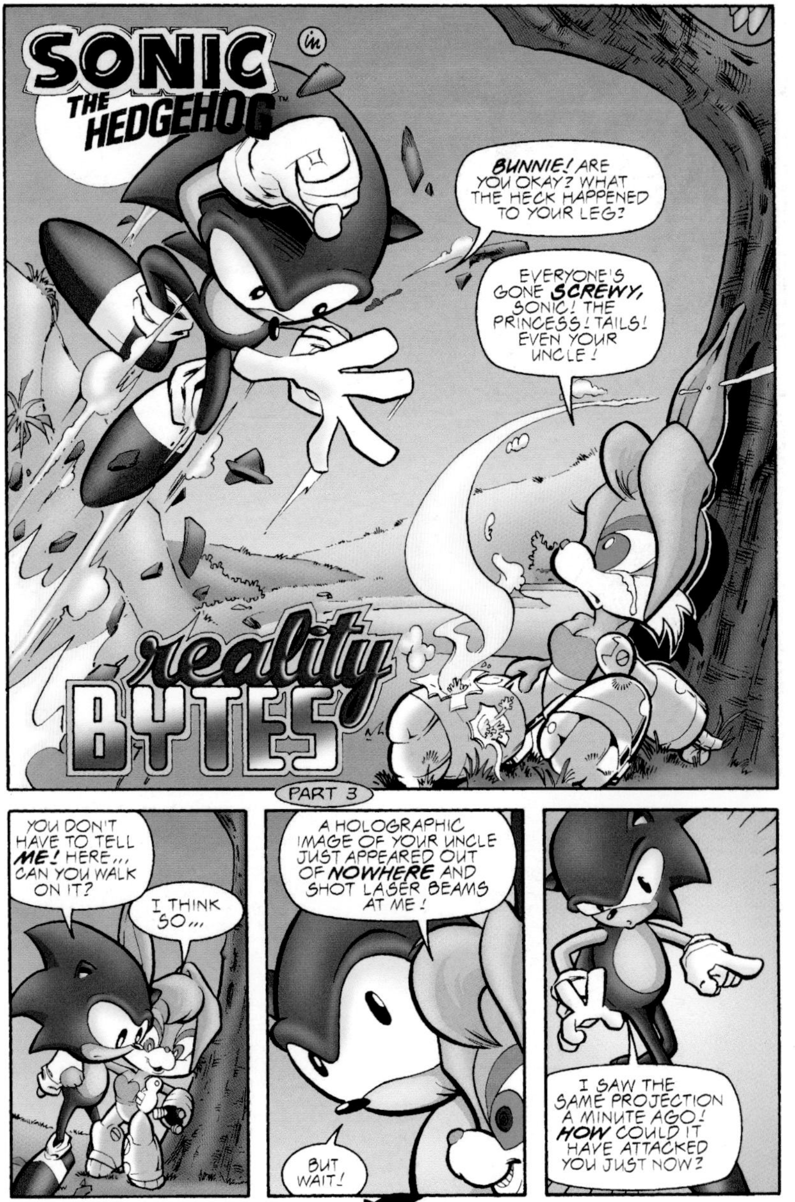
SONIC THE HEDGEHOG in
BUNNIE! ARE YOU OKAY? WHAT THE HECK HAPPENED TO YOUR LEG?
EVERYONE'S GONE SCREWY, SONIC! THE PRINCESS! TAILS! EVEN YOUR UNCLE!
reality BYTES
PART 3
YOU DON'T HAVE TO TELL ME! HERE... CAN YOU WALK ON IT?
I THINK SO...
A HOLOGRAPHIC IMAGE OF YOUR UNCLE JUST APPEARED OUT OF NOWHERE AND SHOT LASER BEAMS AT ME!
BUT WAIT!
I SAW THE SAME PROJECTION A MINUTE AGO! HOW COULD IT HAVE ATTACKED YOU JUST NOW?

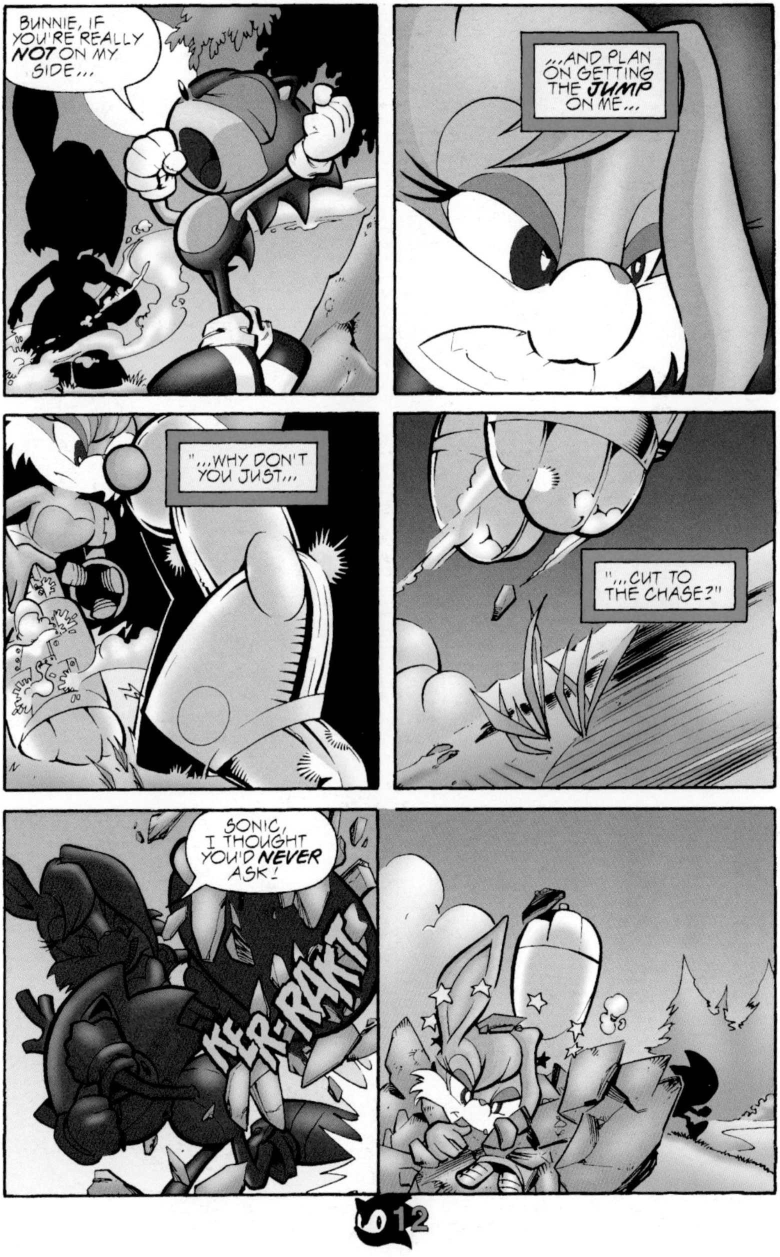
BUNNIE, IF YOU'RE REALLY **NOT** ON MY SIDE...
...AND PLAN ON GETTING THE **JUMP** ON ME...
"...WHY DON'T YOU JUST...
"...CUT TO THE CHASE?"
SONIC, I THOUGHT YOU'D **NEVER** ASK!
KER-RAKT!

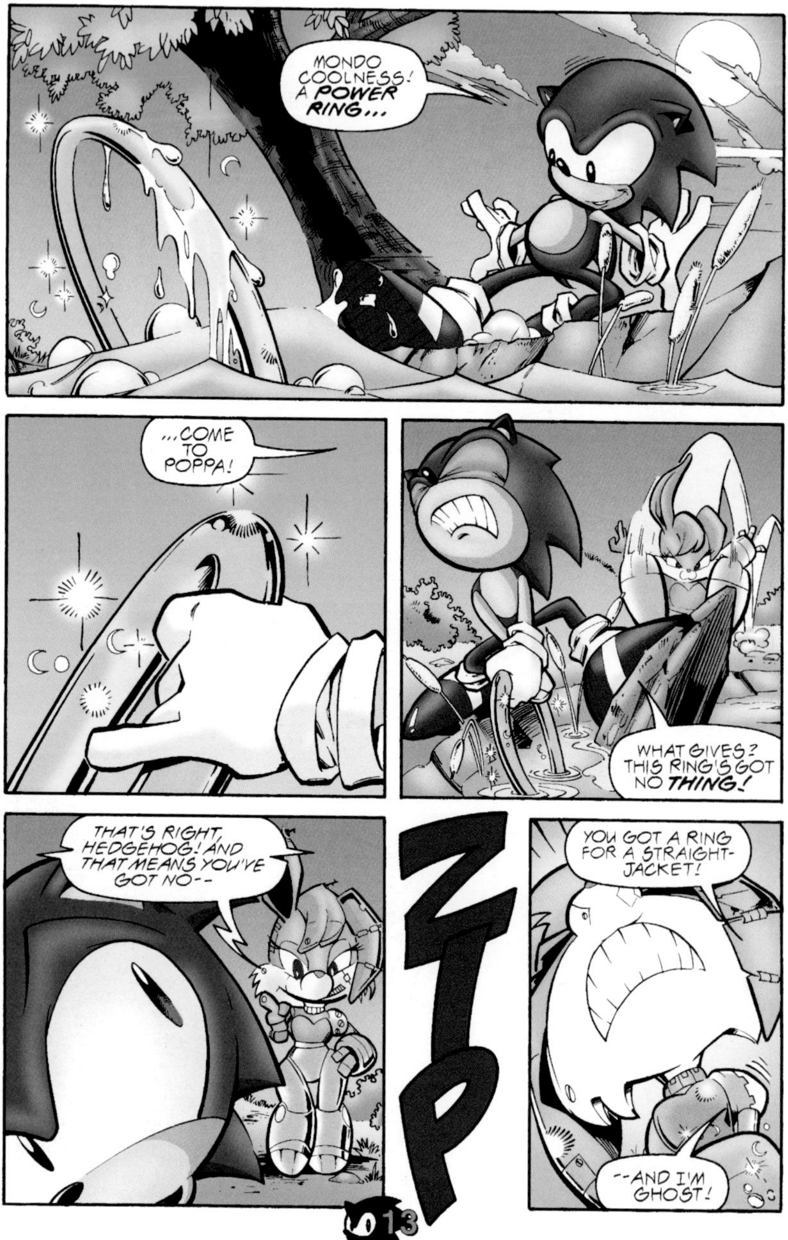
MONDO COOLNESS! A POWER RING...
...COME TO POPPA!
WHAT GIVES? THIS RING'S GOT NO THING!
THAT'S RIGHT, HEDGEHOG! AND THAT MEANS YOU'VE GOT NO--
ZIP
YOU GOT A RING FOR A STRAIGHT-JACKET!
--AND I'M GHOST!

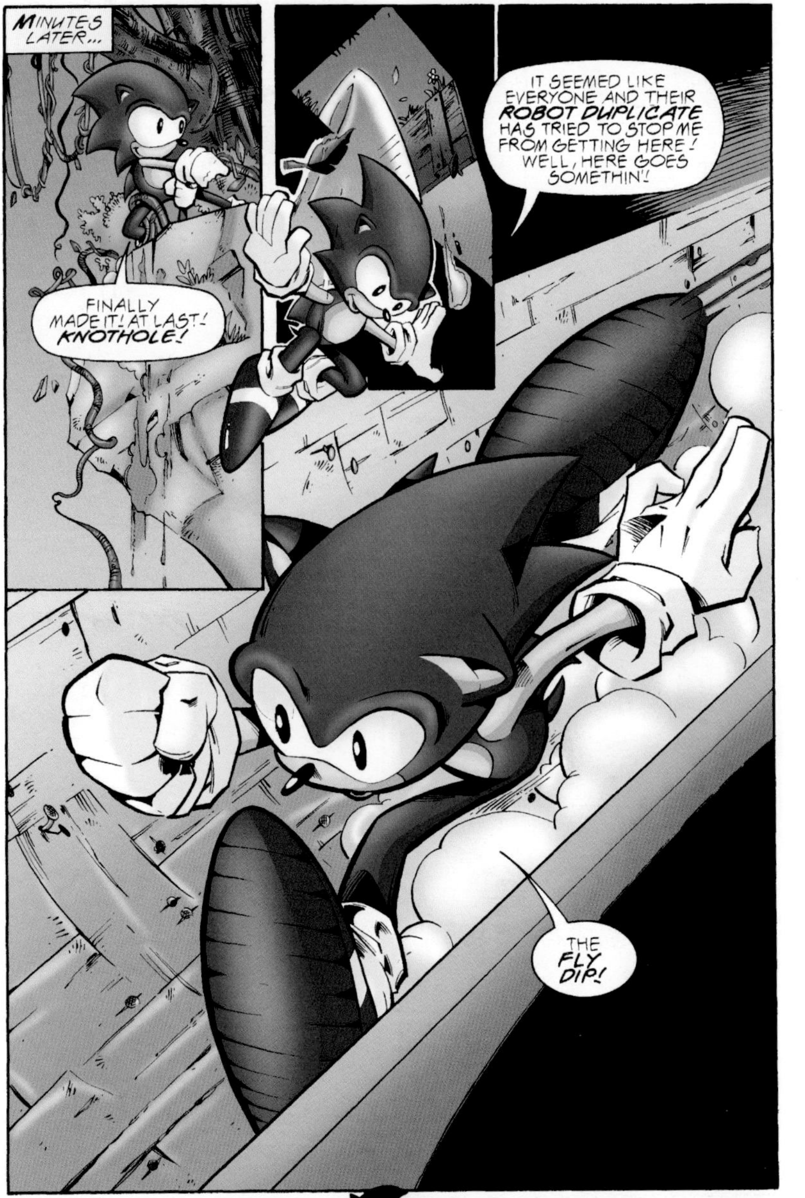
MINUTES LATER...
FINALLY MADE IT! AT LAST! KNOTHOLE!
IT SEEMED LIKE EVERYONE AND THEIR ROBOT DUPLICATE HAS TRIED TO STOP ME FROM GETTING HERE! WELL, HERE GOES SOMETHIN'!
THE FLY DIP!

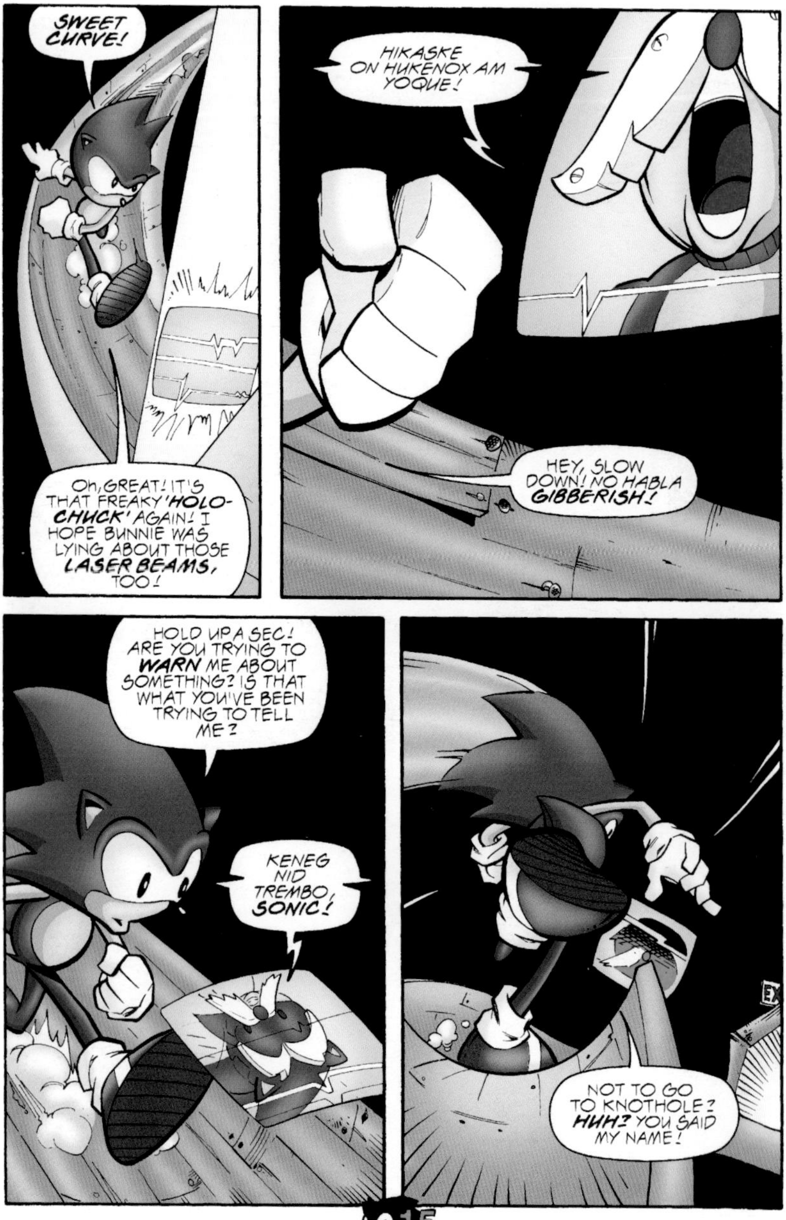
SWEET CURVE!
Oh, GREAT! IT'S THAT FREAKY 'HOLO-CHUCK' AGAIN! I HOPE BUNNIE WAS LYING ABOUT THOSE LASER BEAMS, TOO!
HIKASKE ON HUKENOX AM YOQUE!
HEY, SLOW DOWN! NO HABLA GIBBERISH!
HOLD UP A SEC! ARE YOU TRYING TO WARN ME ABOUT SOMETHING? IS THAT WHAT YOU'VE BEEN TRYING TO TELL ME?
KENEG NID TREMBO, SONIC!
NOT TO GO TO KNOTHOLE? HUH? YOU SAID MY NAME!

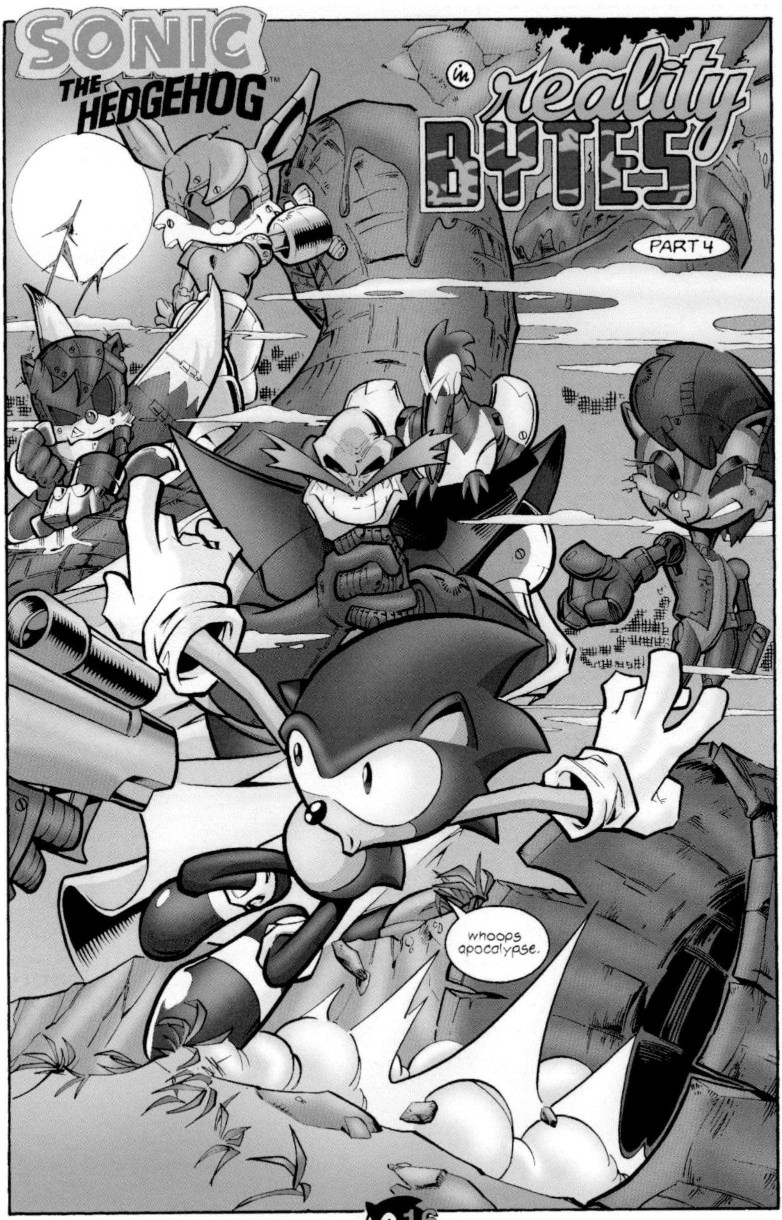
SONIC THE HEDGEHOG™
in reality BYTES
PART 4
whoops apocalypse.

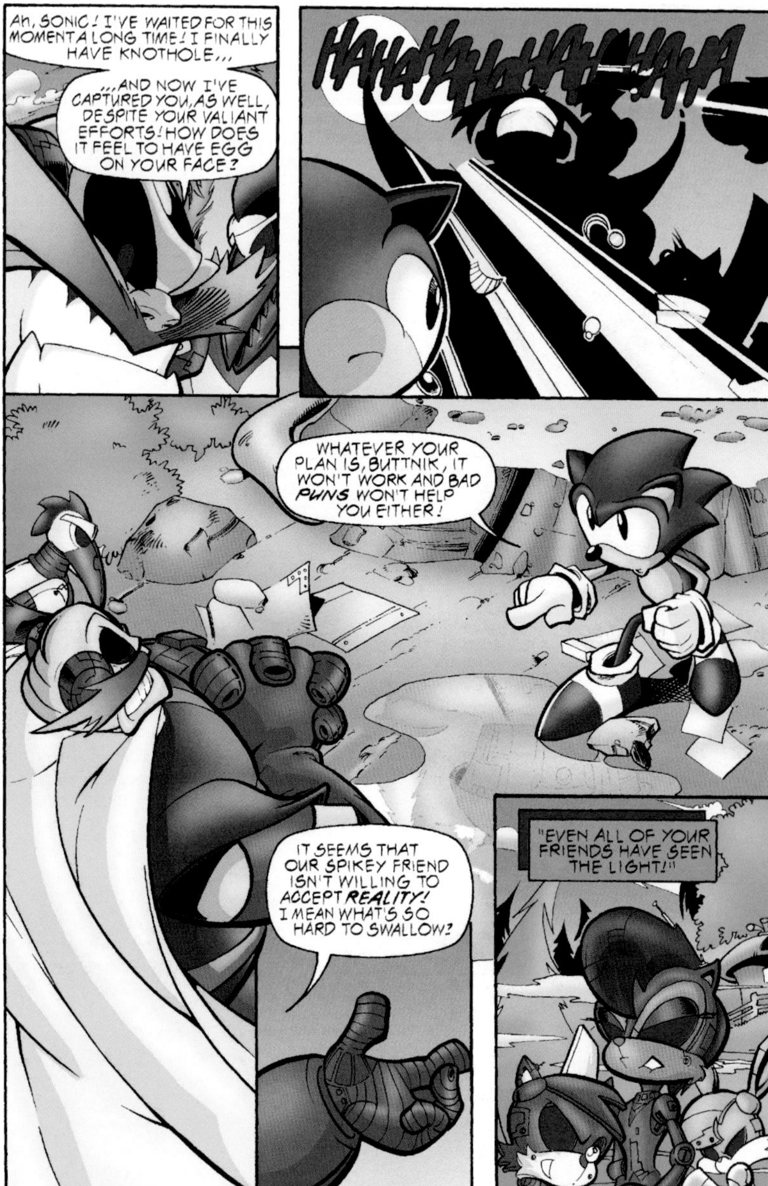
Ah, SONIC! I'VE WAITED FOR THIS MOMENT A LONG TIME! I FINALLY HAVE KNOTHOLE...
...AND NOW I'VE CAPTURED YOU, AS WELL, DESPITE YOUR VALIANT EFFORTS! HOW DOES IT FEEL TO HAVE EGG ON YOUR FACE?
HAHAHAHAHAHAHAHAHA
WHATEVER YOUR PLAN IS, BUTTNIK, IT WON'T WORK AND BAD PUNS WON'T HELP YOU EITHER!
IT SEEMS THAT OUR SPIKEY FRIEND ISN'T WILLING TO ACCEPT REALITY! I MEAN WHAT'S SO HARD TO SWALLOW?
"EVEN ALL OF YOUR FRIENDS HAVE SEEN THE LIGHT!"

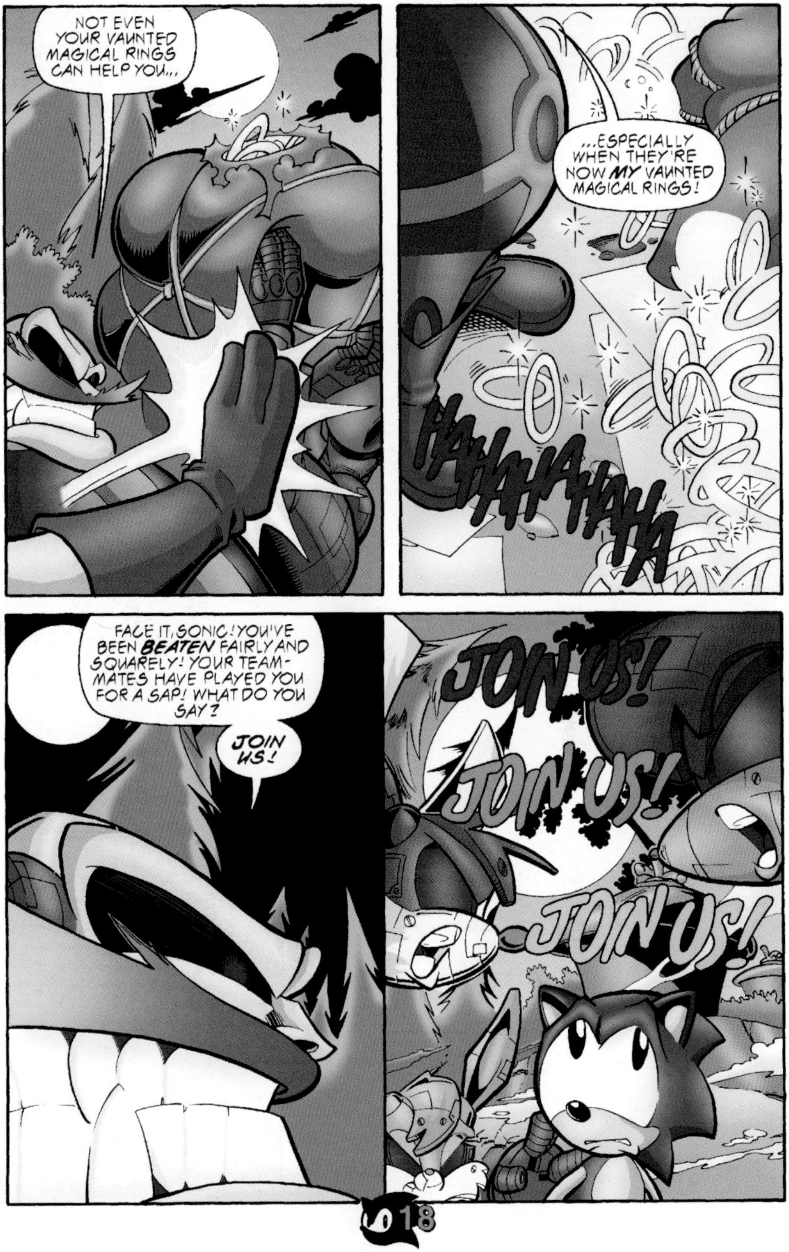
NOT EVEN YOUR VAUNTED MAGICAL RINGS CAN HELP YOU...
...ESPECIALLY WHEN THEY'RE NOW **MY** VAUNTED MAGICAL RINGS!
HAHAHAHAHAHAHA
FACE IT, SONIC! YOU'VE BEEN **BEATEN** FAIRLY AND SQUARELY! YOUR TEAM-MATES HAVE PLAYED YOU FOR A SAP! WHAT DO YOU SAY?
JOIN US!
JOIN US!
JOIN US!
JOIN US!

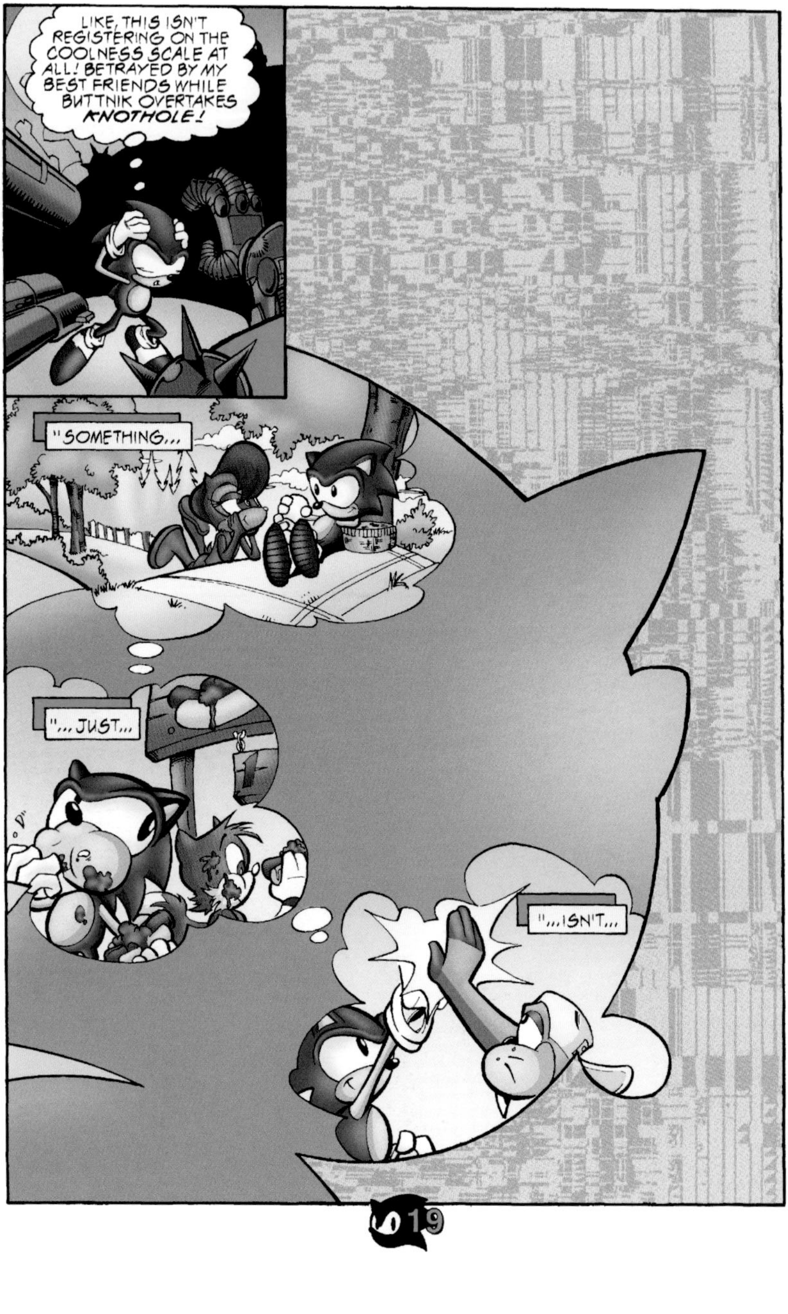
LIKE, THIS ISN'T REGISTERING ON THE COOLNESS SCALE AT ALL! BETRAYED BY MY BEST FRIENDS WHILE BUTTNIK OVERTAKES KNOTHOLE!
"SOMETHING...
"...JUST...
"...ISN'T...

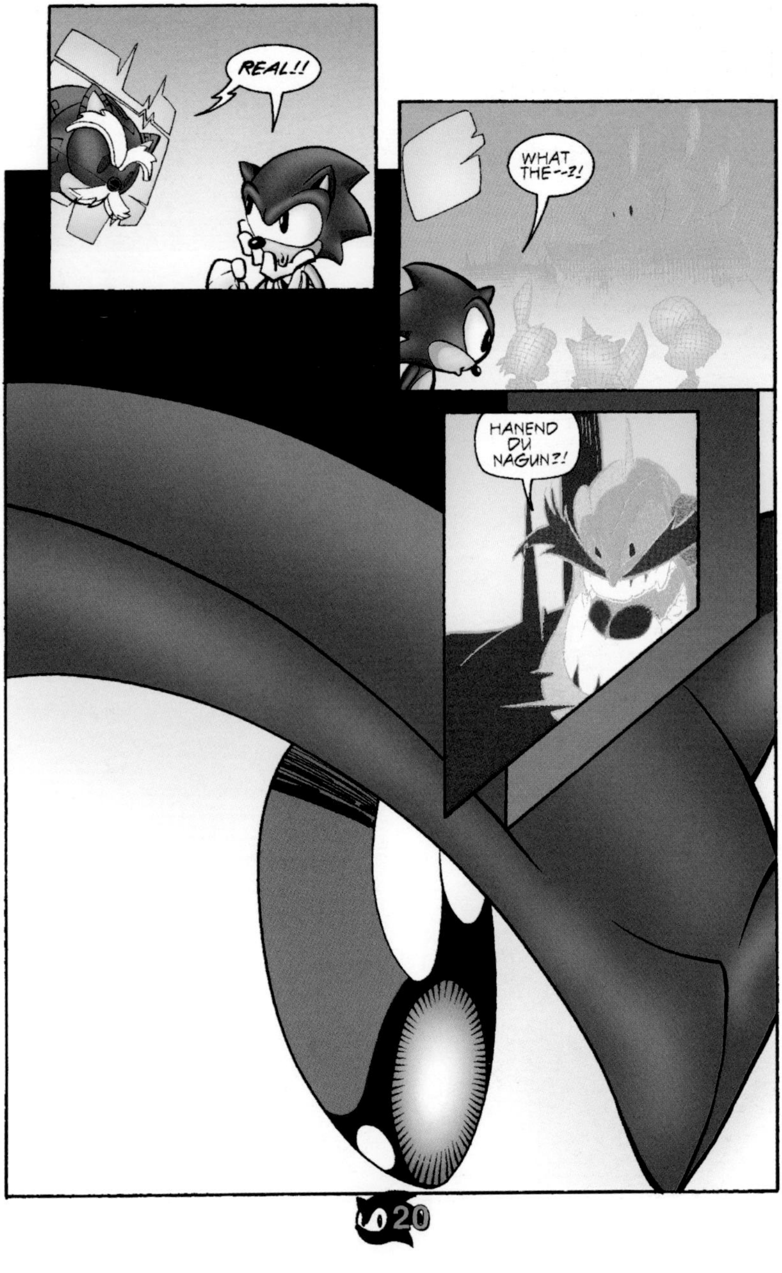
REAL!!
WHAT THE--?!
HANEND DU NAGUN?!

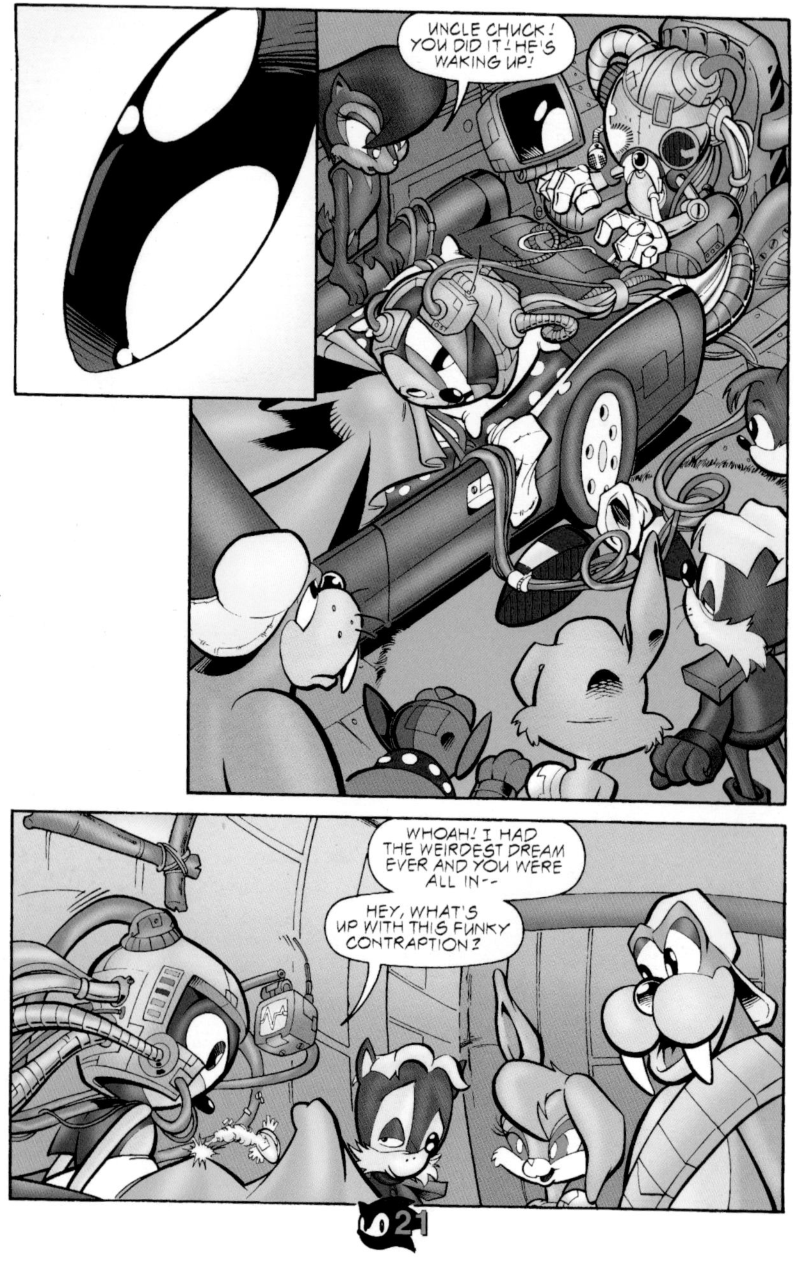
UNCLE CHUCK! YOU DID IT! HE'S WAKING UP!
WHOAH! I HAD THE WEIRDEST DREAM EVER AND YOU WERE ALL IN--
HEY, WHAT'S UP WITH THIS FUNKY CONTRAPTION?

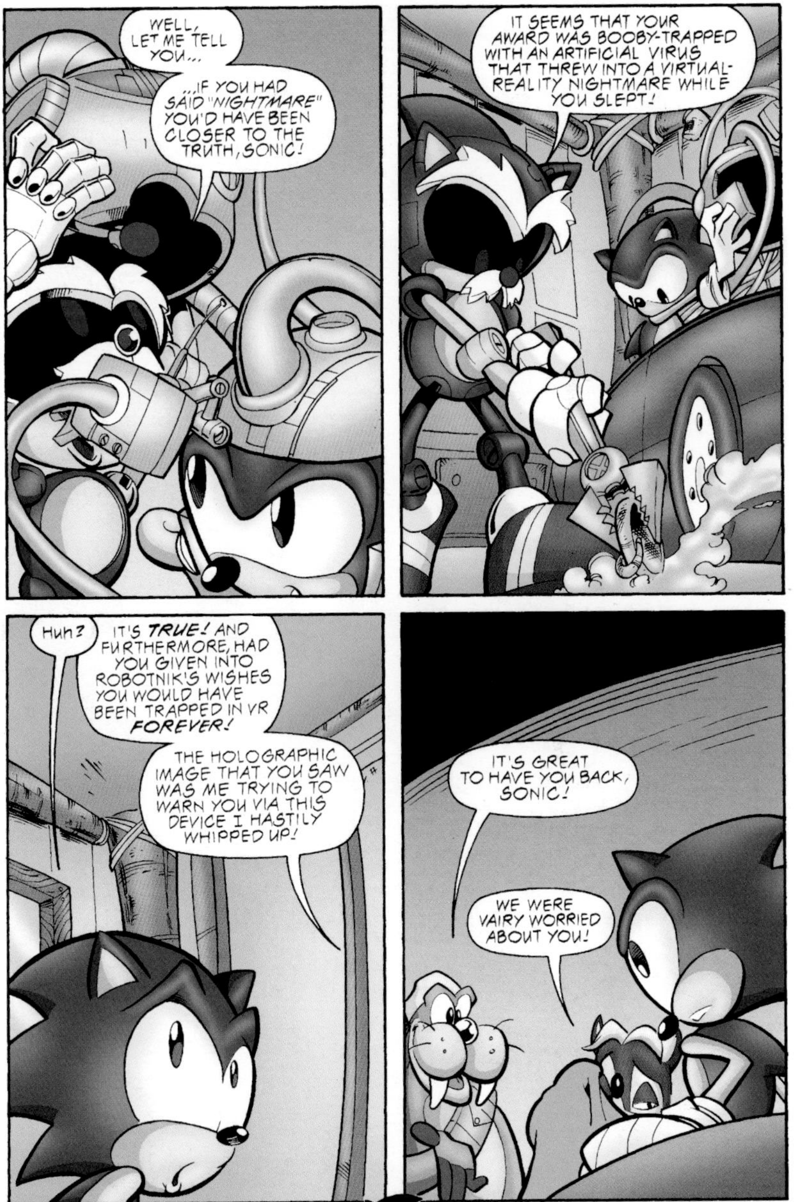
WELL, LET ME TELL YOU...
...IF YOU HAD SAID "NIGHTMARE" YOU'D HAVE BEEN CLOSER TO THE TRUTH, SONIC!
IT SEEMS THAT YOUR AWARD WAS BOOBY-TRAPPED WITH AN ARTIFICIAL VIRUS THAT THREW INTO A VIRTUAL-REALITY NIGHTMARE WHILE YOU SLEPT!
Huh?
IT'S TRUE! AND FURTHERMORE, HAD YOU GIVEN INTO ROBOTNIK'S WISHES YOU WOULD HAVE BEEN TRAPPED IN VR FOREVER!
THE HOLOGRAPHIC IMAGE THAT YOU SAW WAS ME TRYING TO WARN YOU VIA THIS DEVICE I HASTILY WHIPPED UP!
IT'S GREAT TO HAVE YOU BACK, SONIC!
WE WERE VAIRY WORRIED ABOUT YOU!

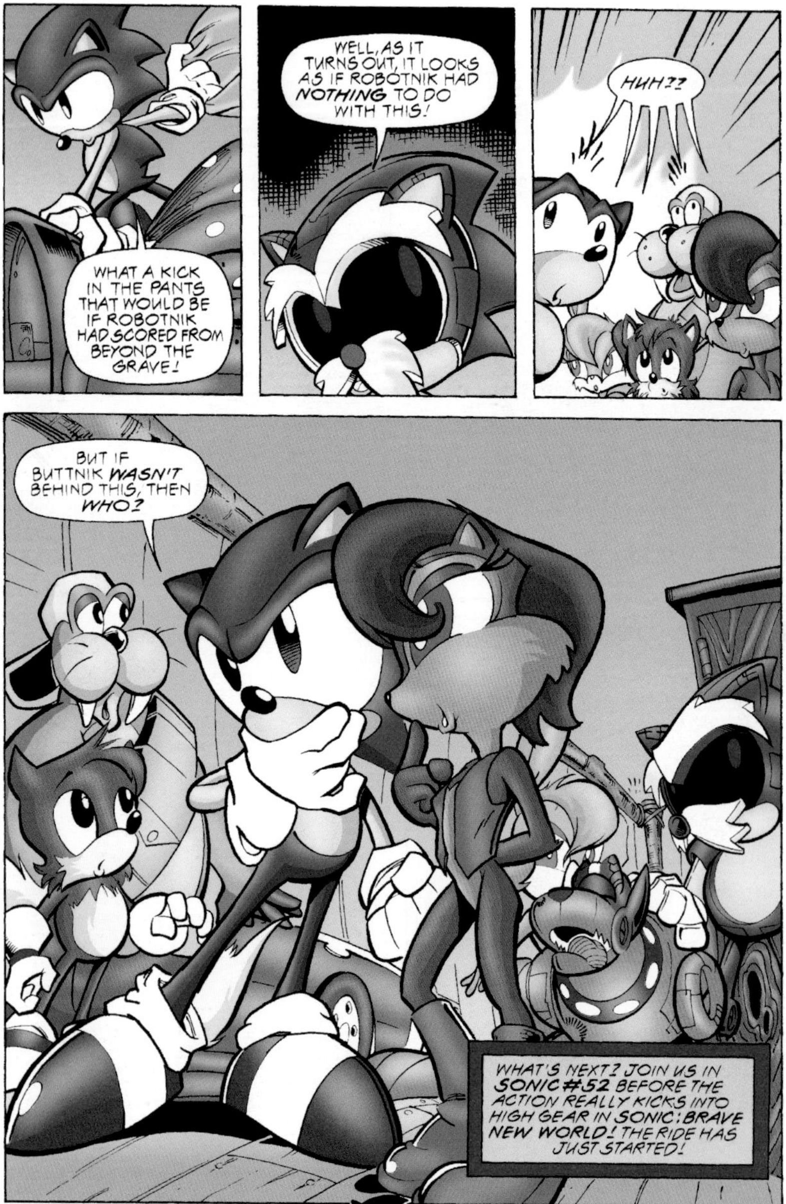
WHAT A KICK IN THE PANTS THAT WOULD BE IF ROBOTNIK HAD SCORED FROM BEYOND THE GRAVE!
WELL, AS IT TURNS OUT, IT LOOKS AS IF ROBOTNIK HAD NOTHING TO DO WITH THIS!
HUH??
BUT IF BUTTNIK WASN'T BEHIND THIS, THEN WHO?
WHAT'S NEXT? JOIN US IN SONIC #52 BEFORE THE ACTION REALLY KICKS INTO HIGH GEAR IN SONIC: BRAVE NEW WORLD! THE RIDE HAS JUST STARTED!

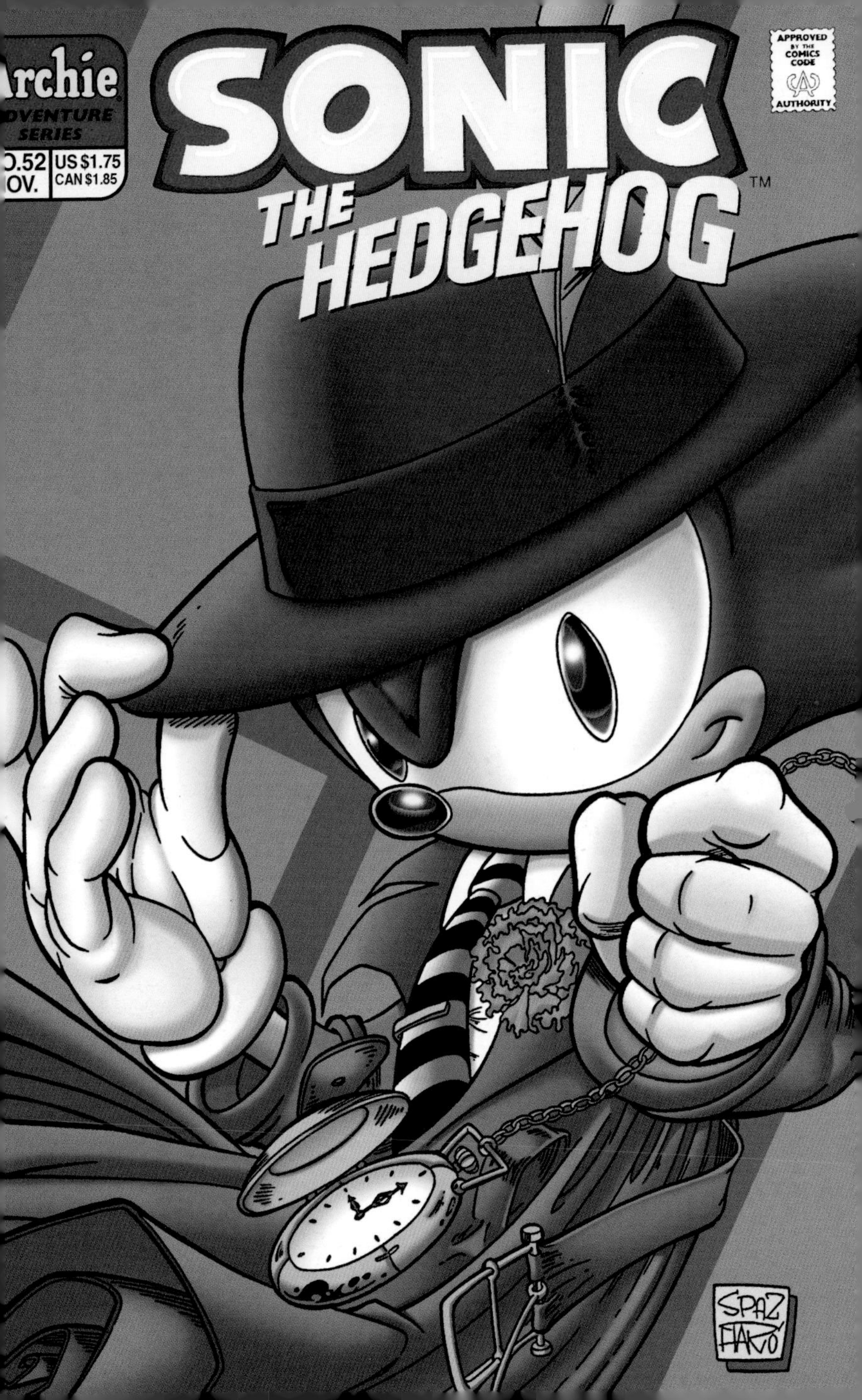
Archie
DVENTURE
SERIES
.52
OV.
US $1.75
CAN $1.85
APPROVED BY THE COMICS CODE AUTHORITY
SONIC
THE HEDGEHOG
TM
SPAZ

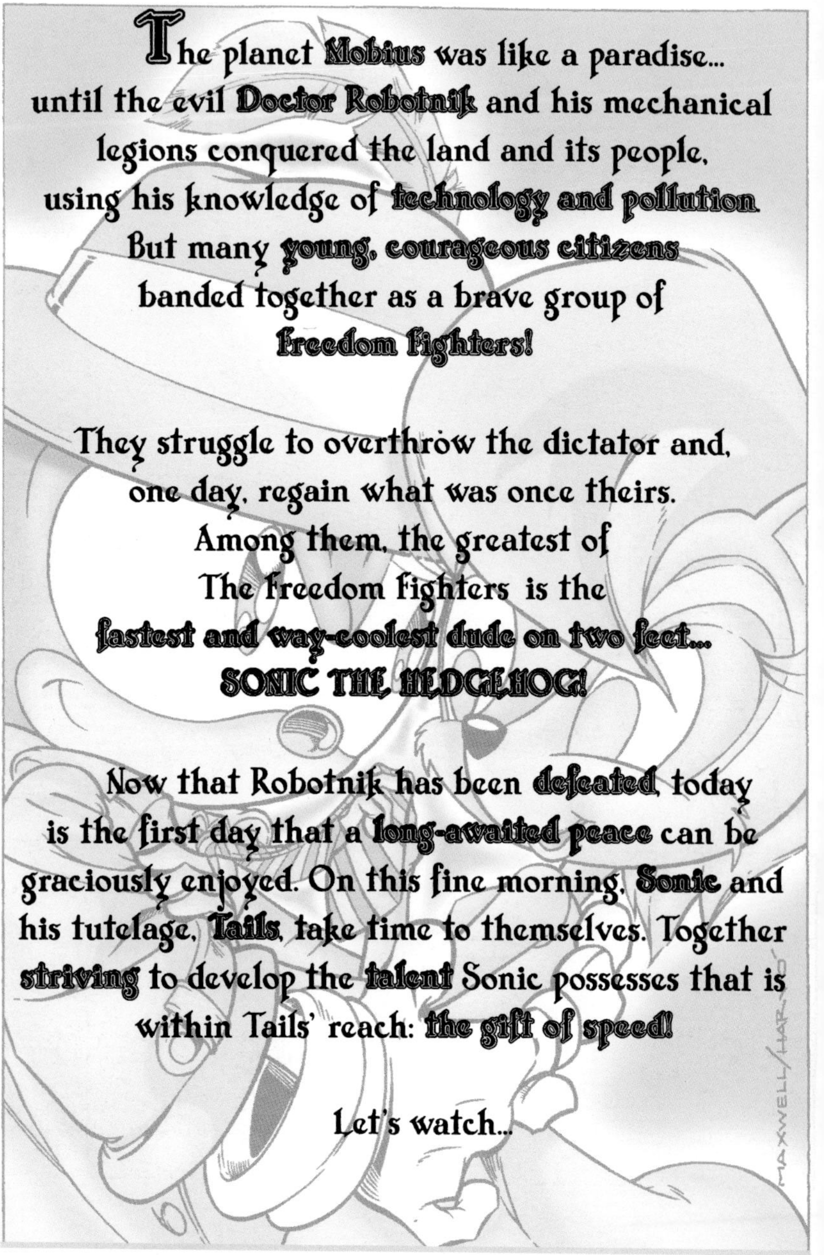

The planet **Mobius** was like a paradise... until the evil **Doctor Robotnik** and his mechanical legions conquered the land and its people, using his knowledge of **technology and pollution**. But many **young, courageous citizens** banded together as a brave group of **freedom fighters!**

They struggle to overthrow the dictator and, one day, regain what was once theirs. Among them, the greatest of The Freedom Fighters is the **fastest and way-coolest dude on two feet... SONIC THE HEDGEHOG!**

Now that Robotnik has been **defeated**, today is the first day that a **long-awaited peace** can be graciously enjoyed. On this fine morning, **Sonic** and his tutelage, **Tails**, take time to themselves. Together **striving** to develop the **talent** Sonic possesses that is within Tails' reach: **the gift of speed!**

Let's watch...

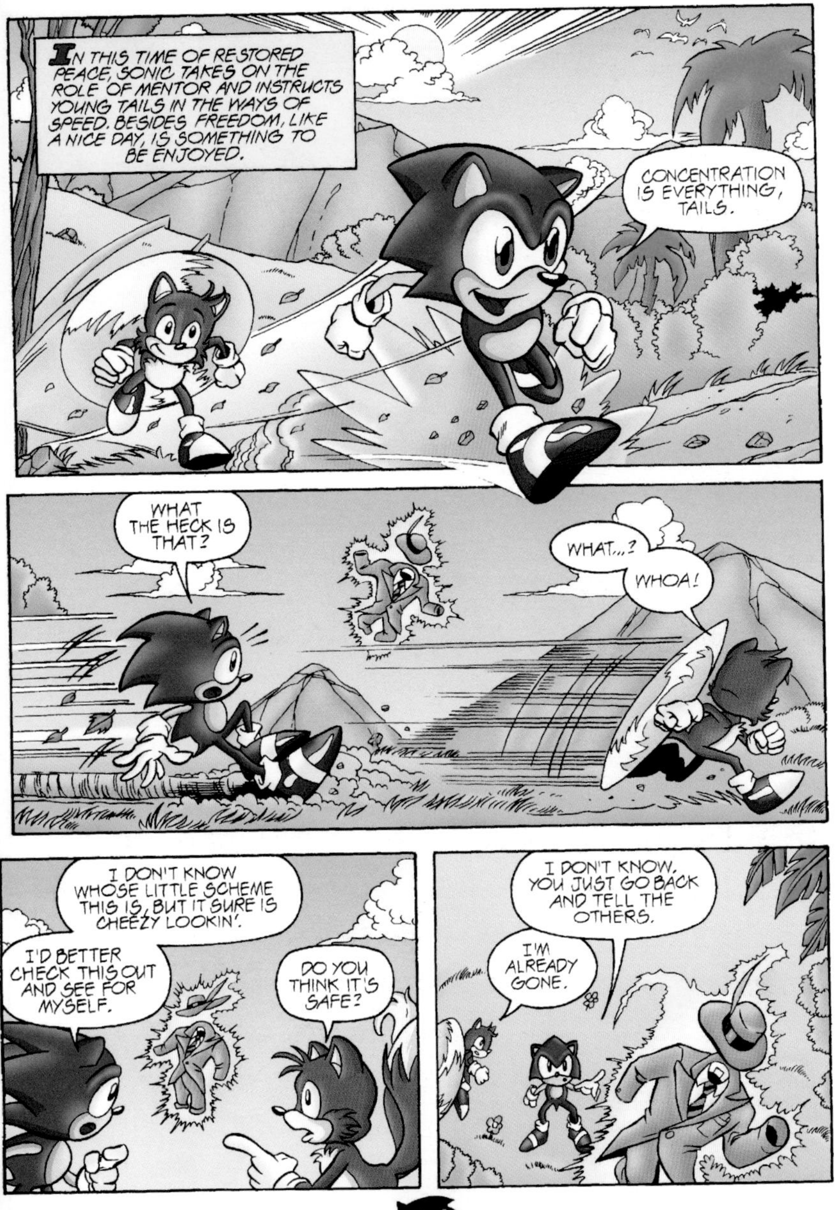
IN THIS TIME OF RESTORED PEACE, SONIC TAKES ON THE ROLE OF MENTOR AND INSTRUCTS YOUNG TAILS IN THE WAYS OF SPEED. BESIDES FREEDOM, LIKE A NICE DAY, IS SOMETHING TO BE ENJOYED.
CONCENTRATION IS EVERYTHING, TAILS.
WHAT THE HECK IS THAT?
WHAT...?
WHOA!
I DON'T KNOW WHOSE LITTLE SCHEME THIS IS, BUT IT SURE IS CHEEZY LOOKIN'.
I'D BETTER CHECK THIS OUT AND SEE FOR MYSELF.
DO YOU THINK IT'S SAFE?
I DON'T KNOW. YOU JUST GO BACK AND TELL THE OTHERS.
I'M ALREADY GONE.

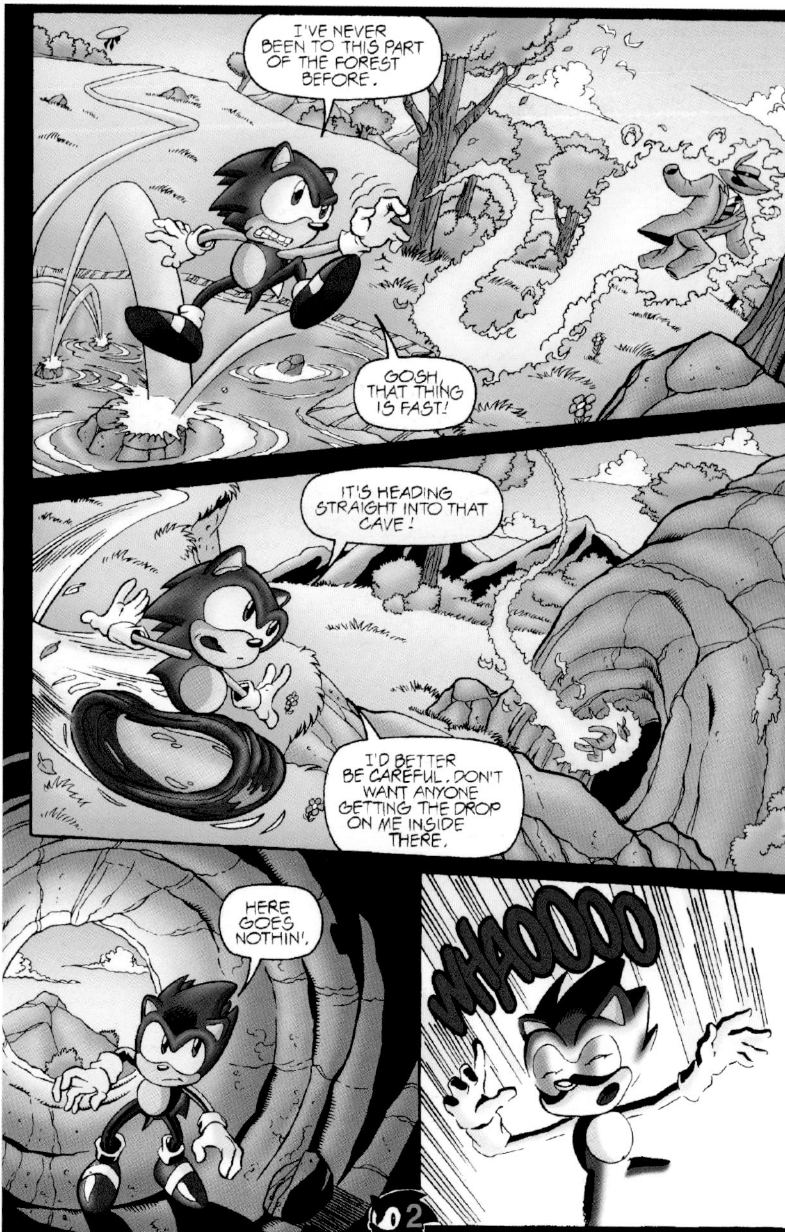

I'VE NEVER BEEN TO THIS PART OF THE FOREST BEFORE.
GOSH, THAT THING IS FAST!
IT'S HEADING STRAIGHT INTO THAT CAVE!
I'D BETTER BE CAREFUL. DON'T WANT ANYONE GETTING THE DROP ON ME INSIDE THERE.
HERE GOES NOTHIN'.
WHAOOOO

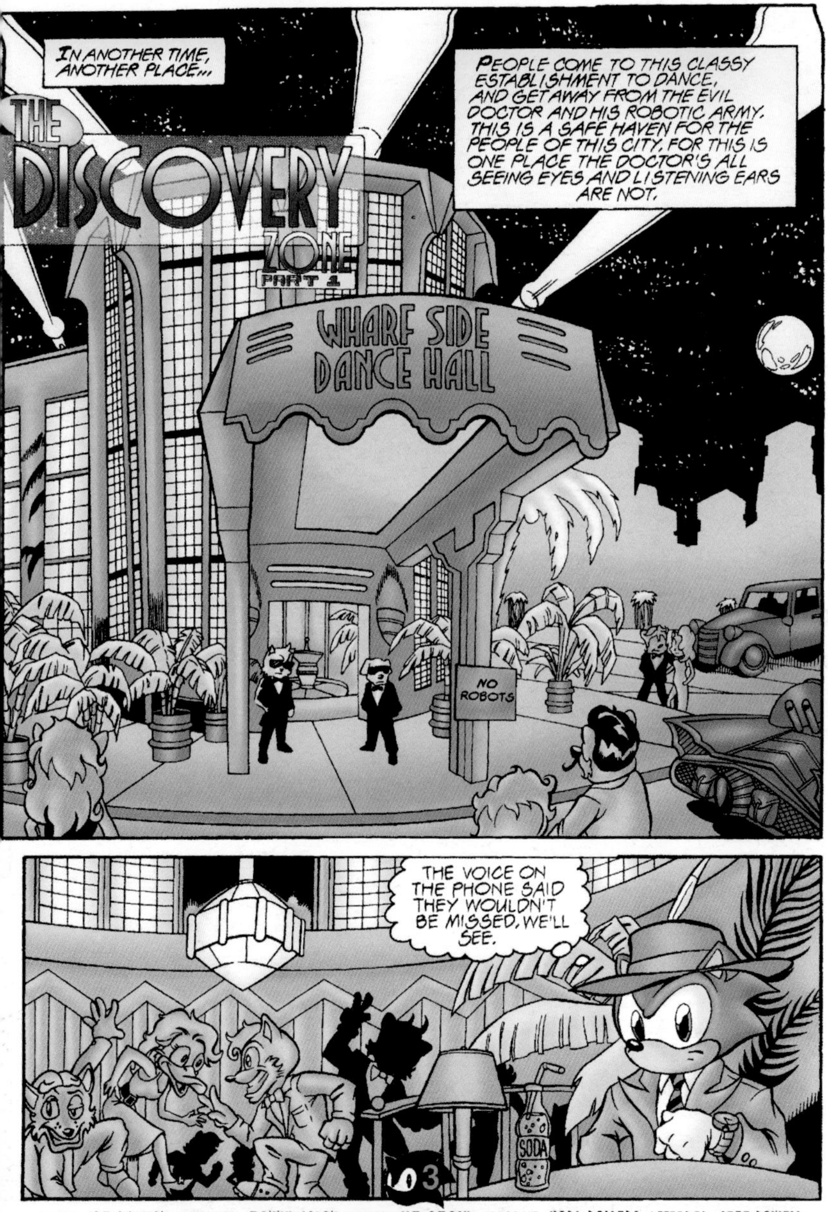
IN ANOTHER TIME, ANOTHER PLACE...
THE DISCOVERY ZONE
PART 1
PEOPLE COME TO THIS CLASSY ESTABLISHMENT TO DANCE, AND GET AWAY FROM THE EVIL DOCTOR AND HIS ROBOTIC ARMY. THIS IS A SAFE HAVEN FOR THE PEOPLE OF THIS CITY, FOR THIS IS ONE PLACE THE DOCTOR'S ALL SEEING EYES AND LISTENING EARS ARE NOT.
WHARF SIDE DANCE HALL
NO ROBOTS
THE VOICE ON THE PHONE SAID THEY WOULDN'T BE MISSED, WE'LL SEE.
SODA
3

◆SCRIPT: TOM ROLSTON◆PENCILER: MANNY GALAN◆INKER: JIM AMASH◆COLORIST: KARL BOLLERS◆LETTERER: JEFF POWELL◆
◆EDITOR: J. FREDDY GABRIE◆MANAGING EDITOR: VICTOR GORELICK◆EDITOR-IN-CHIEF: RICHARD GOLDWATER◆

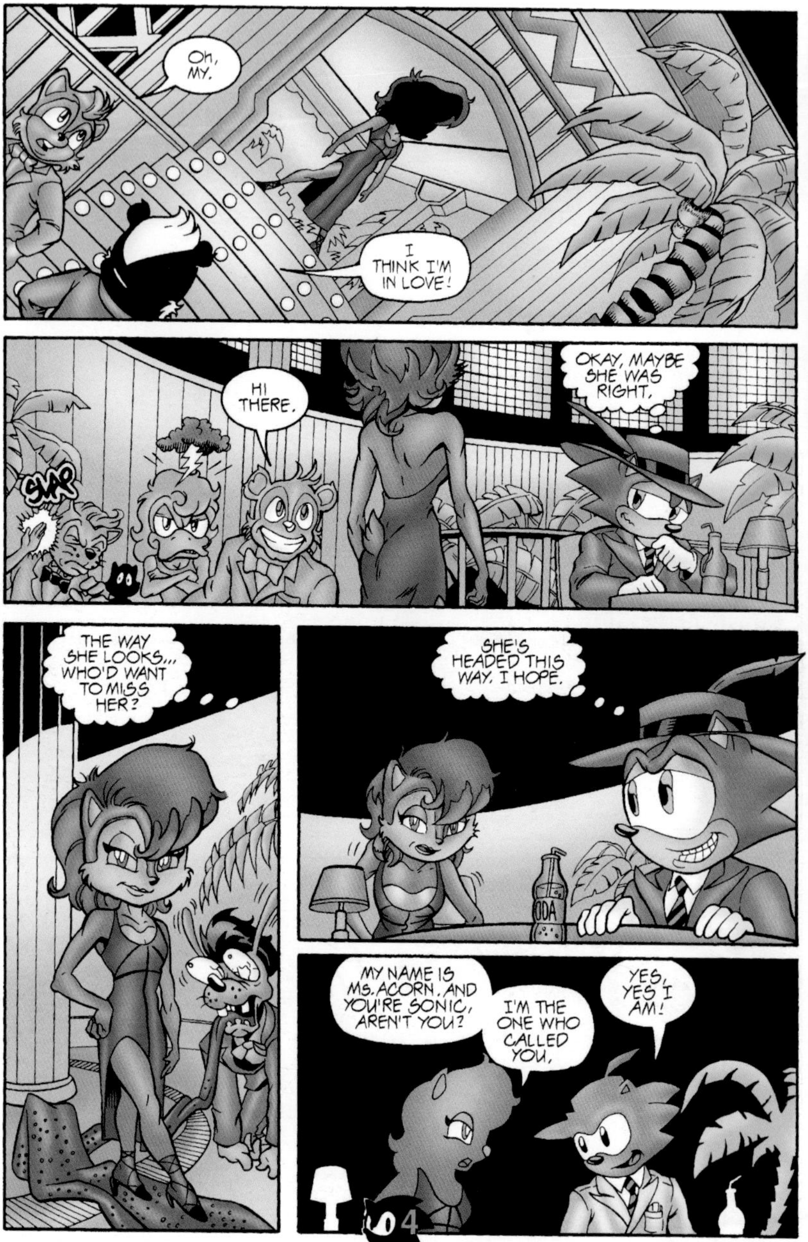

OH, MY.
I THINK I'M IN LOVE!
SNAP
HI THERE.
OKAY, MAYBE SHE WAS RIGHT.
THE WAY SHE LOOKS... WHO'D WANT TO MISS HER?
SHE'S HEADED THIS WAY. I HOPE.
MY NAME IS MS. ACORN, AND YOU'RE SONIC, AREN'T YOU?
I'M THE ONE WHO CALLED YOU.
YES, YES I AM!

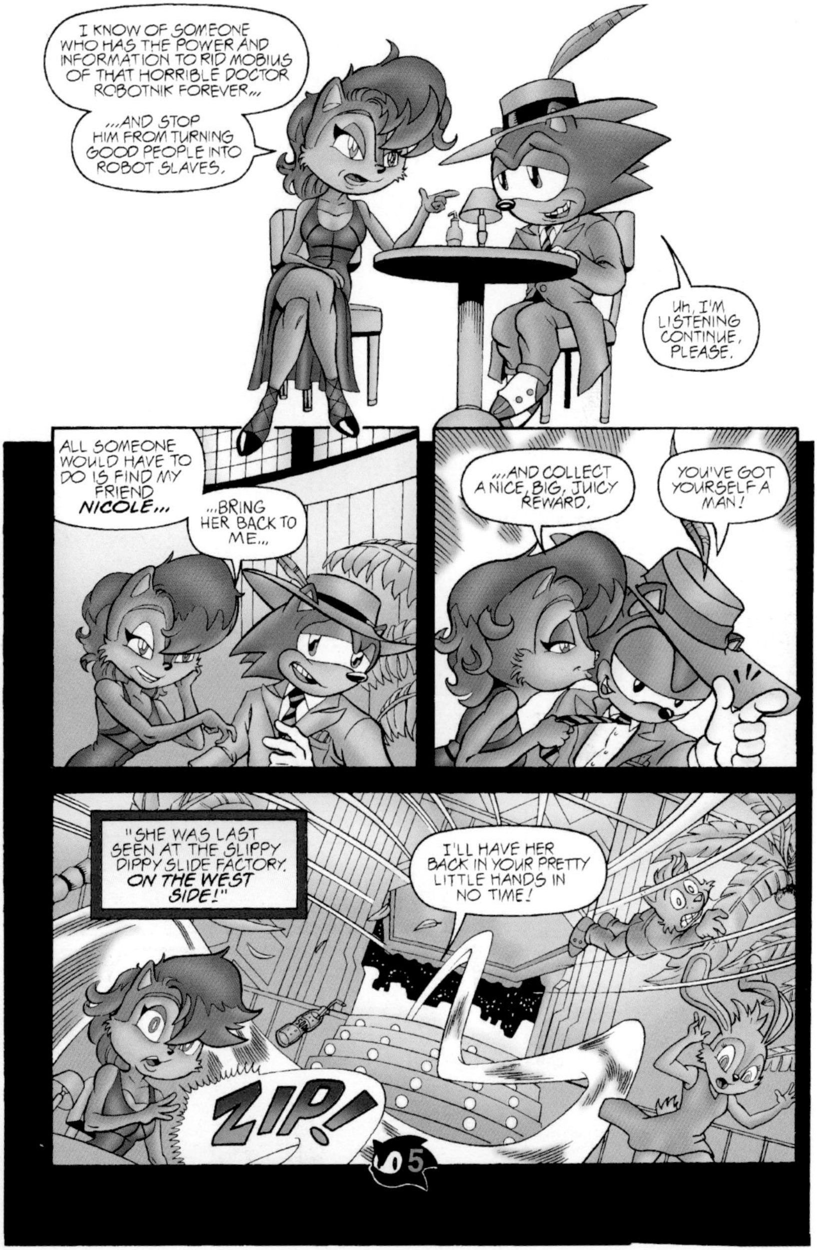
I KNOW OF SOMEONE WHO HAS THE POWER AND INFORMATION TO RID MOBIUS OF THAT HORRIBLE DOCTOR ROBOTNIK FOREVER...
...AND STOP HIM FROM TURNING GOOD PEOPLE INTO ROBOT SLAVES.
Uh, I'M LISTENING CONTINUE, PLEASE.
ALL SOMEONE WOULD HAVE TO DO IS FIND MY FRIEND NICOLE...
...BRING HER BACK TO ME...
...AND COLLECT A NICE, BIG, JUICY REWARD.
YOU'VE GOT YOURSELF A MAN!
"SHE WAS LAST SEEN AT THE SLIPPY DIPPY SLIDE FACTORY. ON THE WEST SIDE!"
I'LL HAVE HER BACK IN YOUR PRETTY LITTLE HANDS IN NO TIME!
ZIP!

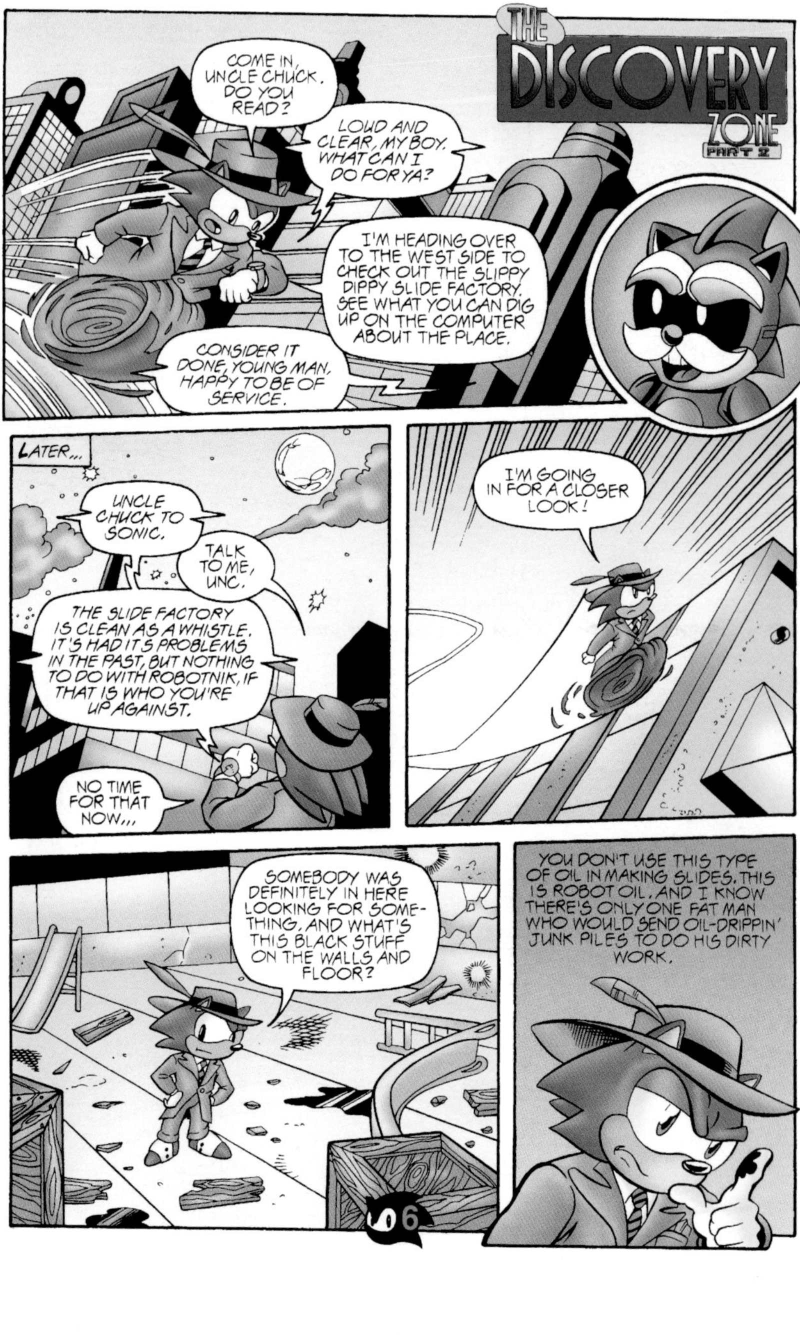
THE DISCOVERY ZONE
PART 2
COME IN, UNCLE CHUCK. DO YOU READ?
LOUD AND CLEAR, MY BOY. WHAT CAN I DO FOR YA?
I'M HEADING OVER TO THE WEST SIDE TO CHECK OUT THE SLIPPY DIPPY SLIDE FACTORY. SEE WHAT YOU CAN DIG UP ON THE COMPUTER ABOUT THE PLACE.
CONSIDER IT DONE, YOUNG MAN. HAPPY TO BE OF SERVICE.
LATER...
UNCLE CHUCK TO SONIC.
TALK TO ME, UNC.
THE SLIDE FACTORY IS CLEAN AS A WHISTLE. IT'S HAD ITS PROBLEMS IN THE PAST, BUT NOTHING TO DO WITH ROBOTNIK, IF THAT IS WHO YOU'RE UP AGAINST.
NO TIME FOR THAT NOW...
I'M GOING IN FOR A CLOSER LOOK!
SOMEBODY WAS DEFINITELY IN HERE LOOKING FOR SOMETHING. AND WHAT'S THIS BLACK STUFF ON THE WALLS AND FLOOR?
YOU DON'T USE THIS TYPE OF OIL IN MAKING SLIDES. THIS IS ROBOT OIL. AND I KNOW THERE'S ONLY ONE FAT MAN WHO WOULD SEND OIL-DRIPPIN' JUNK PILES TO DO HIS DIRTY WORK.

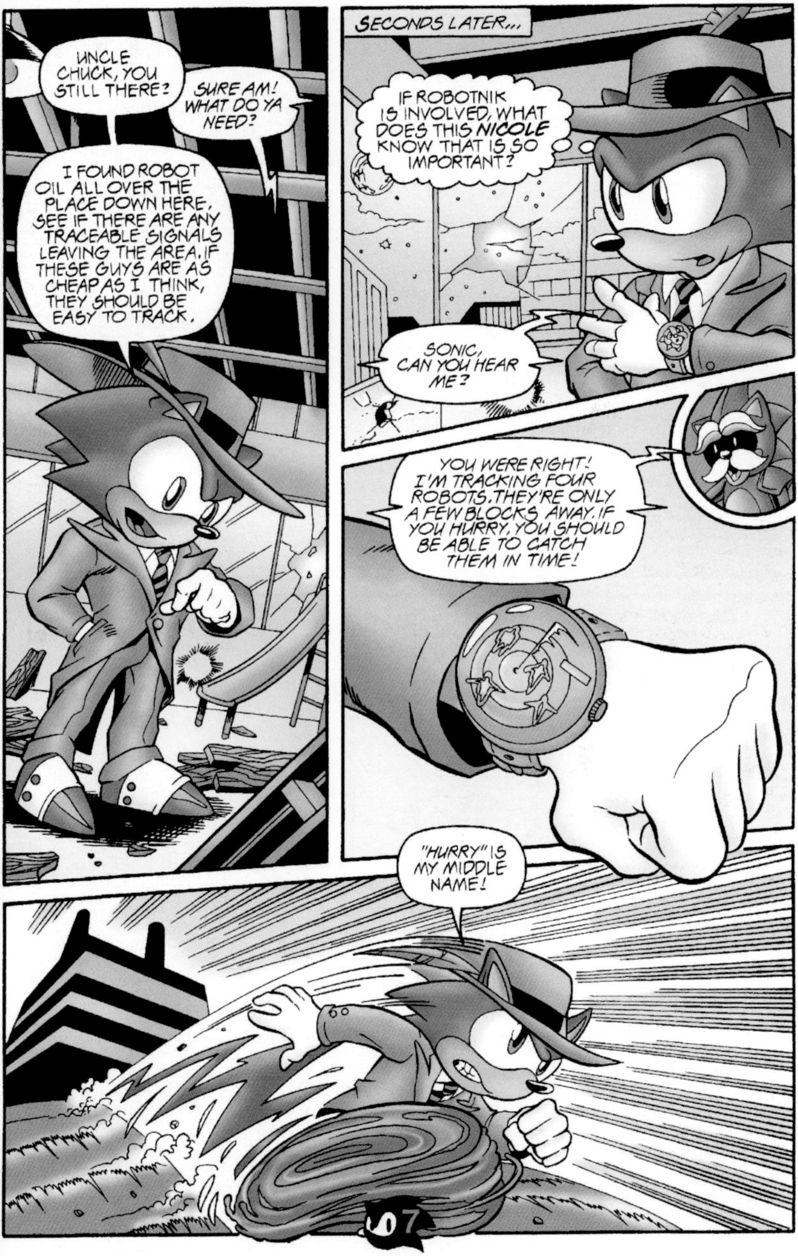
UNCLE CHUCK, YOU STILL THERE?
SURE AM! WHAT DO YA NEED?
I FOUND ROBOT OIL ALL OVER THE PLACE DOWN HERE. SEE IF THERE ARE ANY TRACEABLE SIGNALS LEAVING THE AREA. IF THESE GUYS ARE AS CHEAP AS I THINK, THEY SHOULD BE EASY TO TRACK.
SECONDS LATER...
IF ROBOTNIK IS INVOLVED, WHAT DOES THIS NICOLE KNOW THAT IS SO IMPORTANT?
SONIC, CAN YOU HEAR ME?
YOU WERE RIGHT! I'M TRACKING FOUR ROBOTS. THEY'RE ONLY A FEW BLOCKS AWAY. IF YOU HURRY, YOU SHOULD BE ABLE TO CATCH THEM IN TIME!
"HURRY" IS MY MIDDLE NAME!

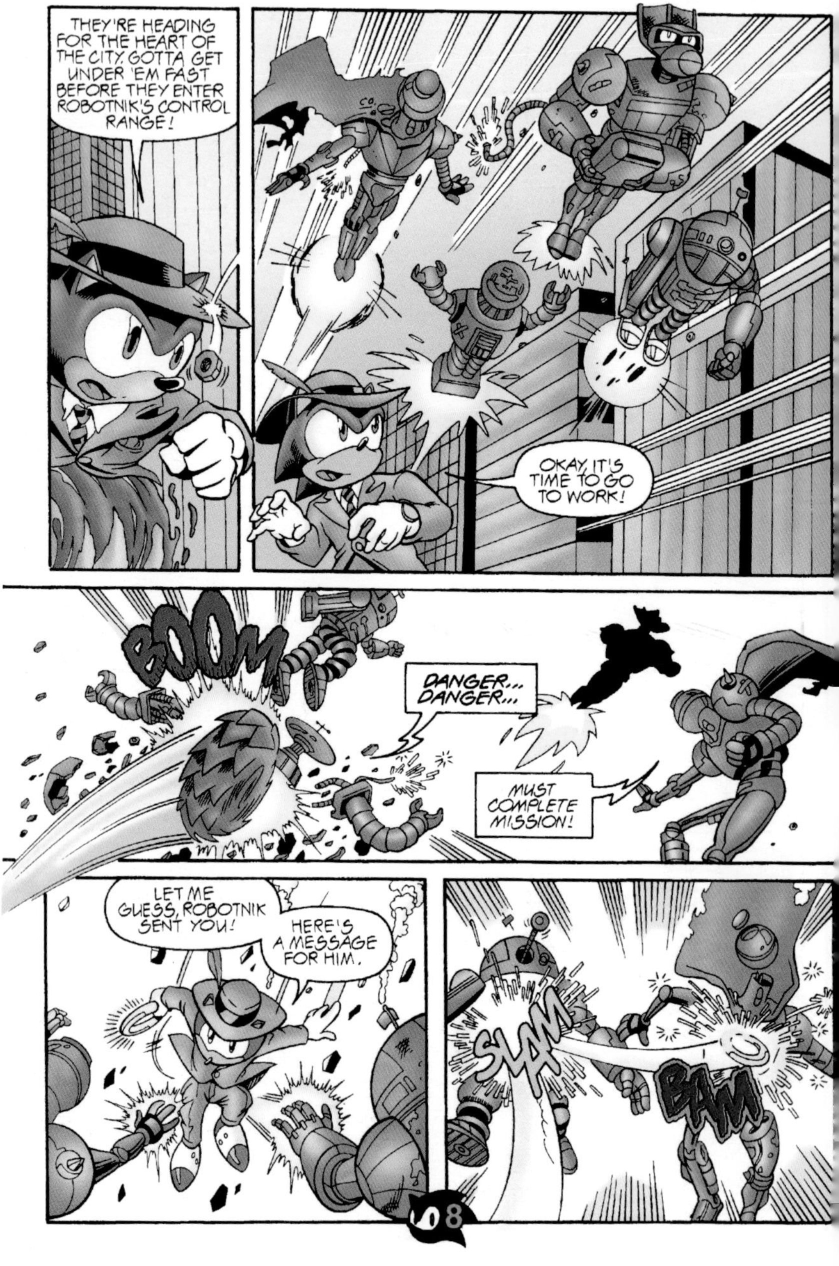
THEY'RE HEADING FOR THE HEART OF THE CITY. GOTTA GET UNDER 'EM FAST BEFORE THEY ENTER ROBOTNIK'S CONTROL RANGE!
OKAY, IT'S TIME TO GO TO WORK!
BOOM
DANGER... DANGER...
MUST COMPLETE MISSION!
LET ME GUESS, ROBOTNIK SENT YOU!
HERE'S A MESSAGE FOR HIM.
SLAM
BAM

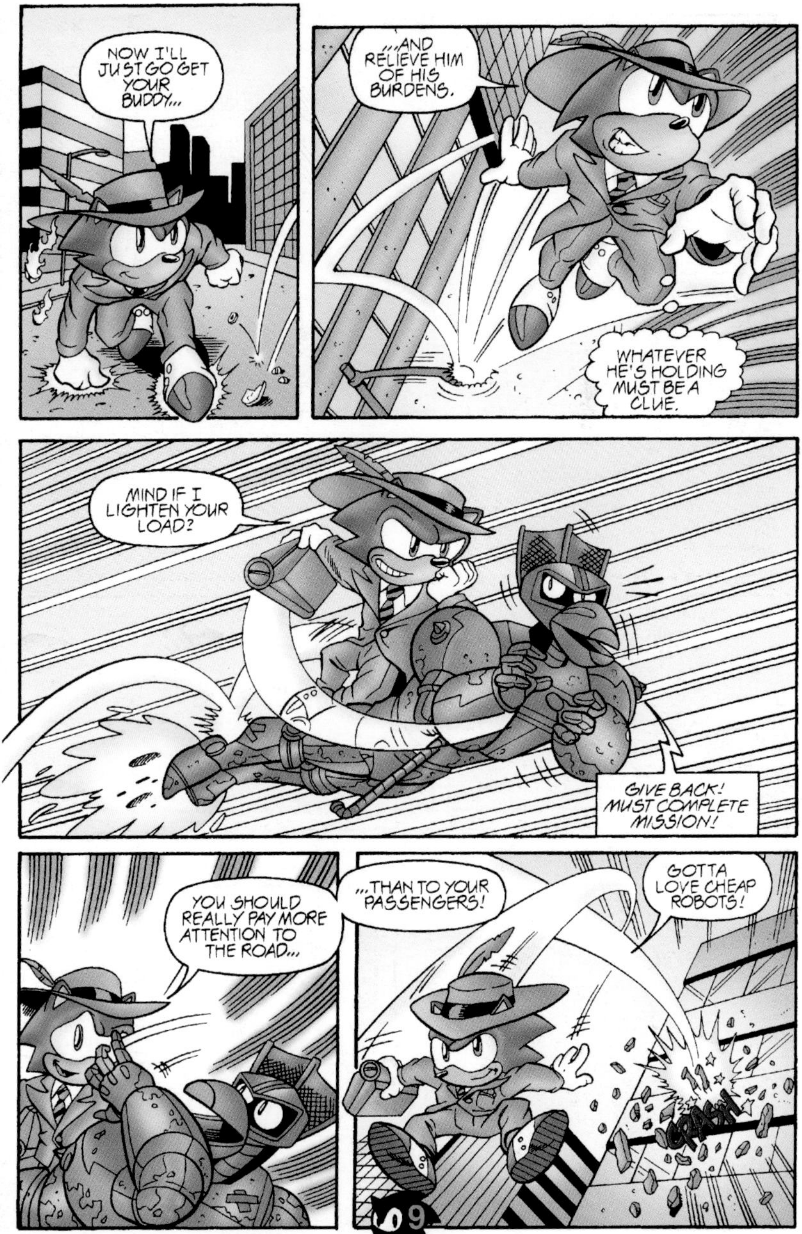
NOW I'LL JUST GO GET YOUR BUDDY...
...AND RELIEVE HIM OF HIS BURDENS.
WHATEVER HE'S HOLDING MUST BE A CLUE.
MIND IF I LIGHTEN YOUR LOAD?
GIVE BACK! MUST COMPLETE MISSION!
YOU SHOULD REALLY PAY MORE ATTENTION TO THE ROAD...
...THAN TO YOUR PASSENGERS!
GOTTA LOVE CHEAP ROBOTS!
CRASH

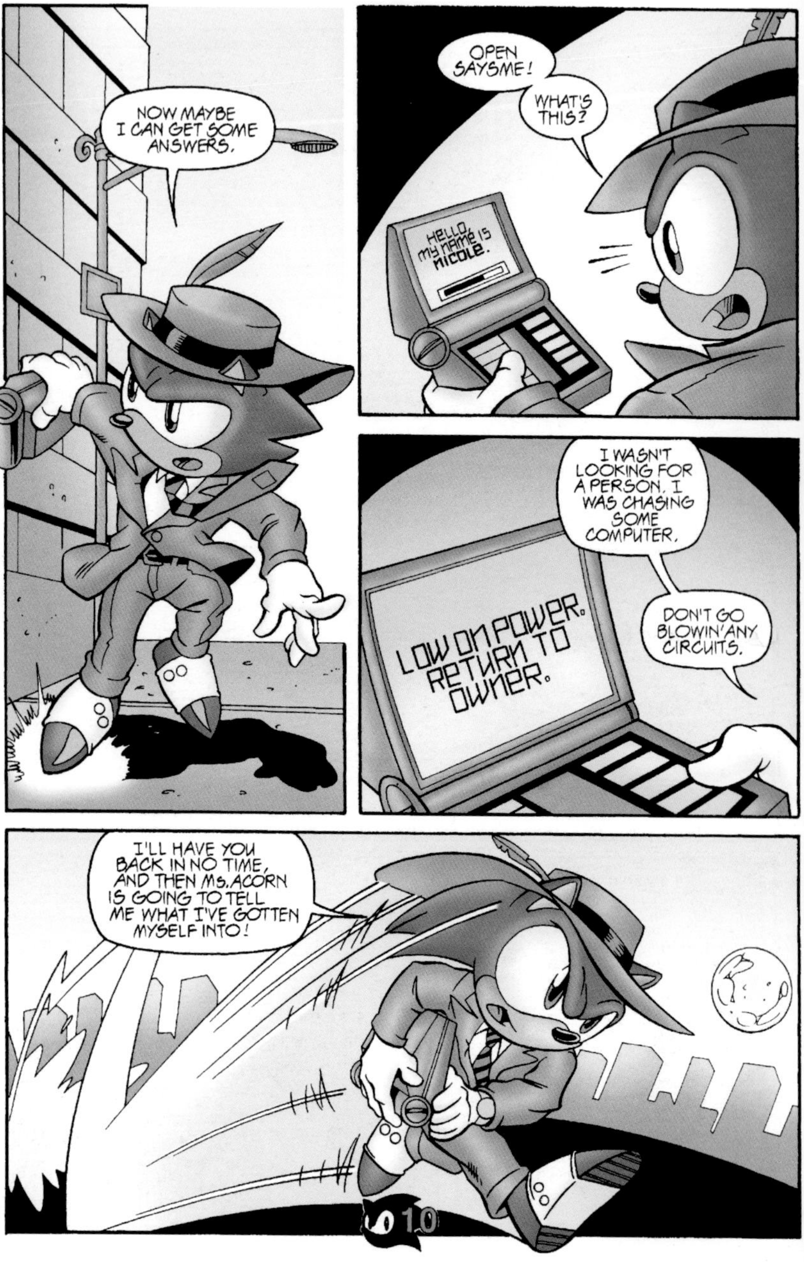
NOW MAYBE I CAN GET SOME ANSWERS.
OPEN SAYSME!
WHAT'S THIS?
HELLO, my name is NICOLE.
I WASN'T LOOKING FOR A PERSON. I WAS CHASING SOME COMPUTER.
LOW ON POWER. RETURN TO OWNER.
DON'T GO BLOWIN' ANY CIRCUITS.
I'LL HAVE YOU BACK IN NO TIME, AND THEN Ms. ACORN IS GOING TO TELL ME WHAT I'VE GOTTEN MYSELF INTO!

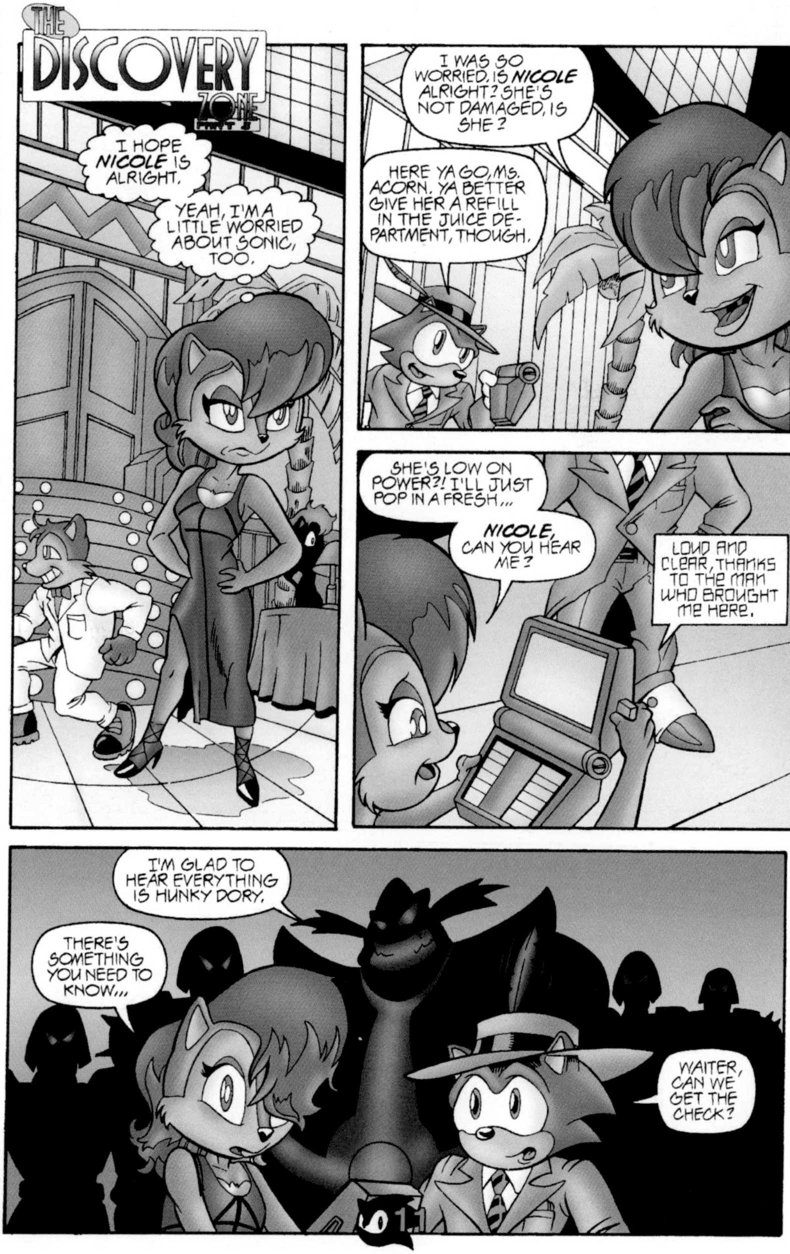
THE DISCOVERY ZONE
I HOPE NICOLE IS ALRIGHT.
YEAH, I'M A LITTLE WORRIED ABOUT SONIC, TOO.
I WAS SO WORRIED. IS NICOLE ALRIGHT? SHE'S NOT DAMAGED, IS SHE?
HERE YA GO, MS. ACORN. YA BETTER GIVE HER A REFILL IN THE JUICE DE-PARTMENT, THOUGH.
SHE'S LOW ON POWER?! I'LL JUST POP IN A FRESH...
NICOLE, CAN YOU HEAR ME?
LOUD AND CLEAR, THANKS TO THE MAN WHO BROUGHT ME HERE.
I'M GLAD TO HEAR EVERYTHING IS HUNKY DORY.
THERE'S SOMETHING YOU NEED TO KNOW...
WAITER, CAN WE GET THE CHECK?

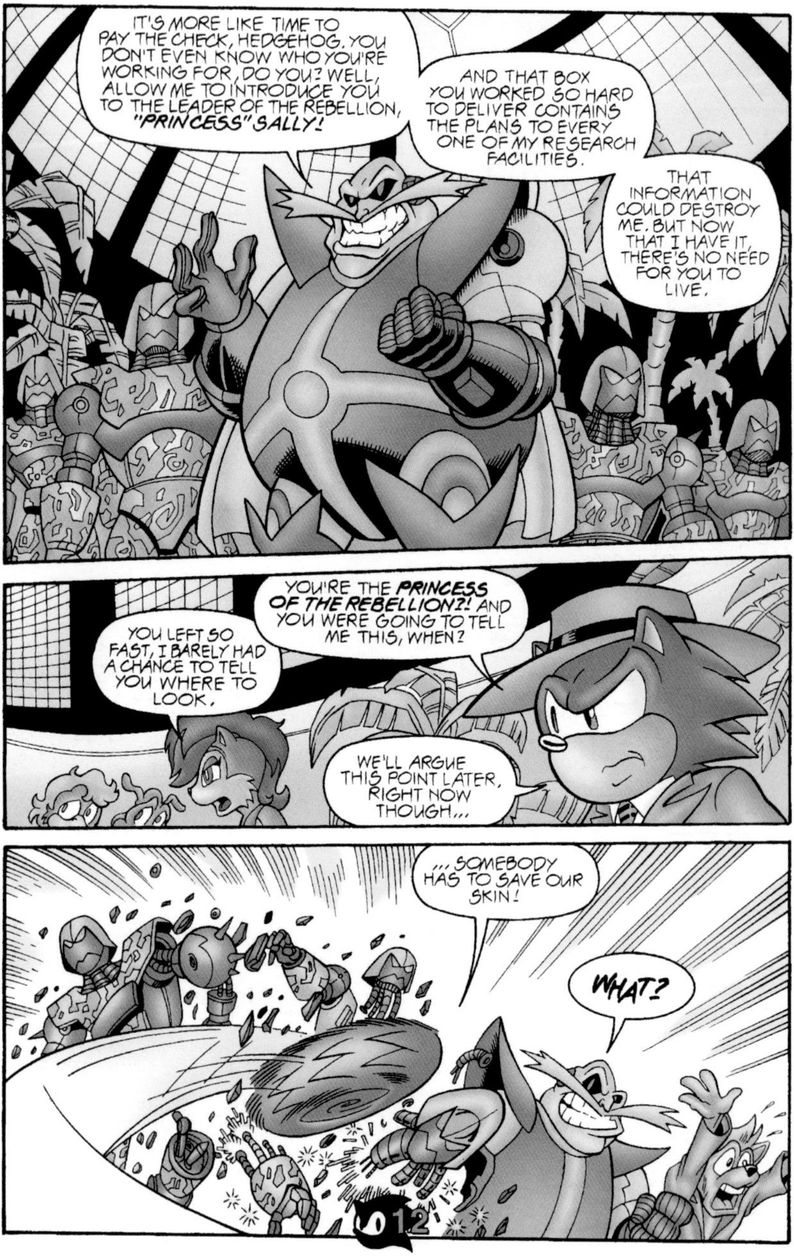
IT'S MORE LIKE TIME TO PAY THE CHECK, HEDGEHOG. YOU DON'T EVEN KNOW WHO YOU'RE WORKING FOR, DO YOU? WELL, ALLOW ME TO INTRODUCE YOU TO THE LEADER OF THE REBELLION, "PRINCESS" SALLY!
AND THAT BOX YOU WORKED SO HARD TO DELIVER CONTAINS THE PLANS TO EVERY ONE OF MY RESEARCH FACILITIES.
THAT INFORMATION COULD DESTROY ME. BUT NOW THAT I HAVE IT, THERE'S NO NEED FOR YOU TO LIVE.
YOU'RE THE PRINCESS OF THE REBELLION?! AND YOU WERE GOING TO TELL ME THIS, WHEN?
YOU LEFT SO FAST, I BARELY HAD A CHANCE TO TELL YOU WHERE TO LOOK.
WE'LL ARGUE THIS POINT LATER, RIGHT NOW THOUGH...
...SOMEBODY HAS TO SAVE OUR SKIN!
WHAT?

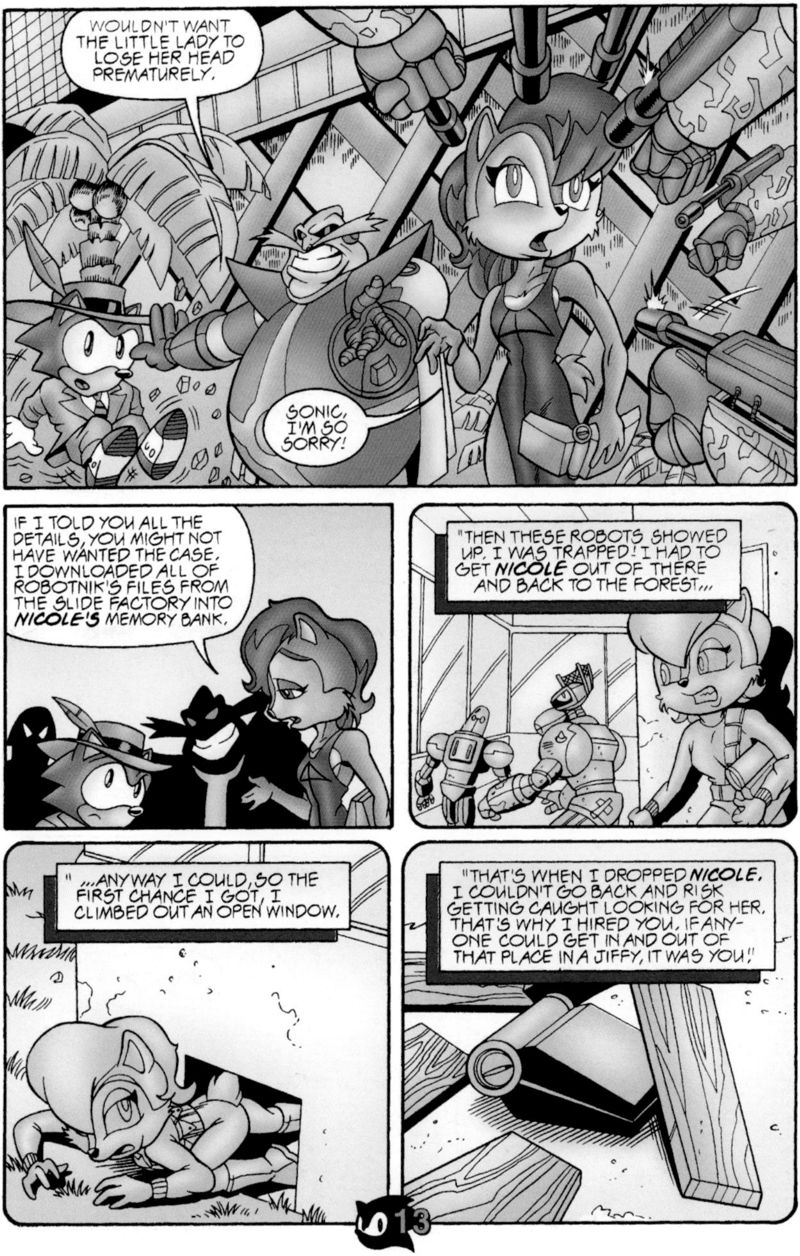
WOULDN'T WANT THE LITTLE LADY TO LOSE HER HEAD PREMATURELY.
SONIC, I'M SO SORRY!
IF I TOLD YOU ALL THE DETAILS, YOU MIGHT NOT HAVE WANTED THE CASE. I DOWNLOADED ALL OF ROBOTNIK'S FILES FROM THE SLIDE FACTORY INTO NICOLE'S MEMORY BANK.
"THEN THESE ROBOTS SHOWED UP. I WAS TRAPPED! I HAD TO GET NICOLE OUT OF THERE AND BACK TO THE FOREST...
"...ANYWAY I COULD, SO THE FIRST CHANCE I GOT, I CLIMBED OUT AN OPEN WINDOW.
"THAT'S WHEN I DROPPED NICOLE. I COULDN'T GO BACK AND RISK GETTING CAUGHT LOOKING FOR HER. THAT'S WHY I HIRED YOU. IF ANYONE COULD GET IN AND OUT OF THAT PLACE IN A JIFFY, IT WAS YOU!"

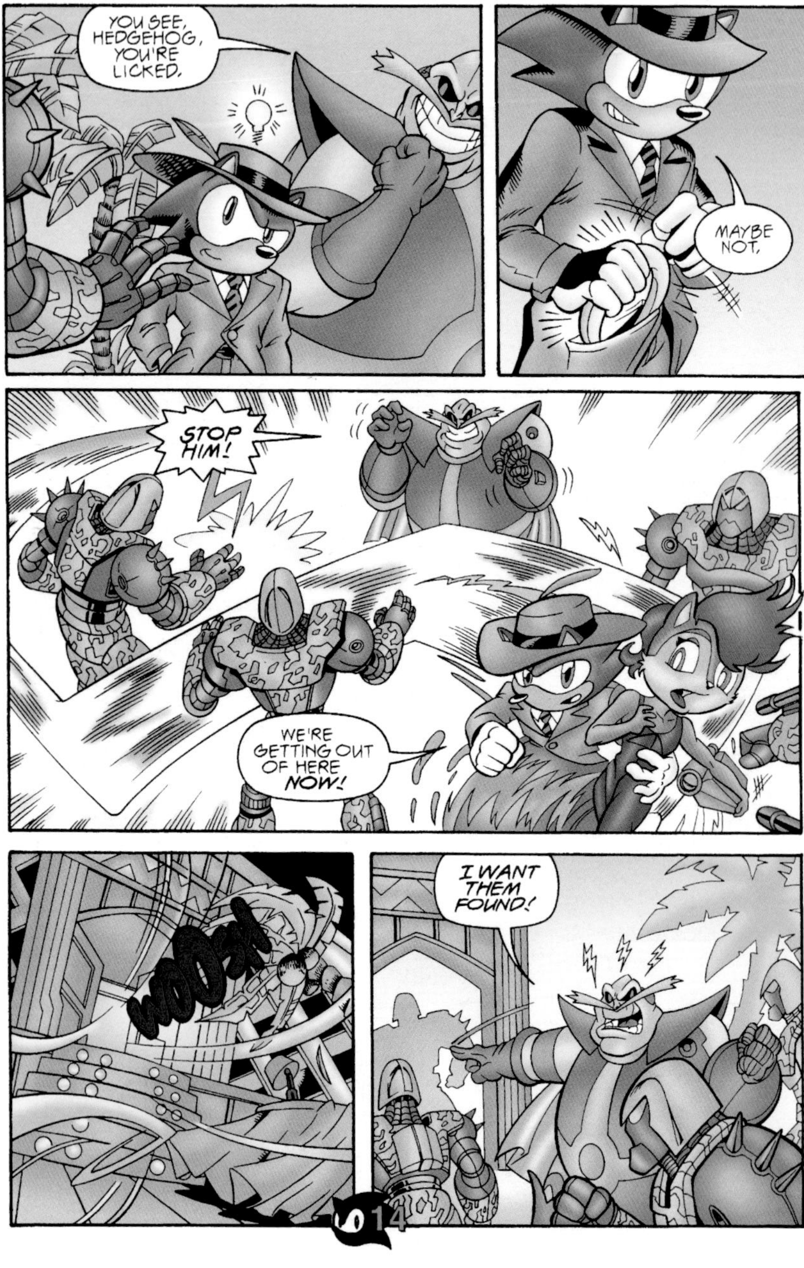
YOU SEE, HEDGEHOG, YOU'RE LICKED.
MAYBE NOT.
STOP HIM!
WE'RE GETTING OUT OF HERE NOW!
I WANT THEM FOUND!

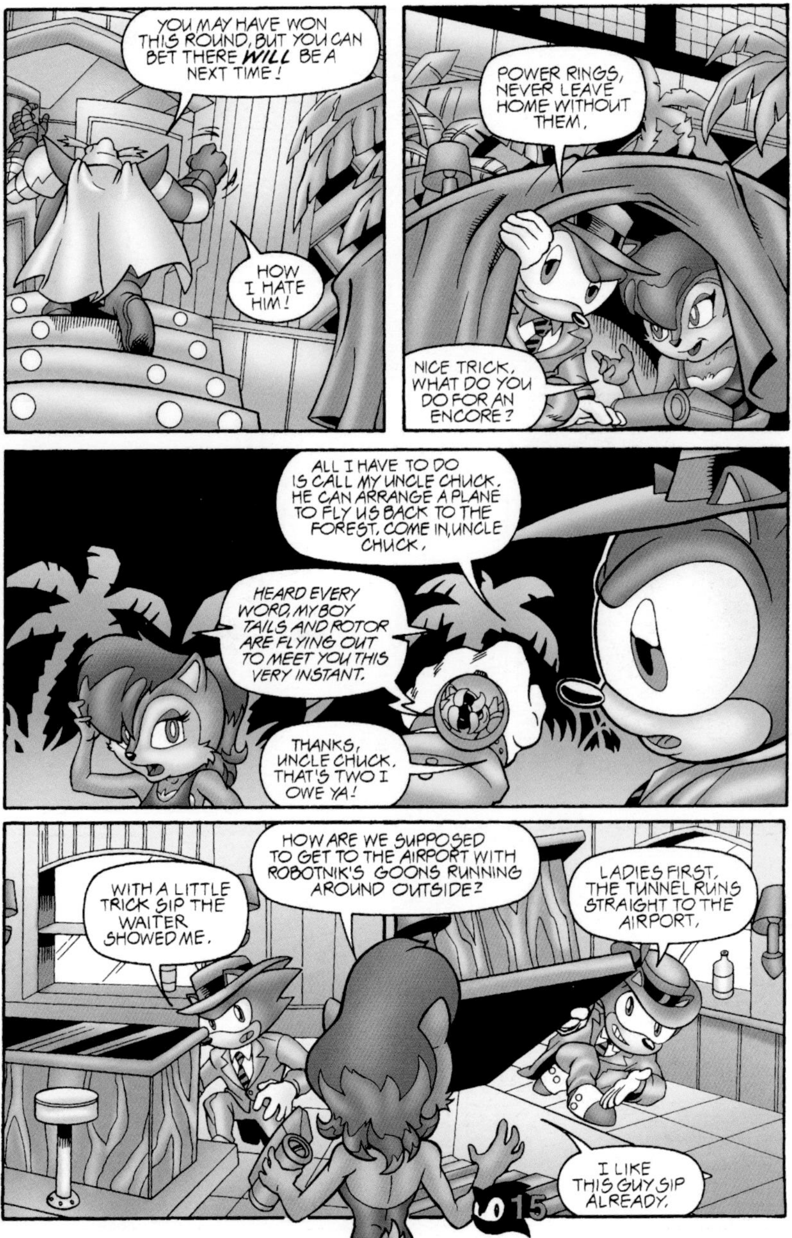
YOU MAY HAVE WON THIS ROUND, BUT YOU CAN BET THERE WILL BE A NEXT TIME!
HOW I HATE HIM!
POWER RINGS, NEVER LEAVE HOME WITHOUT THEM.
NICE TRICK, WHAT DO YOU DO FOR AN ENCORE?
ALL I HAVE TO DO IS CALL MY UNCLE CHUCK. HE CAN ARRANGE A PLANE TO FLY US BACK TO THE FOREST. COME IN, UNCLE CHUCK.
HEARD EVERY WORD, MY BOY. TAILS AND ROTOR ARE FLYING OUT TO MEET YOU THIS VERY INSTANT.
THANKS, UNCLE CHUCK. THAT'S TWO I OWE YA!
HOW ARE WE SUPPOSED TO GET TO THE AIRPORT WITH ROBOTNIK'S GOONS RUNNING AROUND OUTSIDE?
WITH A LITTLE TRICK SIP THE WAITER SHOWED ME.
LADIES FIRST. THE TUNNEL RUNS STRAIGHT TO THE AIRPORT.
I LIKE THIS GUY SIP ALREADY.

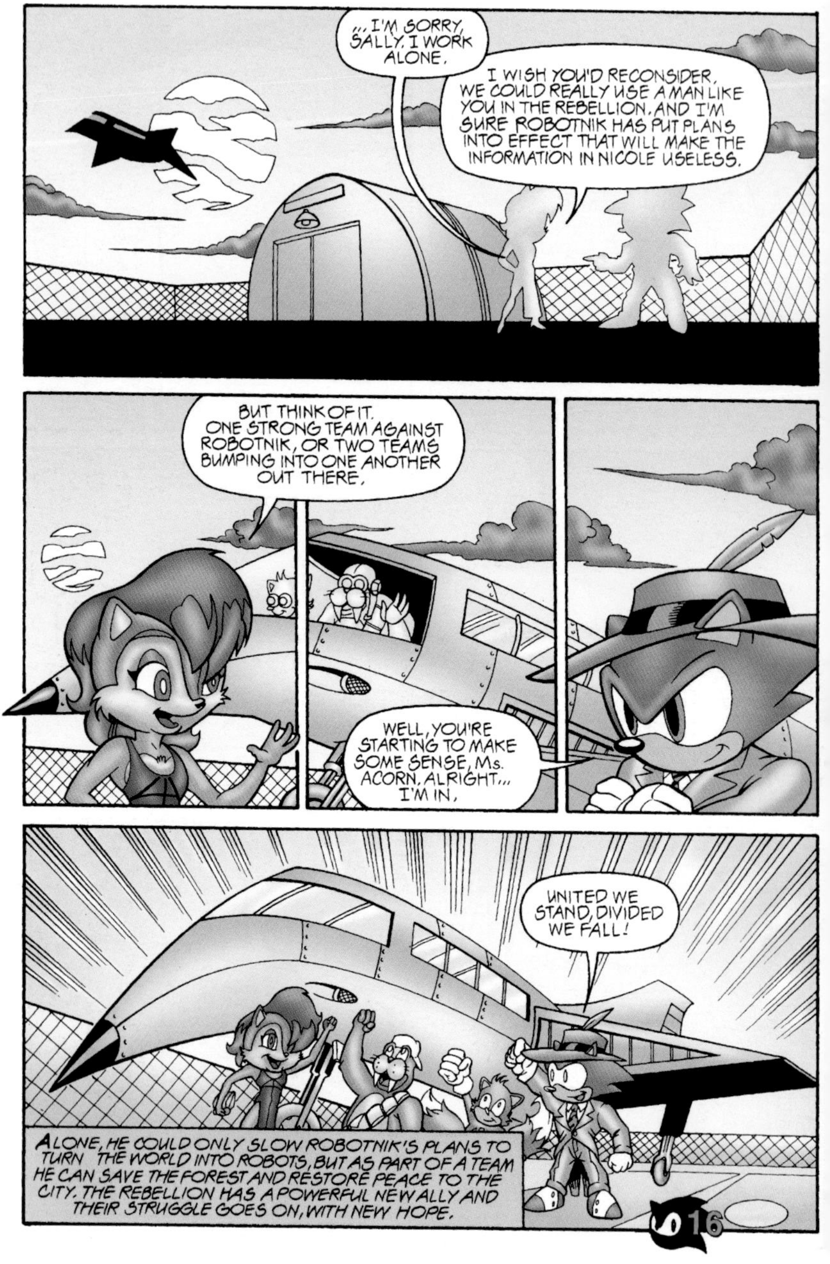
...I'M SORRY, SALLY. I WORK ALONE.
I WISH YOU'D RECONSIDER. WE COULD REALLY USE A MAN LIKE YOU IN THE REBELLION. AND I'M SURE ROBOTNIK HAS PUT PLANS INTO EFFECT THAT WILL MAKE THE INFORMATION IN NICOLE USELESS.
BUT THINK OF IT. ONE STRONG TEAM AGAINST ROBOTNIK, OR TWO TEAMS BUMPING INTO ONE ANOTHER OUT THERE.
WELL, YOU'RE STARTING TO MAKE SOME SENSE, Ms. ACORN. ALRIGHT... I'M IN.
UNITED WE STAND, DIVIDED WE FALL!
ALONE, HE COULD ONLY SLOW ROBOTNIK'S PLANS TO TURN THE WORLD INTO ROBOTS, BUT AS PART OF A TEAM HE CAN SAVE THE FOREST AND RESTORE PEACE TO THE CITY. THE REBELLION HAS A POWERFUL NEW ALLY AND THEIR STRUGGLE GOES ON, WITH NEW HOPE.

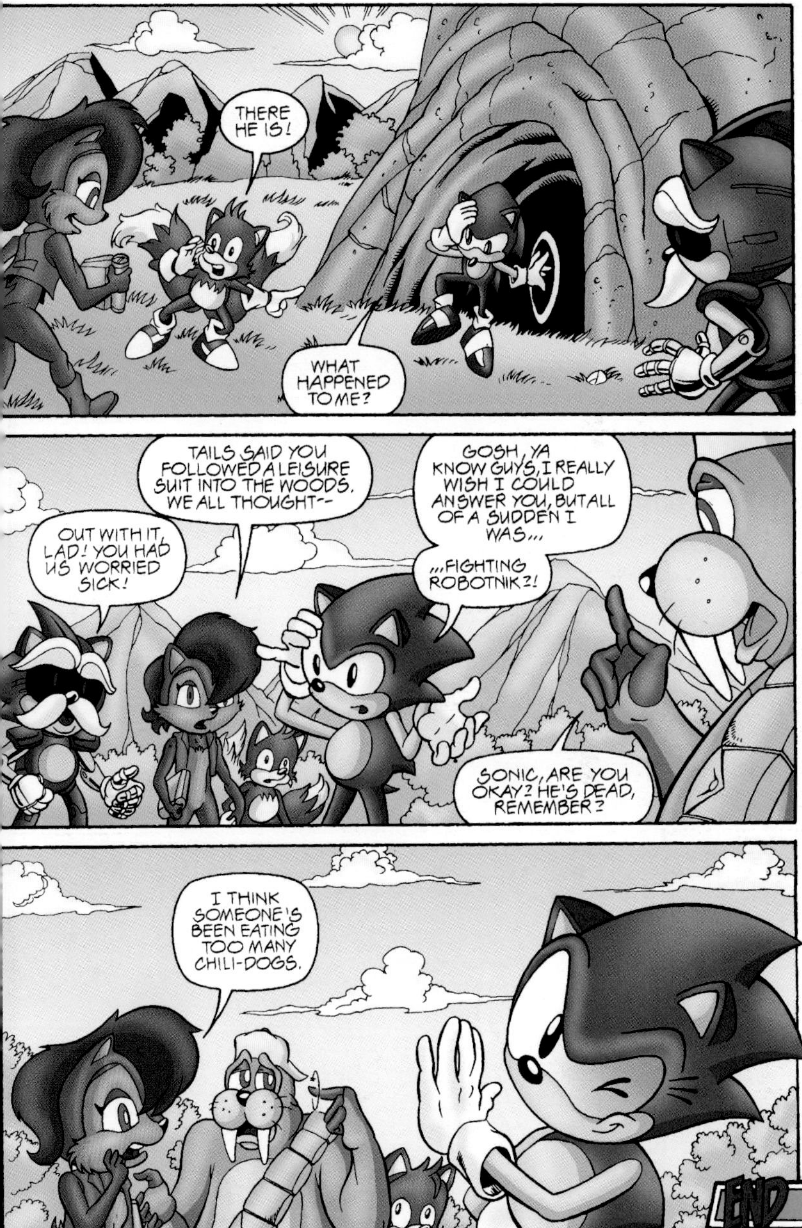

THERE HE IS!
WHAT HAPPENED TO ME?
TAILS SAID YOU FOLLOWED A LEISURE SUIT INTO THE WOODS. WE ALL THOUGHT--
OUT WITH IT, LAD! YOU HAD US WORRIED SICK!
GOSH, YA KNOW GUYS, I REALLY WISH I COULD ANSWER YOU, BUT ALL OF A SUDDEN I WAS...
...FIGHTING ROBOTNIK?!
SONIC, ARE YOU OKAY? HE'S DEAD, REMEMBER?
I THINK SOMEONE'S BEEN EATING TOO MANY CHILI-DOGS.
END

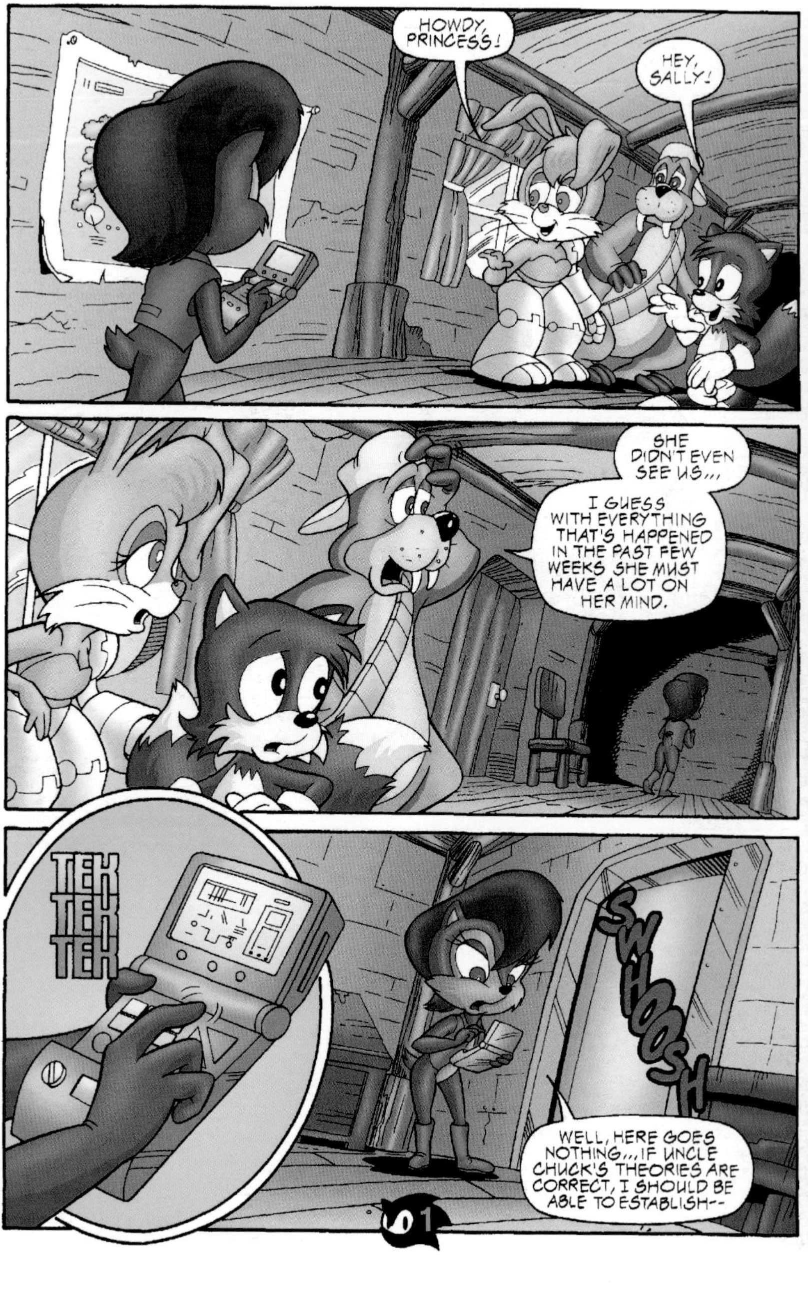
HOWDY, PRINCESS!
HEY, SALLY!
SHE DIDN'T EVEN SEE US...
I GUESS WITH EVERYTHING THAT'S HAPPENED IN THE PAST FEW WEEKS SHE MUST HAVE A LOT ON HER MIND.
TEK TEK TEK
SWHOOSH
WELL, HERE GOES NOTHING...IF UNCLE CHUCK'S THEORIES ARE CORRECT, I SHOULD BE ABLE TO ESTABLISH--

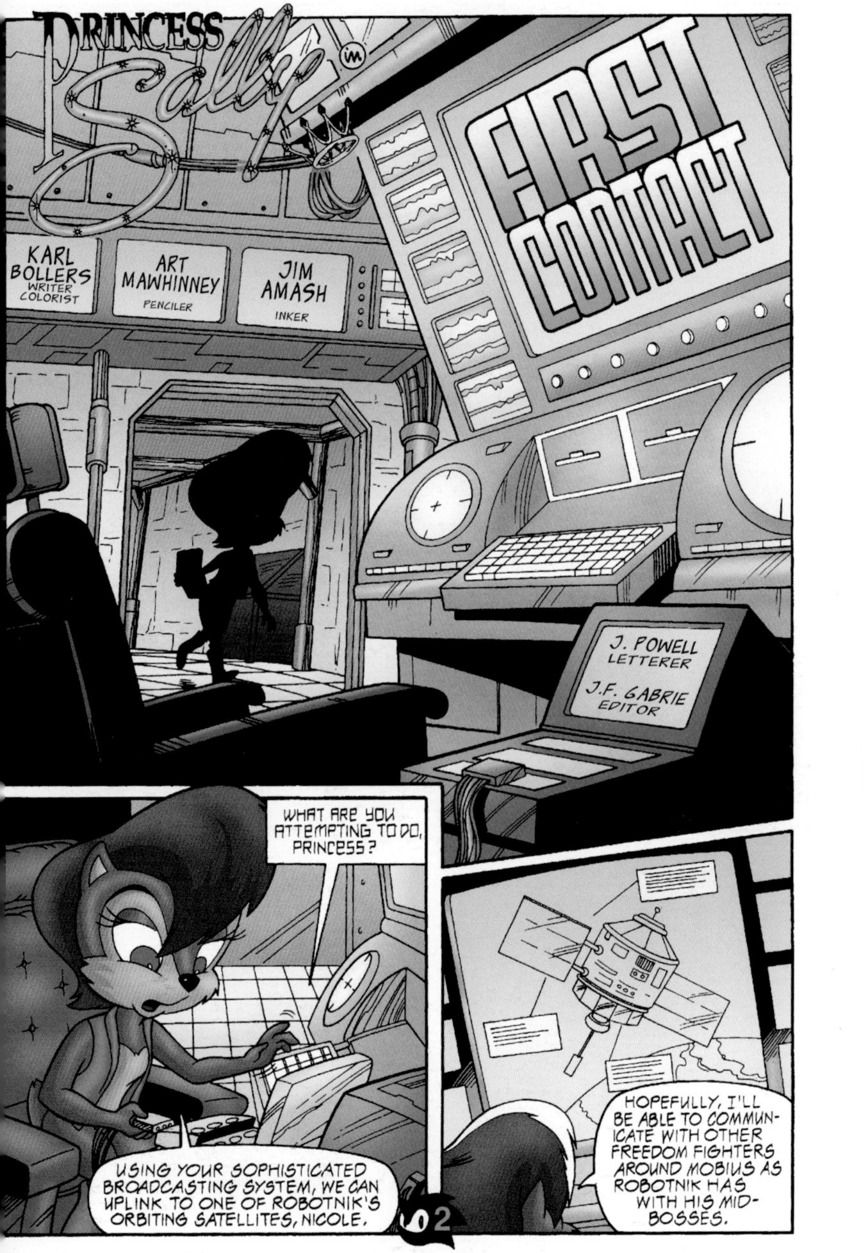
PRINCESS Sally in
FIRST CONTACT
KARL BOLLERS WRITER COLORIST
ART MAWHINNEY PENCILER
JIM AMASH INKER
J. POWELL LETTERER
J.F. GABRIE EDITOR
WHAT ARE YOU ATTEMPTING TO DO, PRINCESS?
USING YOUR SOPHISTICATED BROADCASTING SYSTEM, WE CAN UPLINK TO ONE OF ROBOTNIK'S ORBITING SATELLITES, NICOLE.
HOPEFULLY, I'LL BE ABLE TO COMMUNICATE WITH OTHER FREEDOM FIGHTERS AROUND MOBIUS AS ROBOTNIK HAS WITH HIS MID-BOSSES.

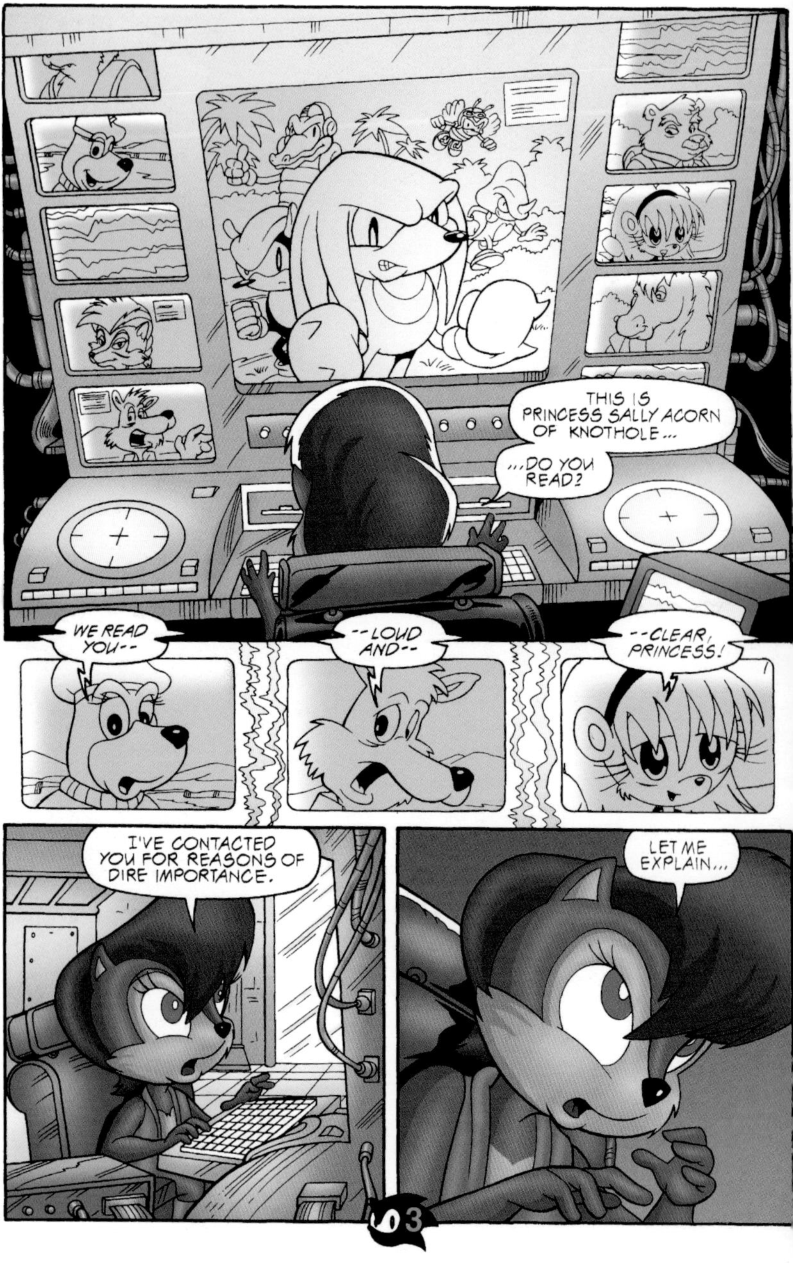
THIS IS PRINCESS SALLY ACORN OF KNOTHOLE...
...DO YOU READ?
WE READ YOU--
--LOUD AND--
--CLEAR, PRINCESS!
I'VE CONTACTED YOU FOR REASONS OF DIRE IMPORTANCE.
LET ME EXPLAIN...

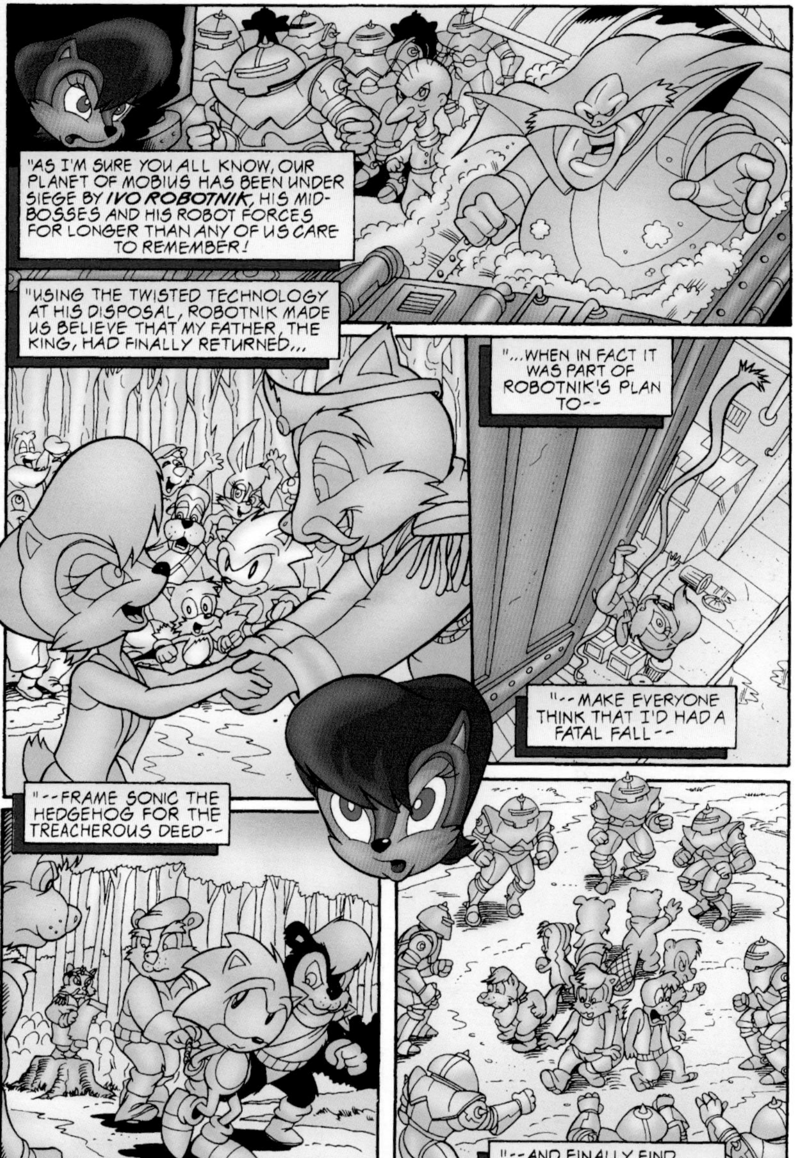
"AS I'M SURE YOU ALL KNOW, OUR PLANET OF MOBIUS HAS BEEN UNDER SIEGE BY IVO ROBOTNIK, HIS MID-BOSSES AND HIS ROBOT FORCES FOR LONGER THAN ANY OF US CARE TO REMEMBER!
"USING THE TWISTED TECHNOLOGY AT HIS DISPOSAL, ROBOTNIK MADE US BELIEVE THAT MY FATHER, THE KING, HAD FINALLY RETURNED...
"...WHEN IN FACT IT WAS PART OF ROBOTNIK'S PLAN TO--
"--MAKE EVERYONE THINK THAT I'D HAD A FATAL FALL--
"--FRAME SONIC THE HEDGEHOG FOR THE TREACHEROUS DEED--
"--AND FINALLY FIND AND ENSLAVE KNOTHOLE VILLAGE!"

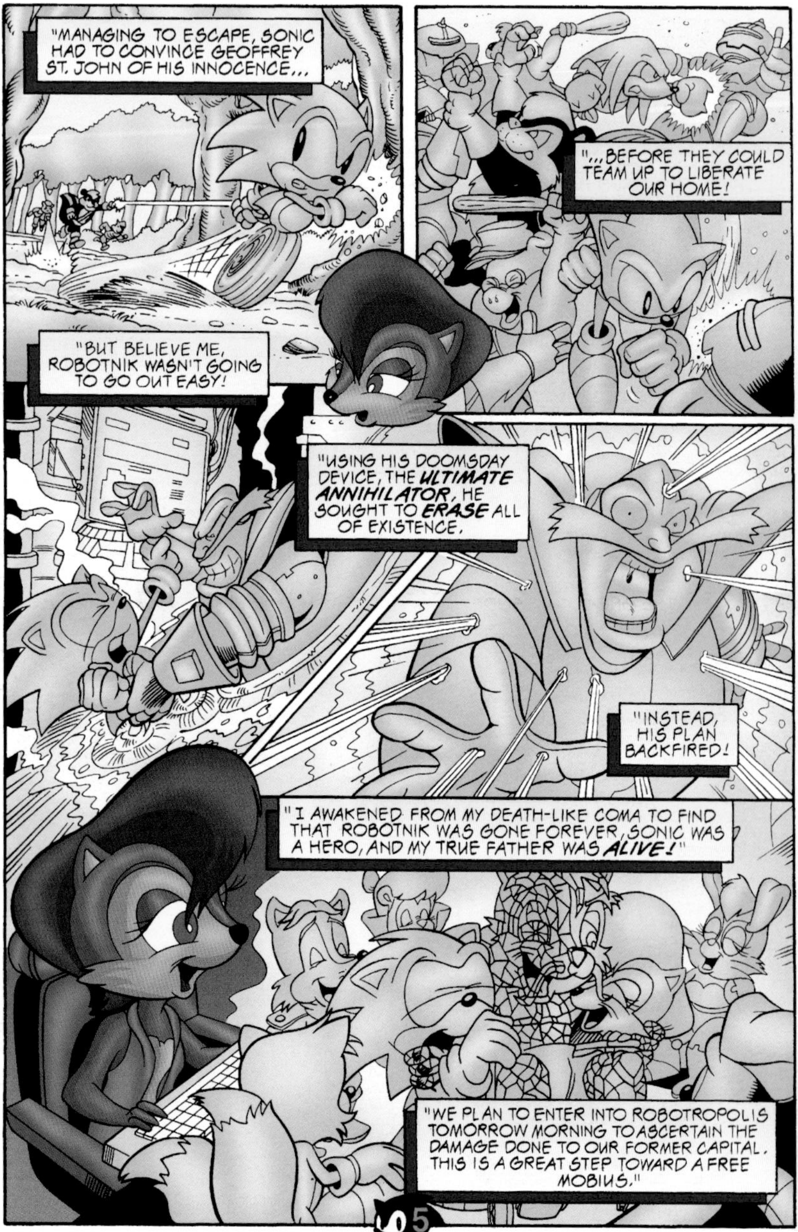
"MANAGING TO ESCAPE, SONIC HAD TO CONVINCE GEOFFREY ST. JOHN OF HIS INNOCENCE...
"...BEFORE THEY COULD TEAM UP TO LIBERATE OUR HOME!
"BUT BELIEVE ME, ROBOTNIK WASN'T GOING TO GO OUT EASY!
"USING HIS DOOMSDAY DEVICE, THE ULTIMATE ANNIHILATOR, HE SOUGHT TO ERASE ALL OF EXISTENCE.
"INSTEAD, HIS PLAN BACKFIRED!
"I AWAKENED FROM MY DEATH-LIKE COMA TO FIND THAT ROBOTNIK WAS GONE FOREVER, SONIC WAS A HERO, AND MY TRUE FATHER WAS ALIVE!"
"WE PLAN TO ENTER INTO ROBOTROPOLIS TOMORROW MORNING TO ASCERTAIN THE DAMAGE DONE TO OUR FORMER CAPITAL. THIS IS A GREAT STEP TOWARD A FREE MOBIUS."

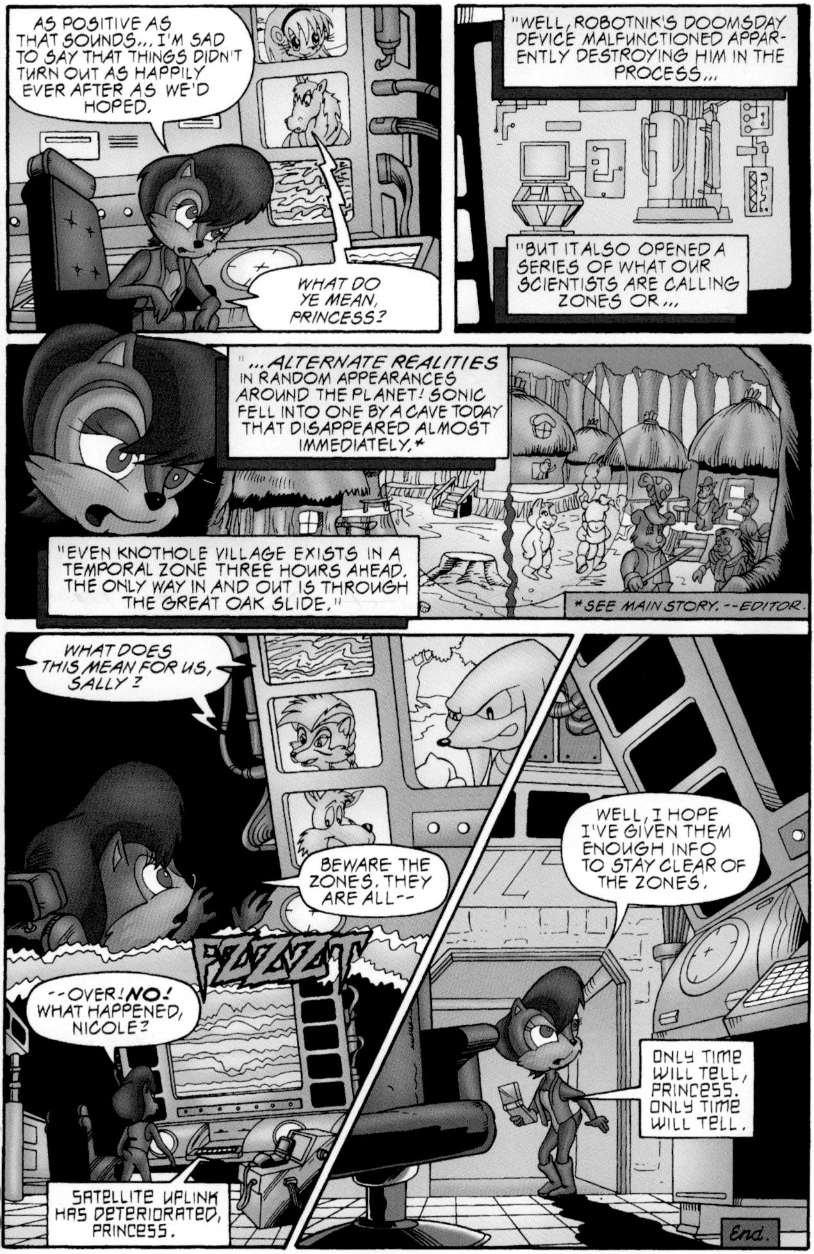

AS POSITIVE AS THAT SOUNDS... I'M SAD TO SAY THAT THINGS DIDN'T TURN OUT AS HAPPILY EVER AFTER AS WE'D HOPED.
WHAT DO YE MEAN, PRINCESS?
"WELL, ROBOTNIK'S DOOMSDAY DEVICE MALFUNCTIONED APPARENTLY DESTROYING HIM IN THE PROCESS...
"BUT IT ALSO OPENED A SERIES OF WHAT OUR SCIENTISTS ARE CALLING ZONES OR...
"...ALTERNATE REALITIES IN RANDOM APPEARANCES AROUND THE PLANET! SONIC FELL INTO ONE BY A CAVE TODAY THAT DISAPPEARED ALMOST IMMEDIATELY.*
"EVEN KNOTHOLE VILLAGE EXISTS IN A TEMPORAL ZONE THREE HOURS AHEAD. THE ONLY WAY IN AND OUT IS THROUGH THE GREAT OAK SLIDE."
*SEE MAIN STORY. --EDITOR.
WHAT DOES THIS MEAN FOR US, SALLY?
BEWARE THE ZONES. THEY ARE ALL--
FZZZZT
--OVER! NO! WHAT HAPPENED, NICOLE?
SATELLITE UPLINK HAS DETERIORATED, PRINCESS.
WELL, I HOPE I'VE GIVEN THEM ENOUGH INFO TO STAY CLEAR OF THE ZONES.
ONLY TIME WILL TELL, PRINCESS. ONLY TIME WILL TELL.
End.

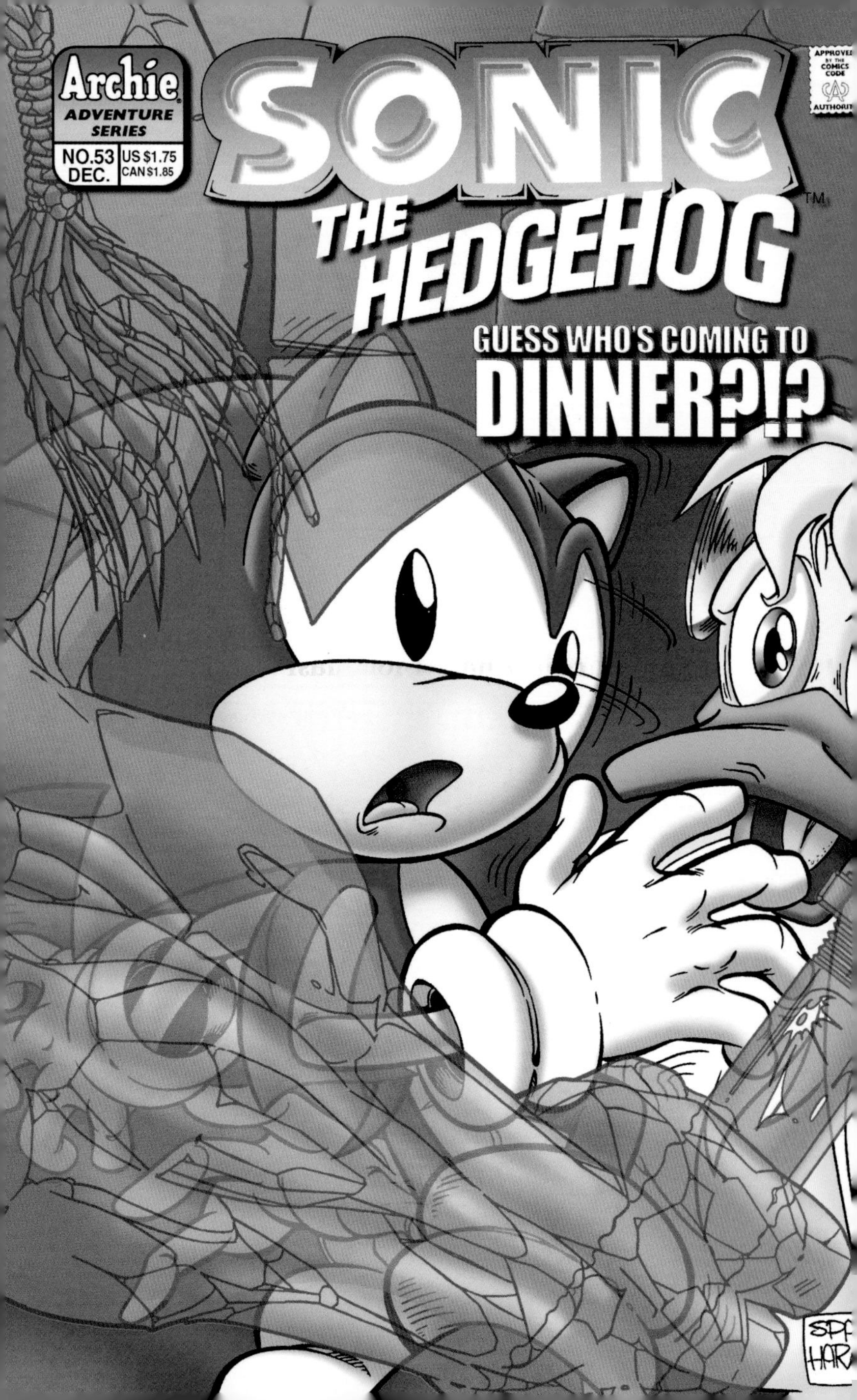

Archie
ADVENTURE SERIES
NO.53 DEC.
US $1.75 CAN $1.85
SONIC THE HEDGEHOG™
GUESS WHO'S COMING TO DINNER?!?
APPROVED BY THE COMICS CODE AUTHORITY

Once a virtual paradise, the planet Mobius was enslaved when conquered by the techno-evil of Doctor Robotnik. In the aftermath, a courageous group of "Freedom Fighters" has risen to restore the order and beauty that was once theirs. The greatest among them is the fastest and way-coolest dude on two feet... SONIC THE HEDGEHOG!

Now war-time has at long last ended and a brave new world has started to emerge. Its emergence, however, isn't easy. Especially in the city of Mobotropolis. Before the Knothole Villagers can transport themselves here, The Freedom Fighters begin their awesome task of dismantling the fiendish devices left by Robotnik as a safety precaution. Little do they know of the secrets they will unleash. Secrets of a past best left forgotten!

Especially for one King Acorn...

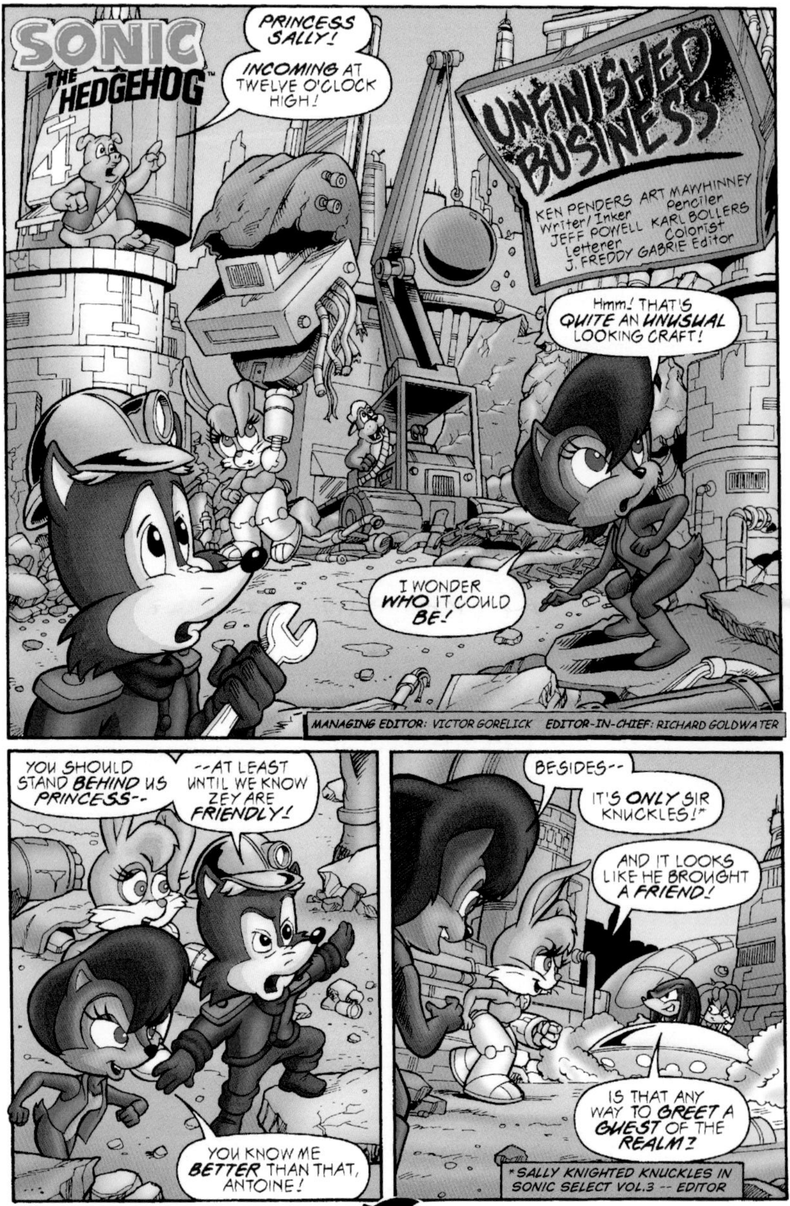
SONIC THE HEDGEHOG
PRINCESS SALLY!
INCOMING AT TWELVE O'CLOCK HIGH!
UNFINISHED BUSINESS
KEN PENDERS Writer/Inker ART MAWHINNEY Penciler JEFF POWELL Letterer KARL BOLLERS Colorist J. FREDDY GABRIE Editor
Hmm! THAT'S QUITE AN UNUSUAL LOOKING CRAFT!
I WONDER WHO IT COULD BE!
MANAGING EDITOR: VICTOR GORELICK EDITOR-IN-CHIEF: RICHARD GOLDWATER
YOU SHOULD STAND BEHIND US PRINCESS--
--AT LEAST UNTIL WE KNOW ZEY ARE FRIENDLY!
YOU KNOW ME BETTER THAN THAT, ANTOINE!
BESIDES--
IT'S ONLY SIR KNUCKLES!*
AND IT LOOKS LIKE HE BROUGHT A FRIEND!
IS THAT ANY WAY TO GREET A GUEST OF THE REALM?
*SALLY KNIGHTED KNUCKLES IN SONIC SELECT VOL.3 -- EDITOR

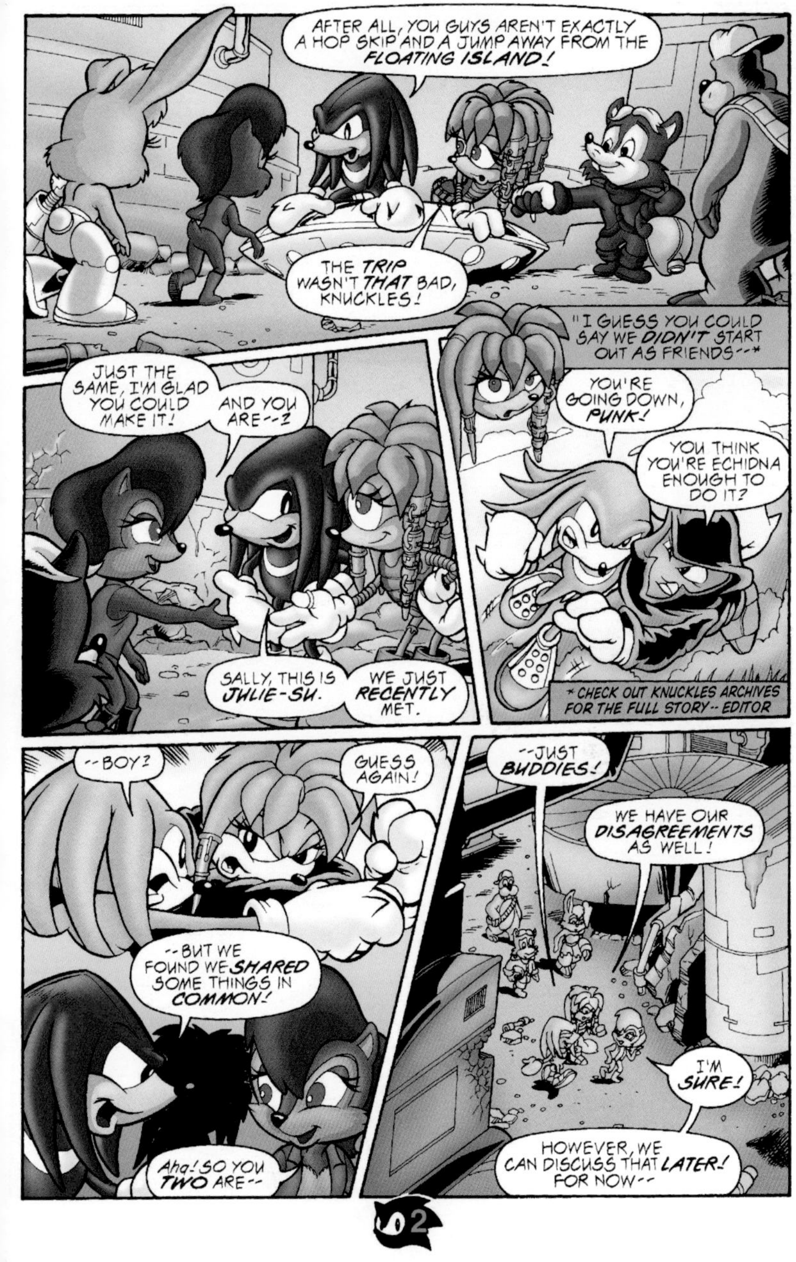
AFTER ALL, YOU GUYS AREN'T EXACTLY A HOP SKIP AND A JUMP AWAY FROM THE FLOATING ISLAND!
THE TRIP WASN'T THAT BAD, KNUCKLES!
JUST THE SAME, I'M GLAD YOU COULD MAKE IT!
AND YOU ARE--?
SALLY, THIS IS JULIE-SU.
WE JUST RECENTLY MET.
"I GUESS YOU COULD SAY WE DIDN'T START OUT AS FRIENDS--*
YOU'RE GOING DOWN, PUNK!
YOU THINK YOU'RE ECHIDNA ENOUGH TO DO IT?
* CHECK OUT KNUCKLES ARCHIVES FOR THE FULL STORY-- EDITOR
--BOY?
GUESS AGAIN!
--BUT WE FOUND WE SHARED SOME THINGS IN COMMON!
Aha! SO YOU TWO ARE--
--JUST BUDDIES!
WE HAVE OUR DISAGREEMENTS AS WELL!
I'M SURE!
HOWEVER, WE CAN DISCUSS THAT LATER! FOR NOW--

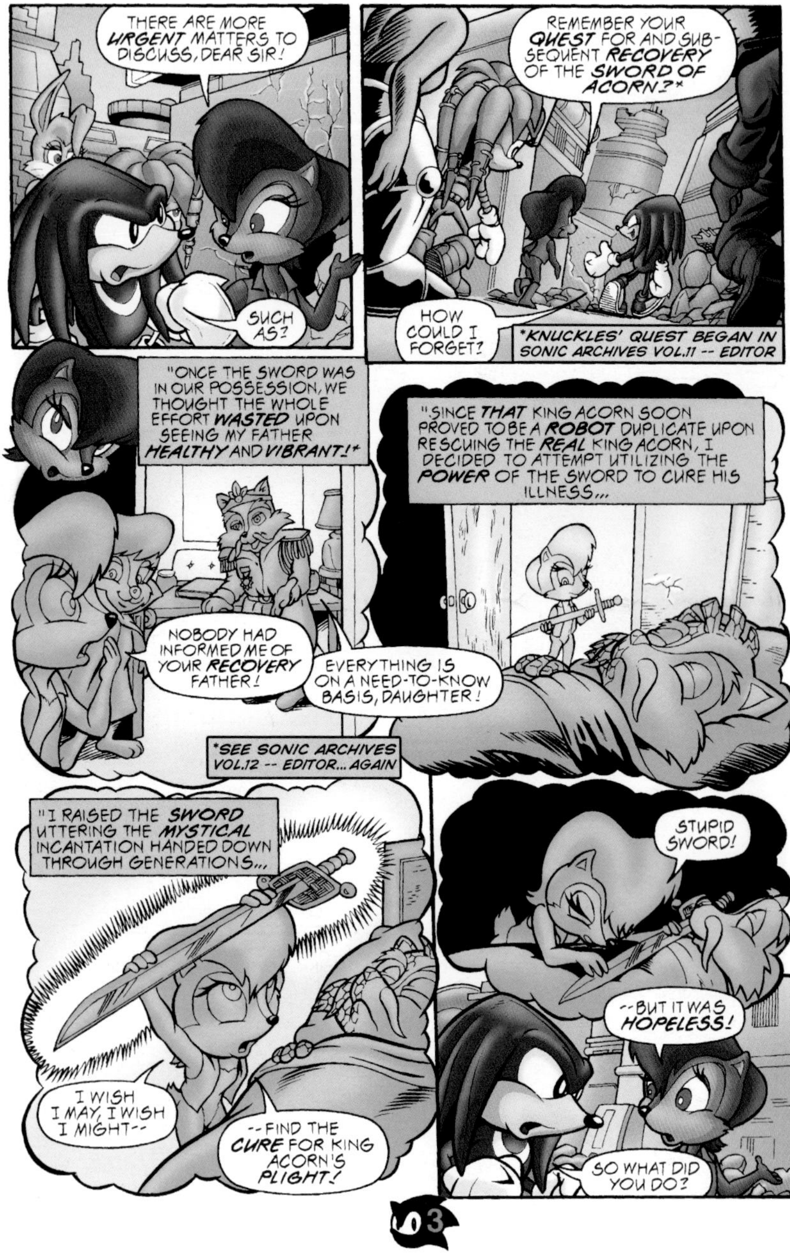
THERE ARE MORE URGENT MATTERS TO DISCUSS, DEAR SIR!
SUCH AS?
REMEMBER YOUR QUEST FOR AND SUB-SEQUENT RECOVERY OF THE SWORD OF ACORN?*
HOW COULD I FORGET?
*KNUCKLES' QUEST BEGAN IN SONIC ARCHIVES VOL.11 -- EDITOR
"ONCE THE SWORD WAS IN OUR POSSESSION, WE THOUGHT THE WHOLE EFFORT WASTED UPON SEEING MY FATHER HEALTHY AND VIBRANT!*
NOBODY HAD INFORMED ME OF YOUR RECOVERY FATHER!
EVERYTHING IS ON A NEED-TO-KNOW BASIS, DAUGHTER!
*SEE SONIC ARCHIVES VOL.12 -- EDITOR... AGAIN
"SINCE THAT KING ACORN SOON PROVED TO BE A ROBOT DUPLICATE UPON RESCUING THE REAL KING ACORN, I DECIDED TO ATTEMPT UTILIZING THE POWER OF THE SWORD TO CURE HIS ILLNESS...
"I RAISED THE SWORD UTTERING THE MYSTICAL INCANTATION HANDED DOWN THROUGH GENERATIONS...
I WISH I MAY, I WISH I MIGHT--
--FIND THE CURE FOR KING ACORN'S PLIGHT!
STUPID SWORD!
--BUT IT WAS HOPELESS!
SO WHAT DID YOU DO?

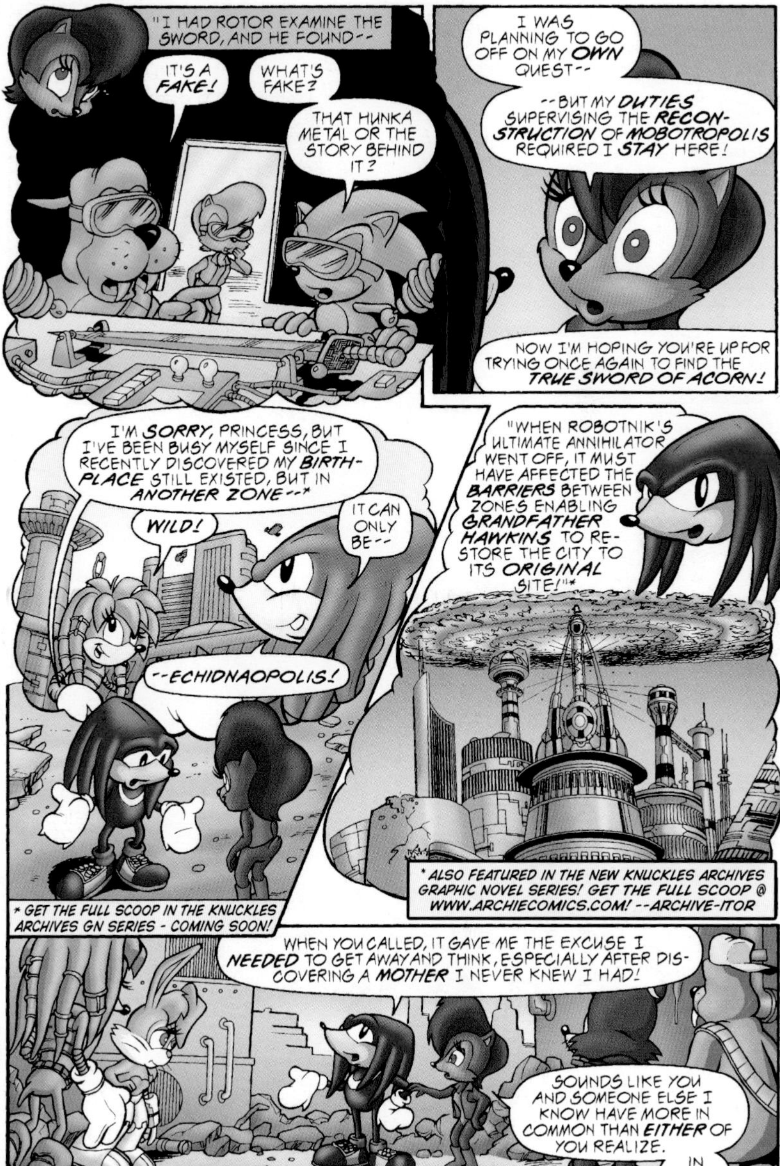
"I HAD ROTOR EXAMINE THE SWORD, AND HE FOUND--
IT'S A FAKE!
WHAT'S FAKE?
THAT HUNKA METAL OR THE STORY BEHIND IT?
I WAS PLANNING TO GO OFF ON MY OWN QUEST--
--BUT MY DUTIES SUPERVISING THE RECONSTRUCTION OF MOBOTROPOLIS REQUIRED I STAY HERE!
NOW I'M HOPING YOU'RE UP FOR TRYING ONCE AGAIN TO FIND THE TRUE SWORD OF ACORN!
I'M SORRY, PRINCESS, BUT I'VE BEEN BUSY MYSELF SINCE I RECENTLY DISCOVERED MY BIRTHPLACE STILL EXISTED, BUT IN ANOTHER ZONE--*
WILD!
IT CAN ONLY BE--
--ECHIDNAOPOLIS!
"WHEN ROBOTNIK'S ULTIMATE ANNIHILATOR WENT OFF, IT MUST HAVE AFFECTED THE BARRIERS BETWEEN ZONES ENABLING GRANDFATHER HAWKINS TO RESTORE THE CITY TO ITS ORIGINAL SITE!"*
* GET THE FULL SCOOP IN THE KNUCKLES ARCHIVES GN SERIES - COMING SOON!
* ALSO FEATURED IN THE NEW KNUCKLES ARCHIVES GRAPHIC NOVEL SERIES! GET THE FULL SCOOP @ WWW.ARCHIECOMICS.COM! --ARCHIVE-ITOR
WHEN YOU CALLED, IT GAVE ME THE EXCUSE I NEEDED TO GET AWAY AND THINK, ESPECIALLY AFTER DISCOVERING A MOTHER I NEVER KNEW I HAD!
SOUNDS LIKE YOU AND SOMEONE ELSE I KNOW HAVE MORE IN COMMON THAN EITHER OF YOU REALIZE.
IN FACT--

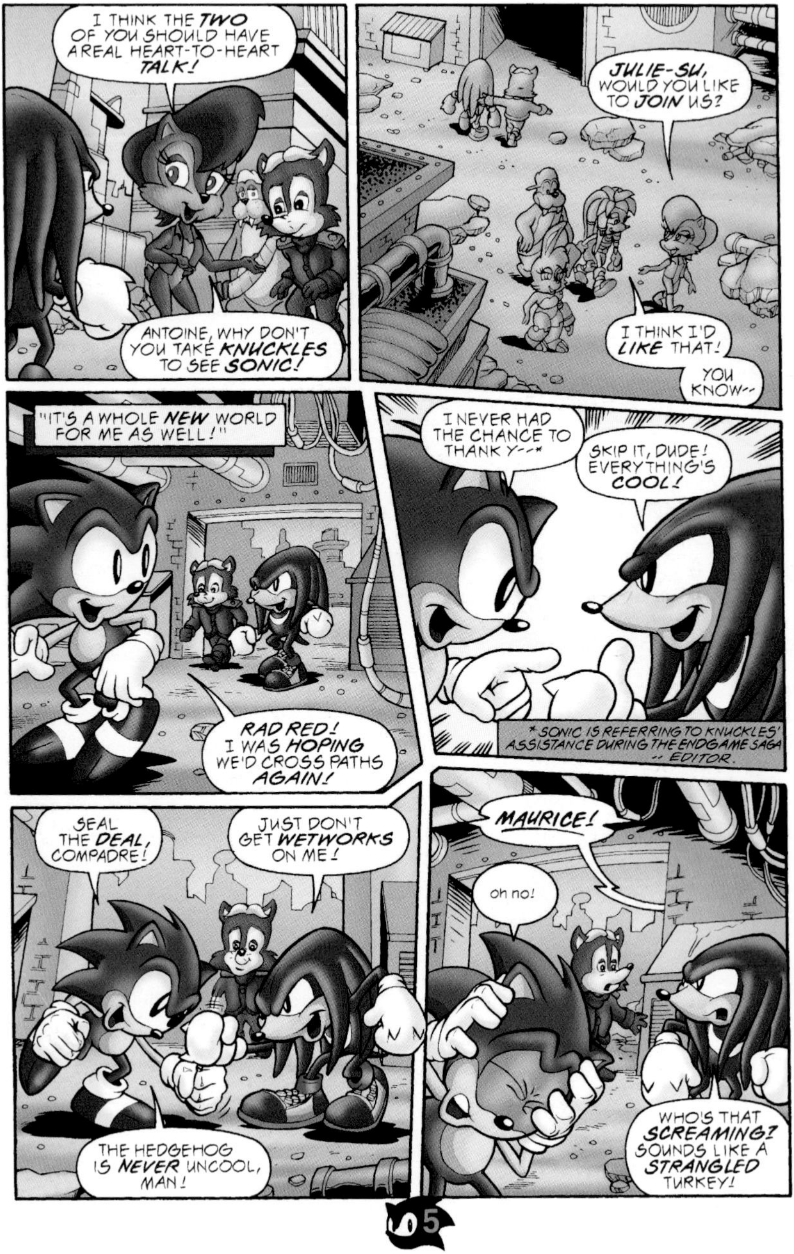
I THINK THE TWO OF YOU SHOULD HAVE A REAL HEART-TO-HEART TALK!
ANTOINE, WHY DON'T YOU TAKE KNUCKLES TO SEE SONIC!
JULIE-SU, WOULD YOU LIKE TO JOIN US?
I THINK I'D LIKE THAT!
YOU KNOW--
"IT'S A WHOLE NEW WORLD FOR ME AS WELL!"
RAD RED! I WAS HOPING WE'D CROSS PATHS AGAIN!
I NEVER HAD THE CHANCE TO THANK Y--*
SKIP IT, DUDE! EVERYTHING'S COOL!
* SONIC IS REFERRING TO KNUCKLES' ASSISTANCE DURING THE ENDGAME SAGA -- EDITOR.
SEAL THE DEAL, COMPADRE!
JUST DON'T GET WETWORKS ON ME!
THE HEDGEHOG IS NEVER UNCOOL, MAN!
MAURICE!
oh no!
WHO'S THAT SCREAMING? SOUNDS LIKE A STRANGLED TURKEY!

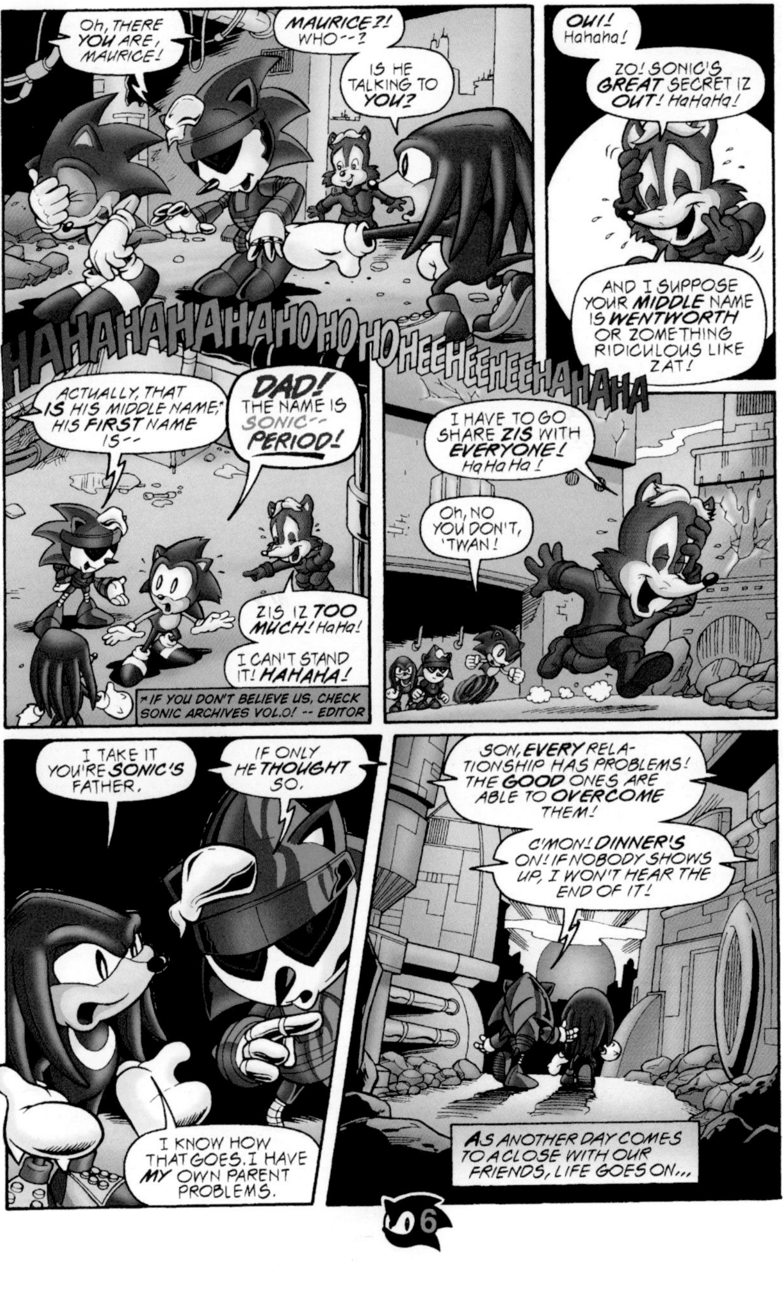

Oh, THERE YOU ARE, MAURICE!
MAURICE?! WHO--?
IS HE TALKING TO YOU?
OUI! Hahaha!
ZO! SONIC'S GREAT SECRET IZ OUT! HaHaHa!
AND I SUPPOSE YOUR MIDDLE NAME IS WENTWORTH OR ZOMETHING RIDICULOUS LIKE ZAT!
HAHAHAHAHAHOHOHOHEEHEEHEEHAHAHA
ACTUALLY, THAT IS HIS MIDDLE NAME;* HIS FIRST NAME IS--
DAD! THE NAME IS SONIC--PERIOD!
ZIS IZ TOO MUCH! HaHa!
I CAN'T STAND IT! HAHAHA!
*IF YOU DON'T BELIEVE US, CHECK SONIC ARCHIVES VOL.0! -- EDITOR
I HAVE TO GO SHARE ZIS WITH EVERYONE! HaHaHa!
Oh, NO YOU DON'T, 'TWAN!
I TAKE IT YOU'RE SONIC'S FATHER.
IF ONLY HE THOUGHT SO.
I KNOW HOW THAT GOES. I HAVE MY OWN PARENT PROBLEMS.
SON, EVERY RELATIONSHIP HAS PROBLEMS! THE GOOD ONES ARE ABLE TO OVERCOME THEM!
C'MON! DINNER'S ON! IF NOBODY SHOWS UP, I WON'T HEAR THE END OF IT!
AS ANOTHER DAY COMES TO A CLOSE WITH OUR FRIENDS, LIFE GOES ON...

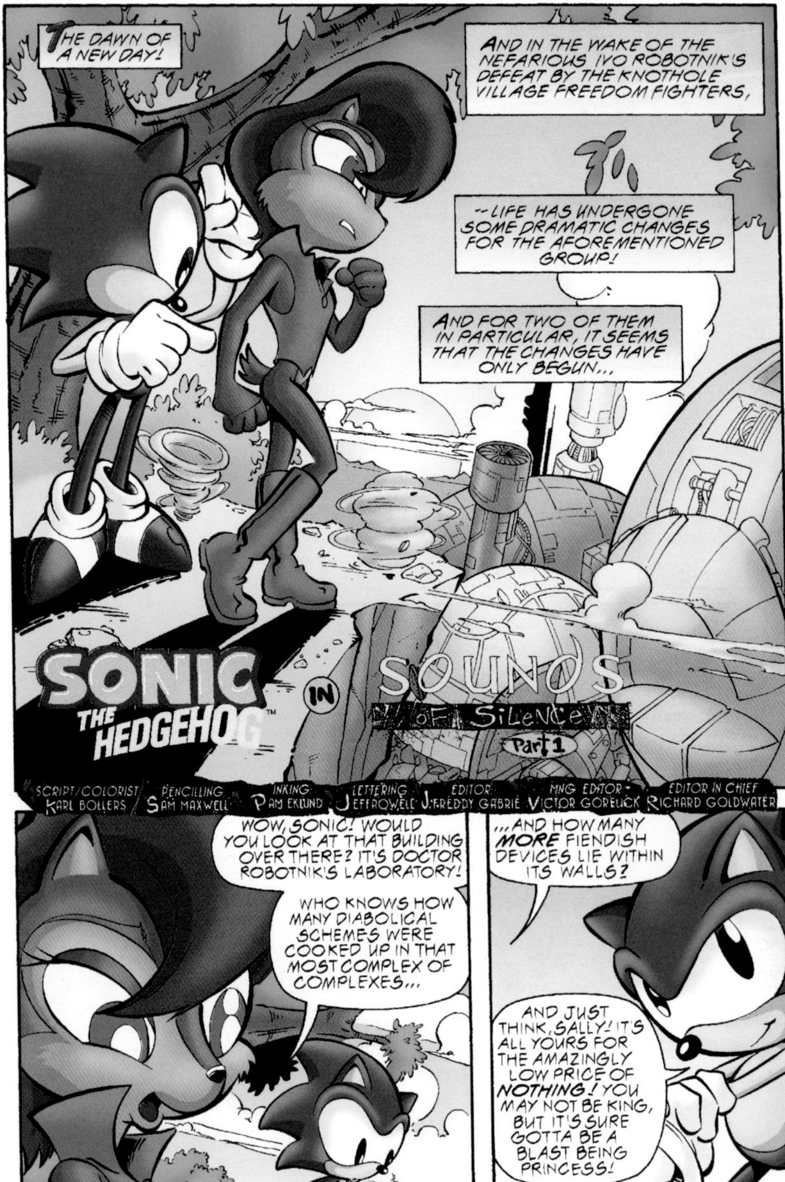
THE DAWN OF A NEW DAY!
AND IN THE WAKE OF THE NEFARIOUS IVO ROBOTNIK'S DEFEAT BY THE KNOTHOLE VILLAGE FREEDOM FIGHTERS,
--LIFE HAS UNDERGONE SOME DRAMATIC CHANGES FOR THE AFOREMENTIONED GROUP!
AND FOR TWO OF THEM IN PARTICULAR, IT SEEMS THAT THE CHANGES HAVE ONLY BEGUN...
SONIC THE HEDGEHOG™ IN SOUNDS OF SILENCE Part 1
SCRIPT/COLORIST KARL BOLLERS
PENCILLING SAM MAXWELL
INKING PAM EKLUND
LETTERING JEFF POWELL
EDITOR J. FREDDY GABRIE
MNG EDITOR VICTOR GORELICK
EDITOR IN CHIEF RICHARD GOLDWATER
WOW, SONIC! WOULD YOU LOOK AT THAT BUILDING OVER THERE? IT'S DOCTOR ROBOTNIK'S LABORATORY!
WHO KNOWS HOW MANY DIABOLICAL SCHEMES WERE COOKED UP IN THAT MOST COMPLEX OF COMPLEXES...
...AND HOW MANY MORE FIENDISH DEVICES LIE WITHIN ITS WALLS?
AND JUST THINK, SALLY! IT'S ALL YOURS FOR THE AMAZINGLY LOW PRICE OF NOTHING! YOU MAY NOT BE KING, BUT IT'S SURE GOTTA BE A BLAST BEING PRINCESS!

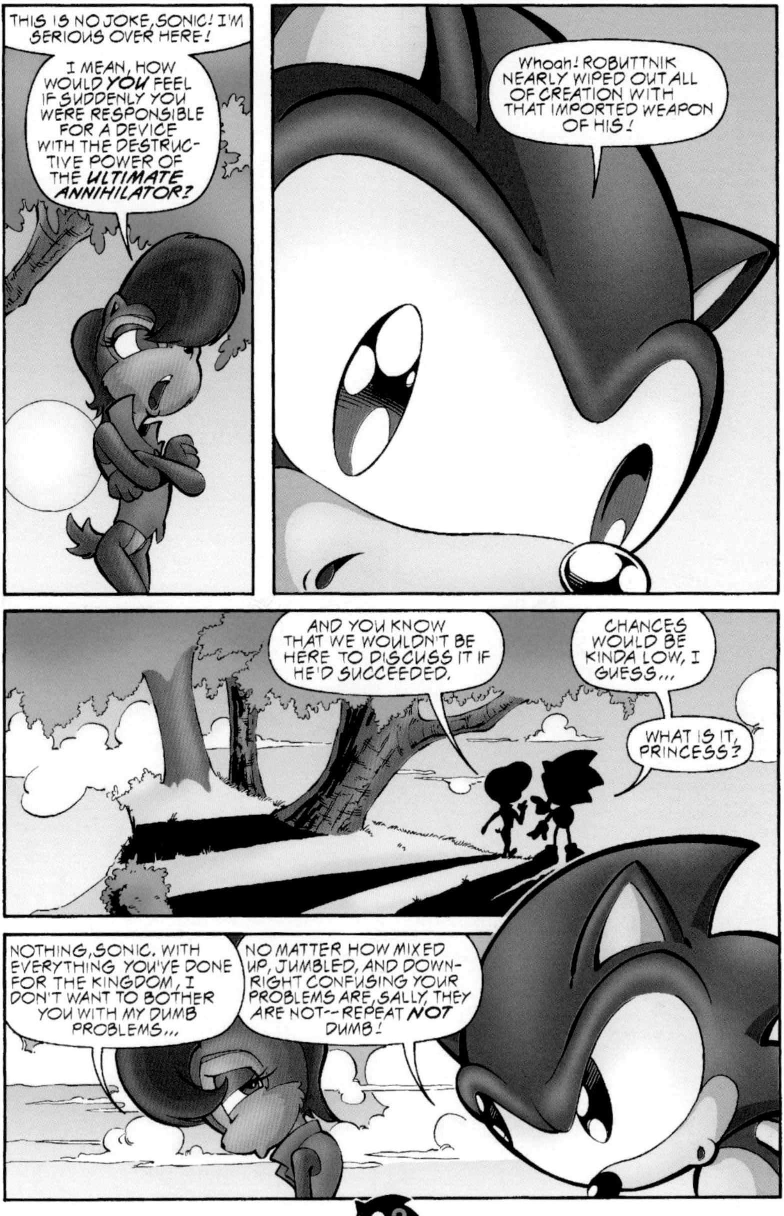
THIS IS NO JOKE, SONIC! I'M SERIOUS OVER HERE!
I MEAN, HOW WOULD YOU FEEL IF SUDDENLY YOU WERE RESPONSIBLE FOR A DEVICE WITH THE DESTRUCTIVE POWER OF THE ULTIMATE ANNIHILATOR?
Whoah! ROBUTTNIK NEARLY WIPED OUT ALL OF CREATION WITH THAT IMPORTED WEAPON OF HIS!
AND YOU KNOW THAT WE WOULDN'T BE HERE TO DISCUSS IT IF HE'D SUCCEEDED.
CHANCES WOULD BE KINDA LOW, I GUESS...
WHAT IS IT, PRINCESS?
NOTHING, SONIC. WITH EVERYTHING YOU'VE DONE FOR THE KINGDOM, I DON'T WANT TO BOTHER YOU WITH MY DUMB PROBLEMS...
NO MATTER HOW MIXED UP, JUMBLED, AND DOWNRIGHT CONFUSING YOUR PROBLEMS ARE, SALLY, THEY ARE NOT--REPEAT NOT DUMB!

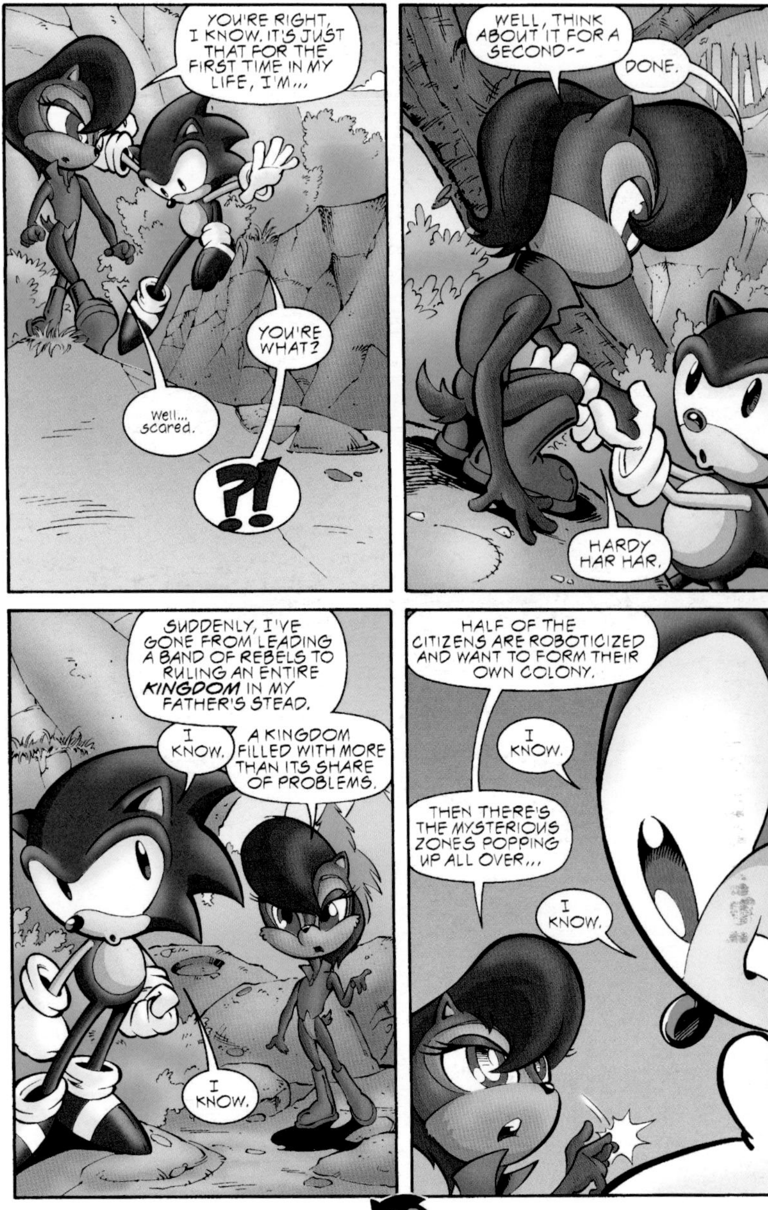
YOU'RE RIGHT, I KNOW. IT'S JUST THAT FOR THE FIRST TIME IN MY LIFE, I'M...
YOU'RE WHAT?
well... scared.
?!
WELL, THINK ABOUT IT FOR A SECOND--
DONE.
HARDY HAR HAR.
SUDDENLY, I'VE GONE FROM LEADING A BAND OF REBELS TO RULING AN ENTIRE KINGDOM IN MY FATHER'S STEAD.
I KNOW.
A KINGDOM FILLED WITH MORE THAN ITS SHARE OF PROBLEMS.
I KNOW.
HALF OF THE CITIZENS ARE ROBOTICIZED AND WANT TO FORM THEIR OWN COLONY.
I KNOW.
THEN THERE'S THE MYSTERIOUS ZONES POPPING UP ALL OVER...
I KNOW.

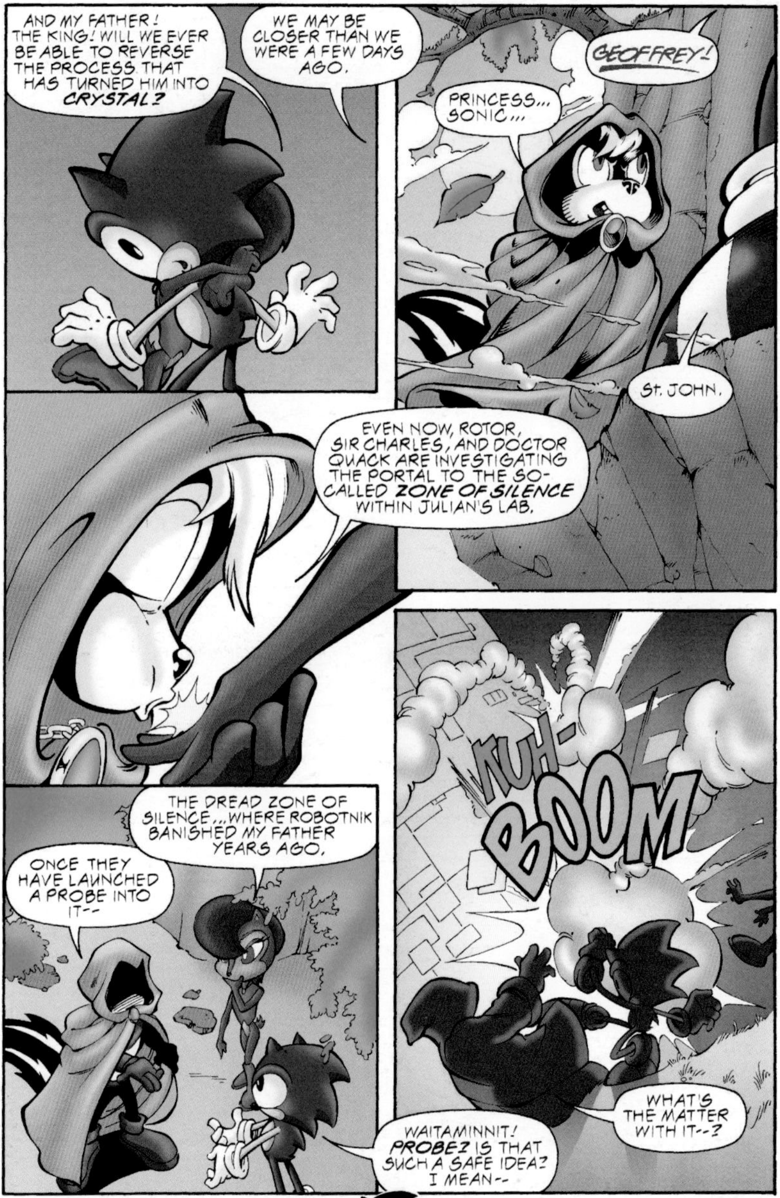
AND MY FATHER! THE KING! WILL WE EVER BE ABLE TO REVERSE THE PROCESS THAT HAS TURNED HIM INTO CRYSTAL?
WE MAY BE CLOSER THAN WE WERE A FEW DAYS AGO.
GEOFFREY!
PRINCESS... SONIC...
St. JOHN.
EVEN NOW, ROTOR, SIR CHARLES, AND DOCTOR QUACK ARE INVESTIGATING THE PORTAL TO THE SO-CALLED ZONE OF SILENCE WITHIN JULIAN'S LAB.
THE DREAD ZONE OF SILENCE...WHERE ROBOTNIK BANISHED MY FATHER YEARS AGO.
ONCE THEY HAVE LAUNCHED A PROBE INTO IT--
WAITAMINNIT! PROBE? IS THAT SUCH A SAFE IDEA? I MEAN--
KUH-BOOM
WHAT'S THE MATTER WITH IT--?

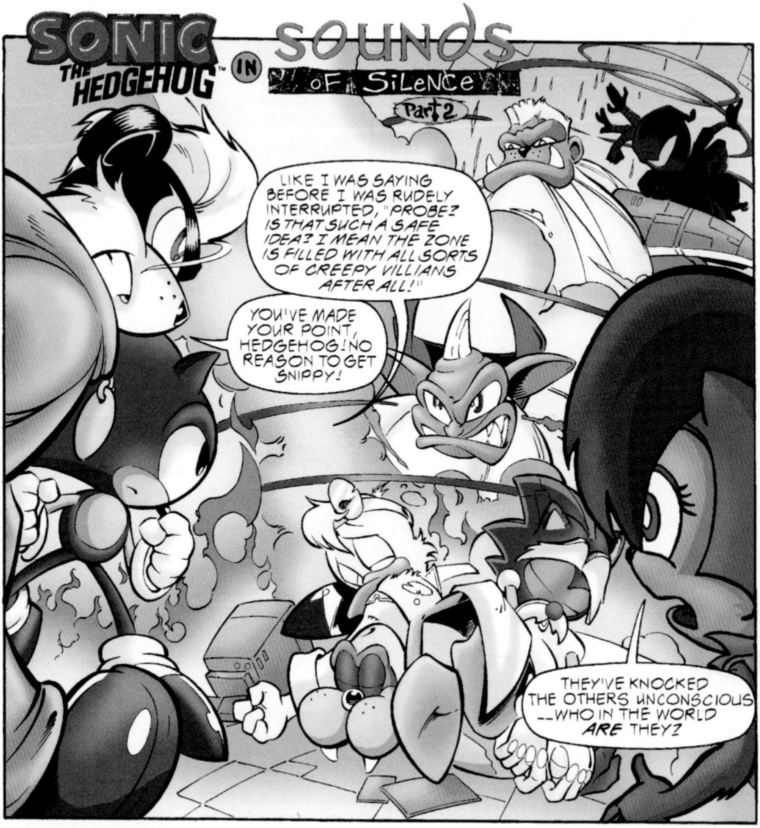
SONIC THE HEDGEHOG IN SOUNDS OF SILENCE
Part 2
LIKE I WAS SAYING BEFORE I WAS RUDELY INTERRUPTED, "PROBE? IS THAT SUCH A SAFE IDEA? I MEAN THE ZONE IS FILLED WITH ALL SORTS OF CREEPY VILLIANS AFTER ALL!"
YOU'VE MADE YOUR POINT, HEDGEHOG! NO REASON TO GET SNIPPY!
THEY'VE KNOCKED THE OTHERS UNCONSCIOUS --WHO IN THE WORLD ARE THEY?

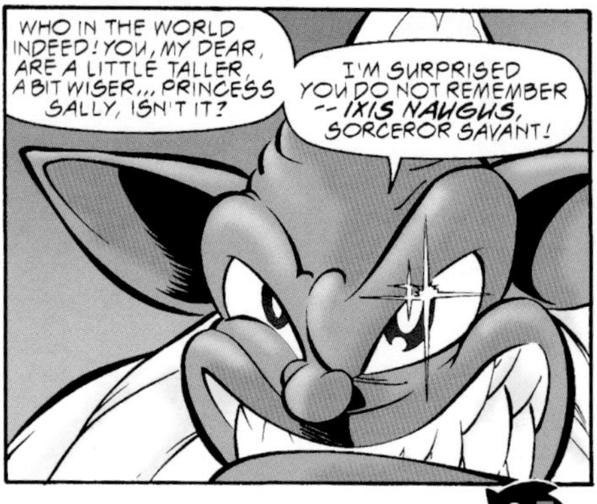
WHO IN THE WORLD INDEED! YOU, MY DEAR, ARE A LITTLE TALLER, A BIT WISER... PRINCESS SALLY, ISN'T IT?
I'M SURPRISED YOU DO NOT REMEMBER -- IXIS NAUGUS, SORCEROR SAVANT!

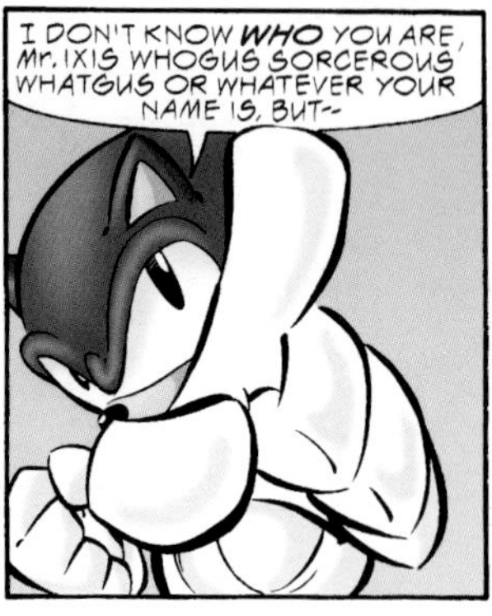
I DON'T KNOW WHO YOU ARE, Mr. IXIS WHOGUS SORCEROUS WHATGUS OR WHATEVER YOUR NAME IS, BUT--

SILENCE! YOU WILL SPEAK WHEN COMMANDED!

FWA-SHAKT

HOLEEEE!

LIKE I WAS SAYING BEFORE I WAS RUDELY INTERRUPTED, "I DON'T KNOW WHO YOU ARE...

"...BUT ANYONE'S WHO'S ALL BUDDY BUDDY WITH WARLORD KODOS IS NO FRIEND OF MINE (AND THAT BLAST WASN'T TOO ENDEARING EITHER)!"

WELL, PERHAPS ANOTHER WILL STIFLE YOU FOREVER!

FWA-SHAKT

YOU'LL HAVE TO HIT ME FIRST, IXE!

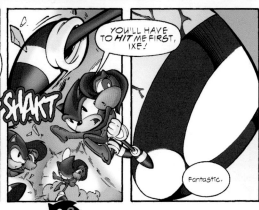

Fantastic.

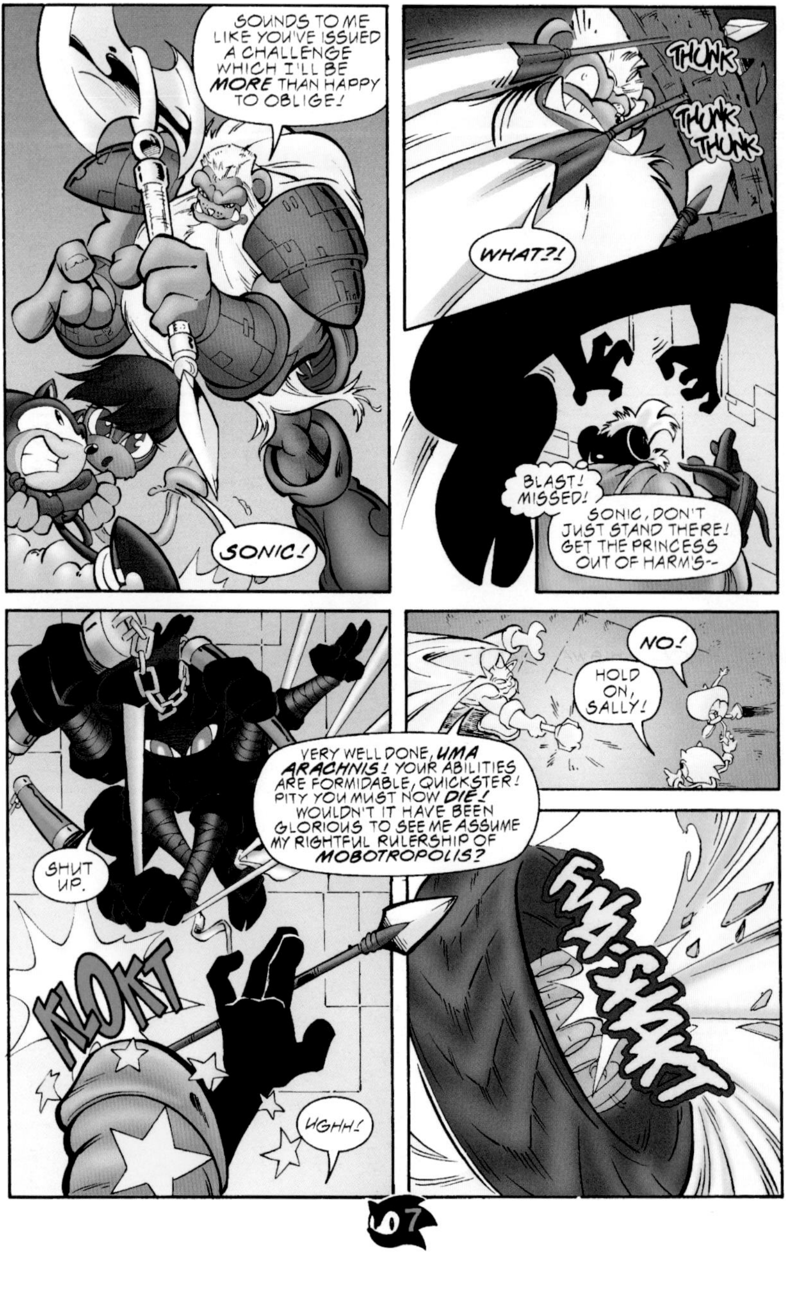
SOUNDS TO ME LIKE YOU'VE ISSUED A CHALLENGE WHICH I'LL BE MORE THAN HAPPY TO OBLIGE!
SONIC!
THUNK
THUNK THUNK
WHAT?!
BLAST! MISSED!
SONIC, DON'T JUST STAND THERE! GET THE PRINCESS OUT OF HARM'S--
VERY WELL DONE, UMA ARACHNIS! YOUR ABILITIES ARE FORMIDABLE, QUICKSTER! PITY YOU MUST NOW DIE! WOULDN'T IT HAVE BEEN GLORIOUS TO SEE ME ASSUME MY RIGHTFUL RULERSHIP OF MOBOTROPOLIS?
SHUT UP.
KLOKT
UGHH!
NO!
HOLD ON, SALLY!
FWA-SHAK!

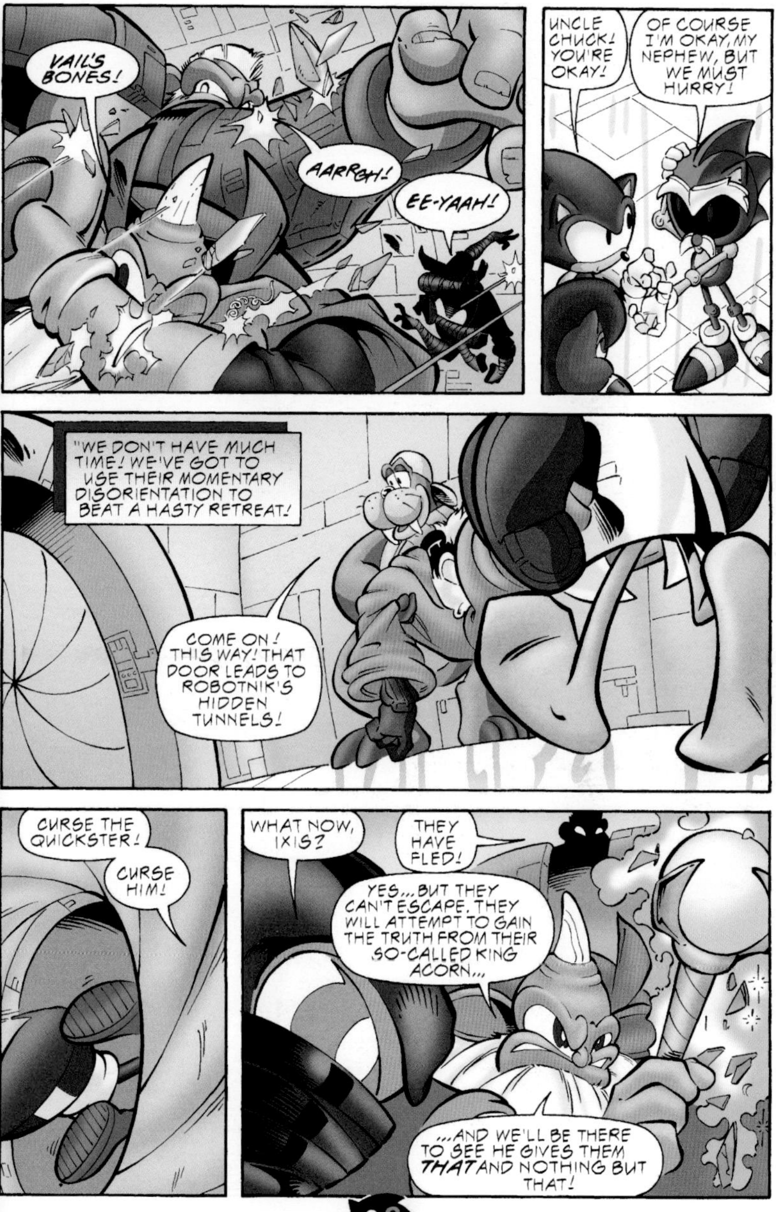
VAIL'S BONES!
AARRGH!
EE-YAAH!
UNCLE CHUCK! YOU'RE OKAY!
OF COURSE I'M OKAY, MY NEPHEW, BUT WE MUST HURRY!
"WE DON'T HAVE MUCH TIME! WE'VE GOT TO USE THEIR MOMENTARY DISORIENTATION TO BEAT A HASTY RETREAT!
COME ON! THIS WAY! THAT DOOR LEADS TO ROBOTNIK'S HIDDEN TUNNELS!
CURSE THE QUICKSTER!
CURSE HIM!
WHAT NOW, IXIS?
THEY HAVE FLED!
YES... BUT THEY CAN'T ESCAPE. THEY WILL ATTEMPT TO GAIN THE TRUTH FROM THEIR SO-CALLED KING ACORN...
...AND WE'LL BE THERE TO SEE HE GIVES THEM *THAT* AND NOTHING BUT THAT!

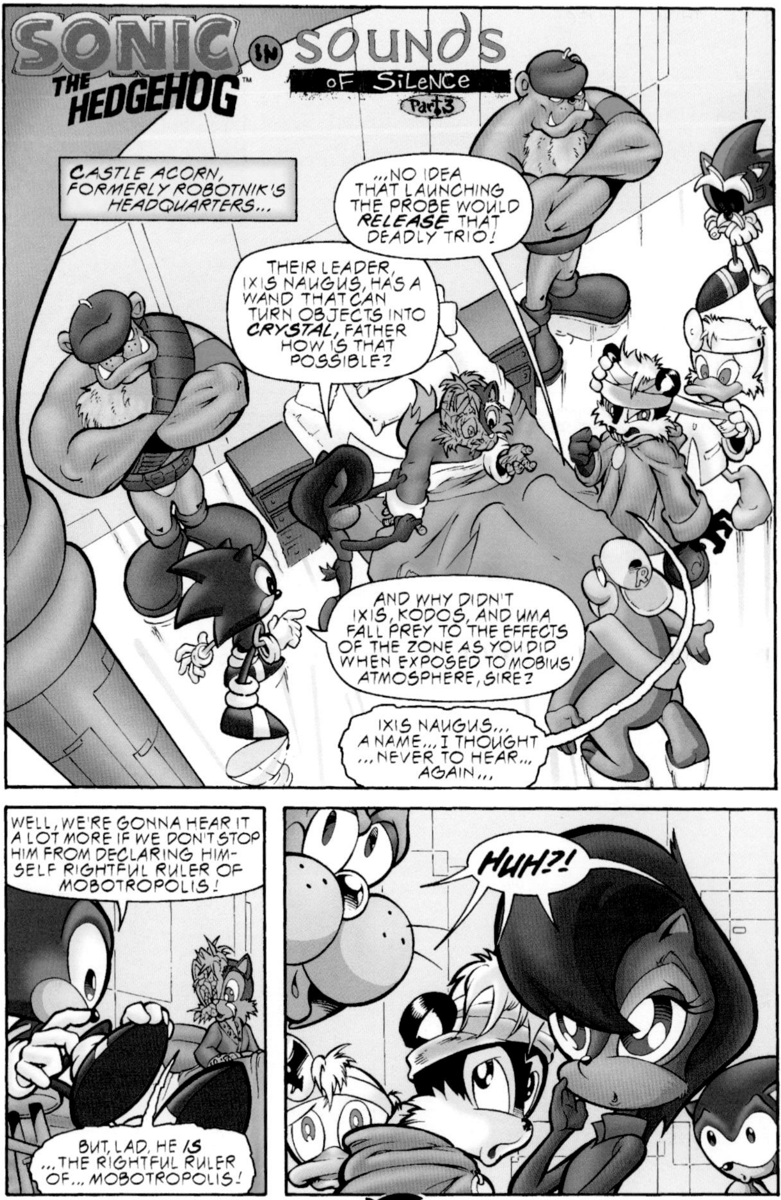
SONIC THE HEDGEHOG™
IN SOUNDS OF SILENCE
Part 3
CASTLE ACORN, FORMERLY ROBOTNIK'S HEADQUARTERS...
...NO IDEA THAT LAUNCHING THE PROBE WOULD RELEASE THAT DEADLY TRIO!
THEIR LEADER, IXIS NAUGUS, HAS A WAND THAT CAN TURN OBJECTS INTO CRYSTAL, FATHER. HOW IS THAT POSSIBLE?
AND WHY DIDN'T IXIS, KODOS, AND UMA FALL PREY TO THE EFFECTS OF THE ZONE AS YOU DID WHEN EXPOSED TO MOBIUS' ATMOSPHERE, SIRE?
IXIS NAUGUS... A NAME... I THOUGHT ...NEVER TO HEAR... AGAIN...
WELL, WE'RE GONNA HEAR IT A LOT MORE IF WE DON'T STOP HIM FROM DECLARING HIM-SELF RIGHTFUL RULER OF MOBOTROPOLIS!
BUT, LAD, HE IS ...THE RIGHTFUL RULER OF... MOBOTROPOLIS!
HUH?!

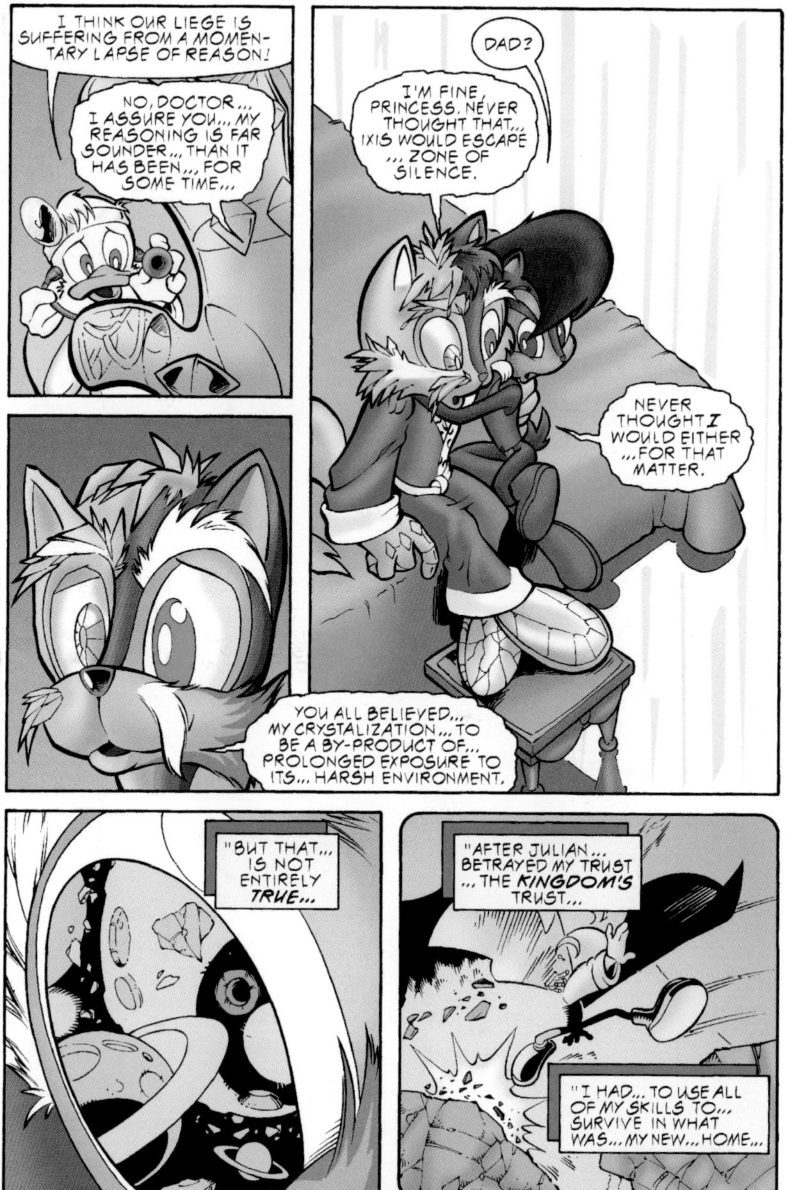
I THINK OUR LIEGE IS SUFFERING FROM A MOMENTARY LAPSE OF REASON!
NO, DOCTOR... I ASSURE YOU... MY REASONING IS FAR SOUNDER... THAN IT HAS BEEN... FOR SOME TIME...
DAD?
I'M FINE, PRINCESS. NEVER THOUGHT THAT... IXIS WOULD ESCAPE ... ZONE OF SILENCE.
NEVER THOUGHT *I* WOULD EITHER ...FOR THAT MATTER.
YOU ALL BELIEVED... MY CRYSTALIZATION... TO BE A BY-PRODUCT OF... PROLONGED EXPOSURE TO ITS... HARSH ENVIRONMENT.
"BUT THAT... IS NOT ENTIRELY ***TRUE...***
"AFTER JULIAN... BETRAYED MY TRUST ... THE ***KINGDOM'S*** TRUST...
"I HAD... TO USE ALL OF MY SKILLS TO... SURVIVE IN WHAT WAS... MY NEW... HOME...

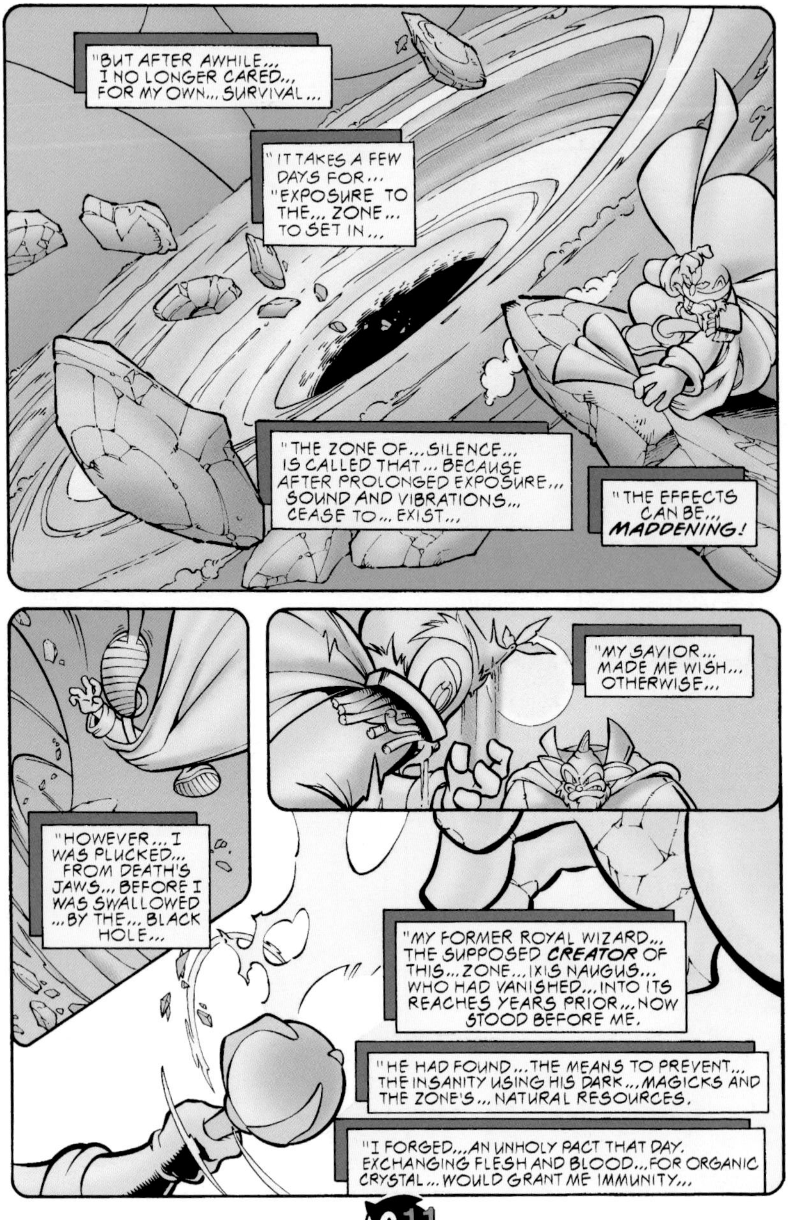
"BUT AFTER AWHILE... I NO LONGER CARED... FOR MY OWN... SURVIVAL...
"IT TAKES A FEW DAYS FOR... "EXPOSURE TO THE... ZONE... TO SET IN...
"THE ZONE OF... SILENCE... IS CALLED THAT... BECAUSE AFTER PROLONGED EXPOSURE... SOUND AND VIBRATIONS... CEASE TO... EXIST...
"THE EFFECTS CAN BE... MADDENING!
"HOWEVER... I WAS PLUCKED... FROM DEATH'S JAWS... BEFORE I WAS SWALLOWED ...BY THE... BLACK HOLE...
"MY SAVIOR... MADE ME WISH... OTHERWISE...
"MY FORMER ROYAL WIZARD... THE SUPPOSED CREATOR OF THIS... ZONE... IXIS NAUGUS... WHO HAD VANISHED... INTO ITS REACHES YEARS PRIOR... NOW STOOD BEFORE ME.
"HE HAD FOUND... THE MEANS TO PREVENT... THE INSANITY USING HIS DARK... MAGICKS AND THE ZONE'S... NATURAL RESOURCES.
"I FORGED... AN UNHOLY PACT THAT DAY. EXCHANGING FLESH AND BLOOD... FOR ORGANIC CRYSTAL... WOULD GRANT ME IMMUNITY...

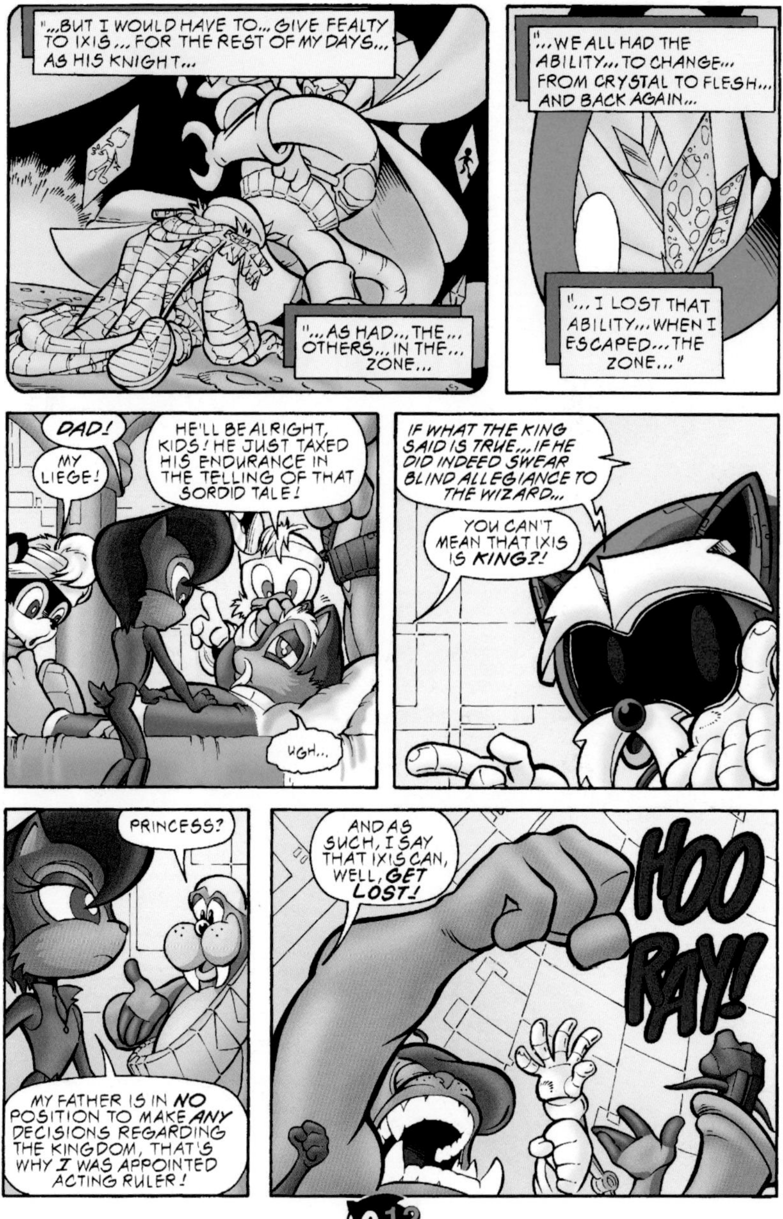
"...BUT I WOULD HAVE TO... GIVE FEALTY TO IXIS... FOR THE REST OF MY DAYS... AS HIS KNIGHT...
"...AS HAD... THE... OTHERS... IN THE... ZONE...
"...WE ALL HAD THE ABILITY... TO CHANGE... FROM CRYSTAL TO FLESH... AND BACK AGAIN...
"...I LOST THAT ABILITY... WHEN I ESCAPED... THE ZONE..."
DAD!
MY LIEGE!
HE'LL BE ALRIGHT, KIDS! HE JUST TAXED HIS ENDURANCE IN THE TELLING OF THAT SORDID TALE!
UGH...
IF WHAT THE KING SAID IS TRUE... IF HE DID INDEED SWEAR BLIND ALLEGIANCE TO THE WIZARD...
YOU CAN'T MEAN THAT IXIS IS KING?!
PRINCESS?
MY FATHER IS IN NO POSITION TO MAKE ANY DECISIONS REGARDING THE KINGDOM, THAT'S WHY I WAS APPOINTED ACTING RULER!
AND AS SUCH, I SAY THAT IXIS CAN, WELL, GET LOST!
HOO RAY!

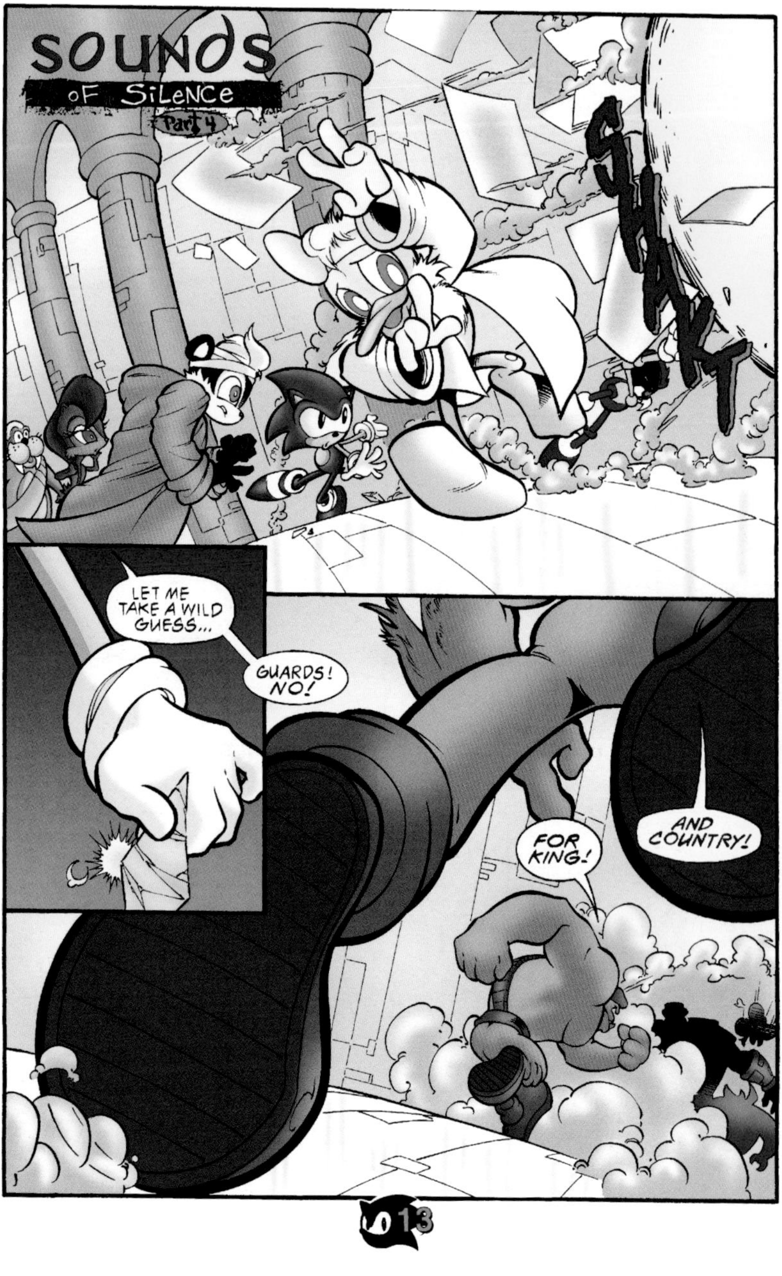
SOUNDS
OF SILENCE
Part 4
SHAKE
LET ME TAKE A WILD GUESS...
GUARDS! NO!
FOR KING!
AND COUNTRY!

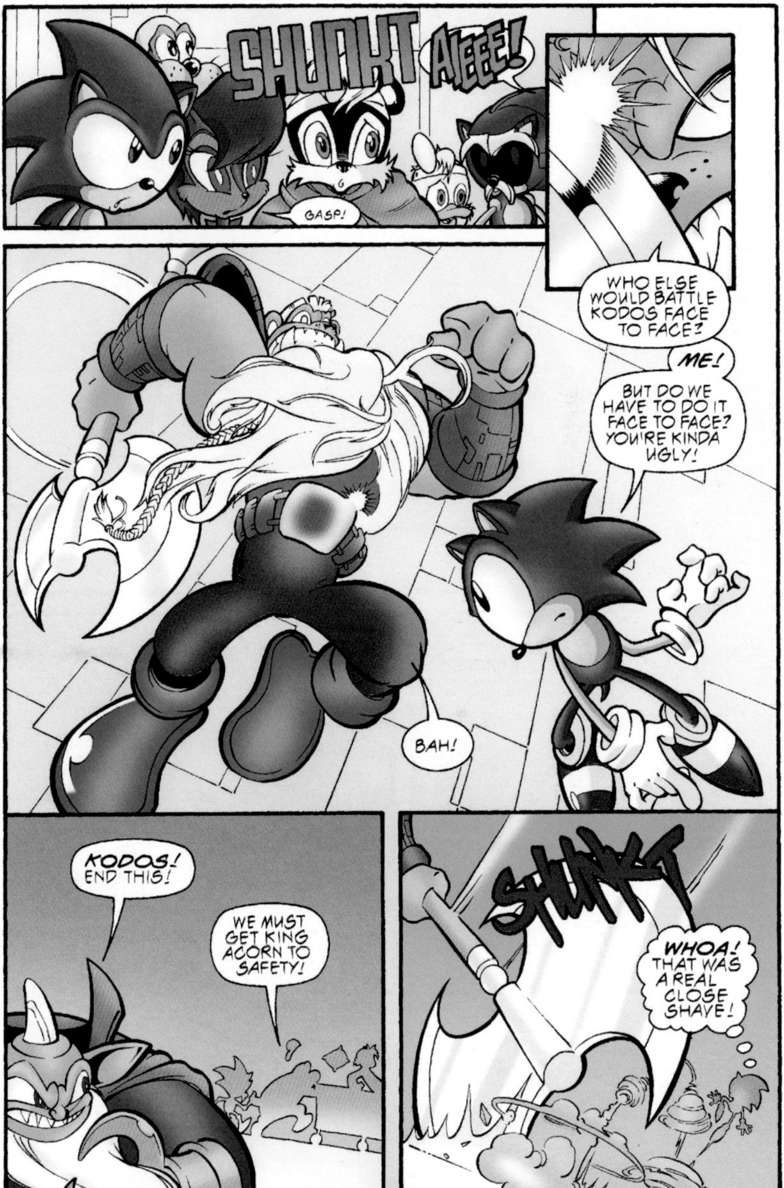
SHUNKT
AIEEE!
GASP!
WHO ELSE WOULD BATTLE KODOS FACE TO FACE?
ME!
BUT DO WE HAVE TO DO IT FACE TO FACE? YOU'RE KINDA UGLY!
BAH!
KODOS! END THIS!
WE MUST GET KING ACORN TO SAFETY!
SHUNKT
WHOA! THAT WAS A REAL CLOSE SHAVE!

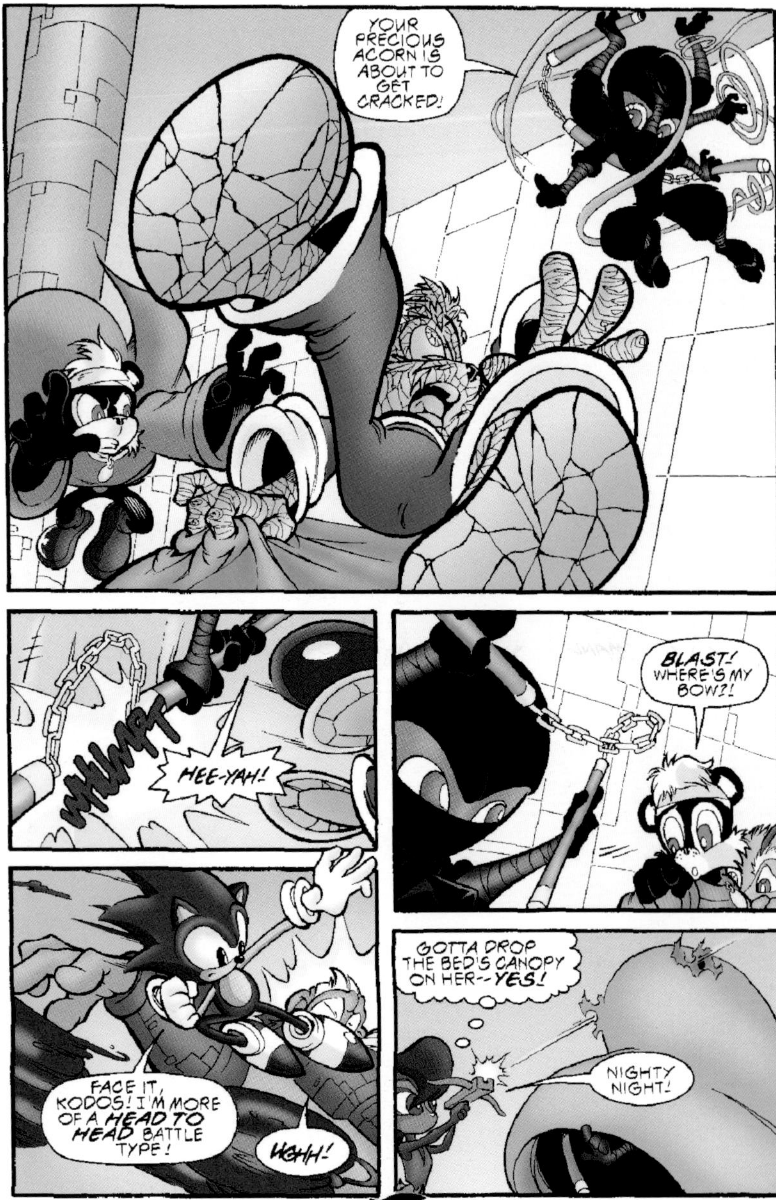
YOUR PRECIOUS ACORN IS ABOUT TO GET CRACKED!
WHUMPF
HEE-YAH!
BLAST! WHERE'S MY BOW?!
FACE IT, KODOS! I'M MORE OF A HEAD TO HEAD BATTLE TYPE!
UGHH!
GOTTA DROP THE BED'S CANOPY ON HER--YES!
NIGHTY NIGHT!

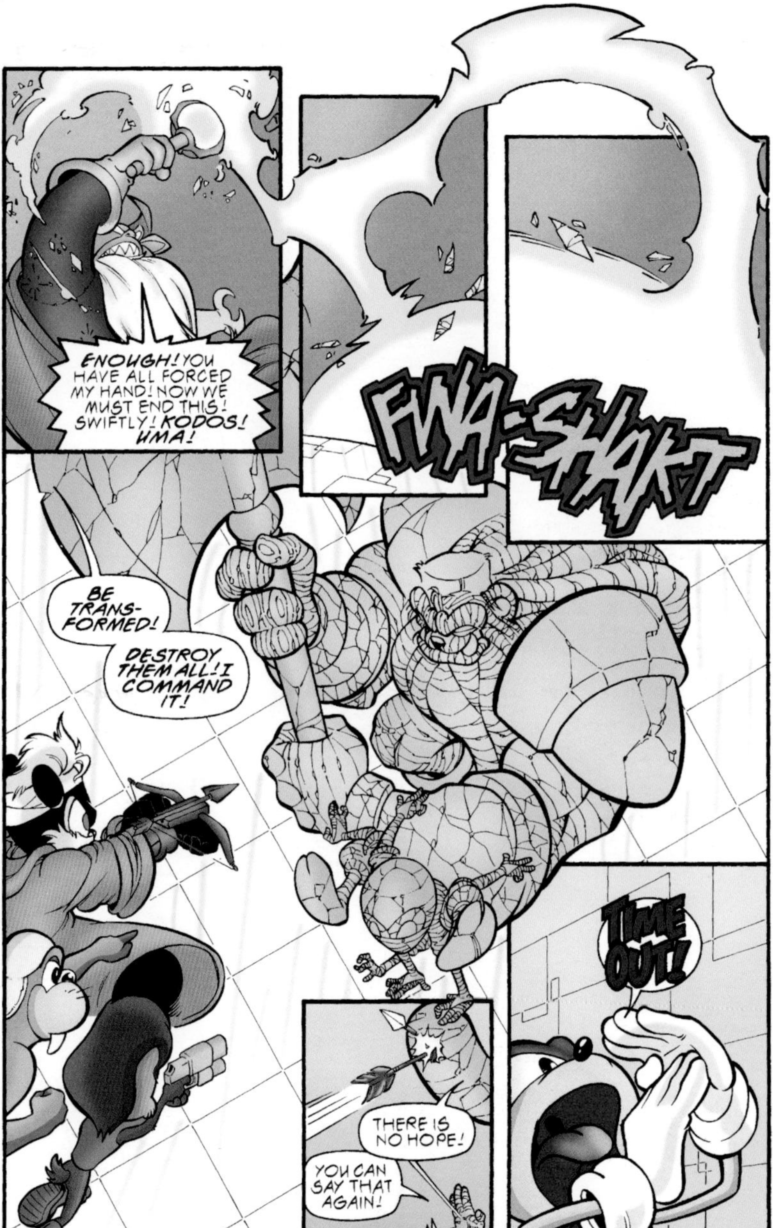
ENOUGH! YOU HAVE ALL FORCED MY HAND! NOW WE MUST END THIS! SWIFTLY! KODOS! UMA!
FWA-SHAKT
BE TRANS-FORMED!
DESTROY THEM ALL! I COMMAND IT!
THERE IS NO HOPE!
YOU CAN SAY THAT AGAIN!
TIME OUT!

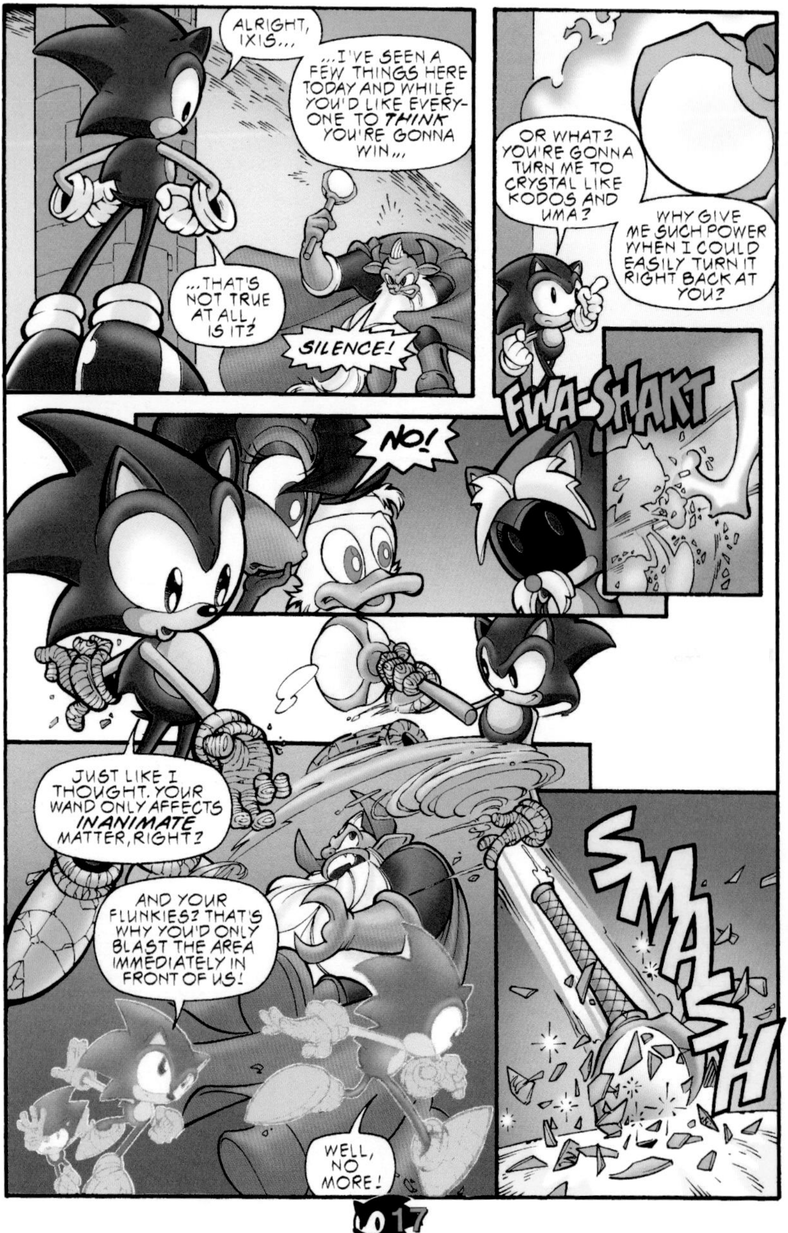
ALRIGHT, IXIS...
...I'VE SEEN A FEW THINGS HERE TODAY AND WHILE YOU'D LIKE EVERY-ONE TO THINK YOU'RE GONNA WIN...
...THAT'S NOT TRUE AT ALL, IS IT?
SILENCE!
OR WHAT? YOU'RE GONNA TURN ME TO CRYSTAL LIKE KODOS AND UMA?
WHY GIVE ME SUCH POWER WHEN I COULD EASILY TURN IT RIGHT BACK AT YOU?
FWA-SHAKT
NO!
JUST LIKE I THOUGHT. YOUR WAND ONLY AFFECTS INANIMATE MATTER, RIGHT?
AND YOUR FLUNKIES? THAT'S WHY YOU'D ONLY BLAST THE AREA IMMEDIATELY IN FRONT OF US!
WELL, NO MORE!
SMASH

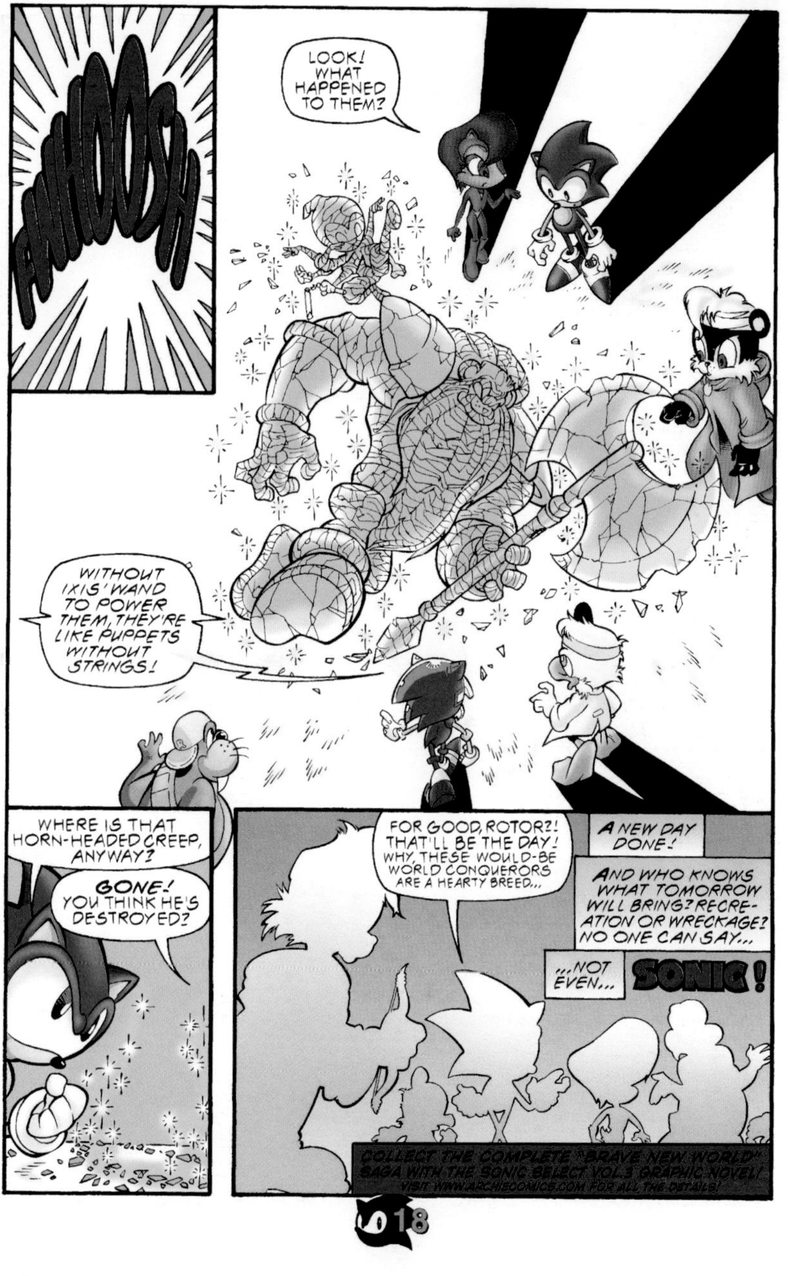
FWHOOSH
LOOK! WHAT HAPPENED TO THEM?
WITHOUT IXIS' WAND TO POWER THEM, THEY'RE LIKE PUPPETS WITHOUT STRINGS!
WHERE IS THAT HORN-HEADED CREEP, ANYWAY?
GONE! YOU THINK HE'S DESTROYED?
FOR GOOD, ROTOR?! THAT'LL BE THE DAY! WHY, THESE WOULD-BE WORLD CONQUERORS ARE A HEARTY BREED...
A NEW DAY DONE!
AND WHO KNOWS WHAT TOMORROW WILL BRING? RECRE-ATION OR WRECKAGE? NO ONE CAN SAY...
...NOT EVEN...
SONIC!
COLLECT THE COMPLETE "BRAVE NEW WORLD" SAGA WITH THE SONIC SELECT VOL.3 GRAPHIC NOVEL!
VISIT WWW.ARCHIECOMICS.COM FOR ALL THE DETAILS!

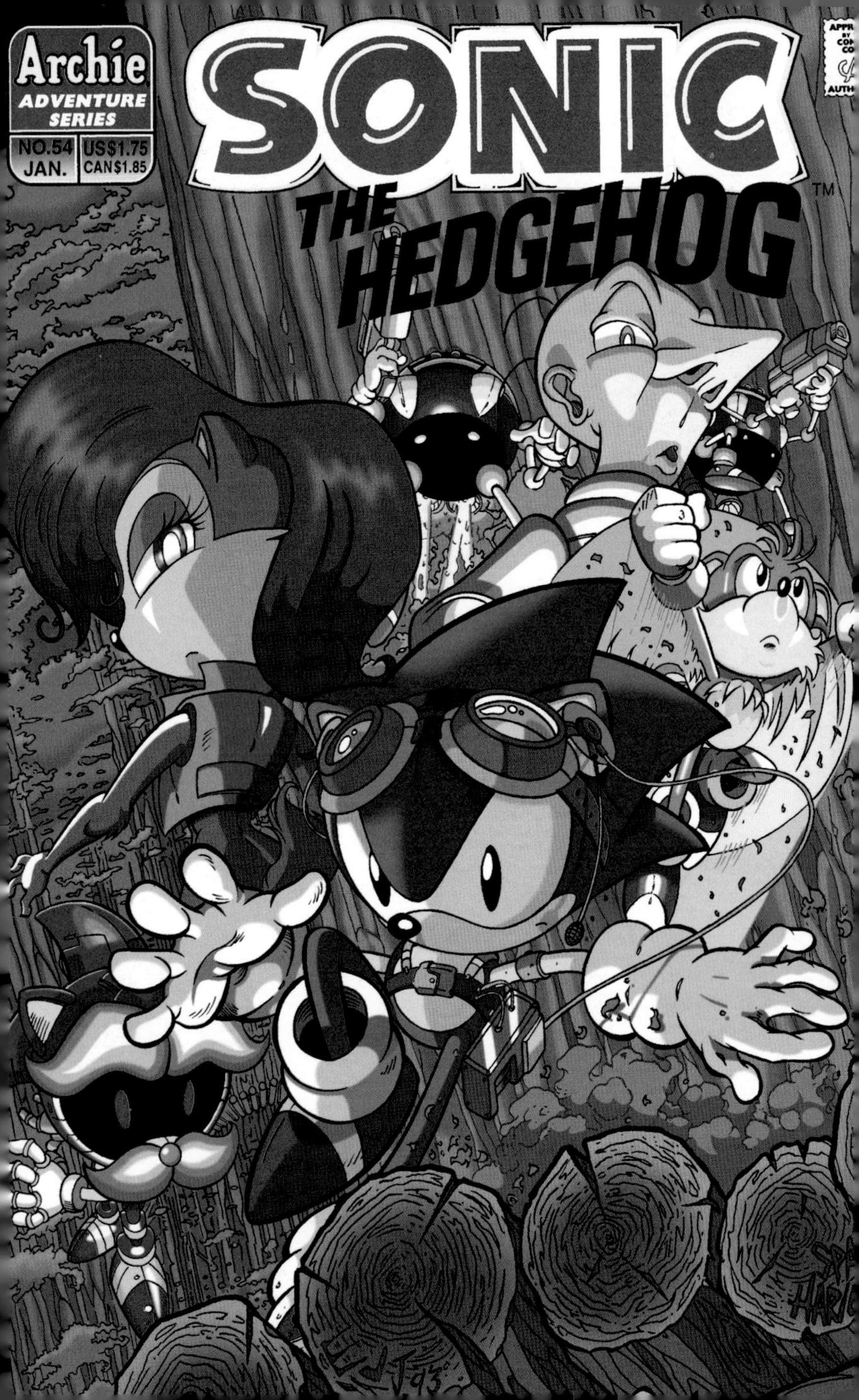
Archie
ADVENTURE SERIES
NO.54
JAN.
US$1.75
CAN$1.85
SONIC
THE HEDGEHOG™

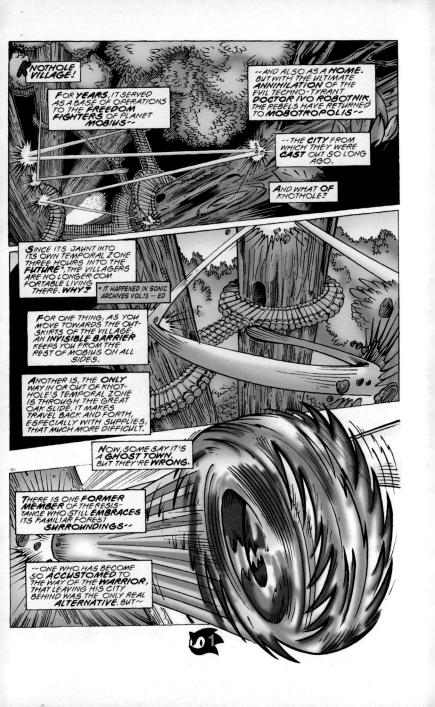

KNOTHOLE VILLAGE!

FOR **YEARS**, IT SERVED AS A BASE OF OPERATIONS TO THE **FREEDOM FIGHTERS** OF PLANET **MOBIUS**--

--AND ALSO AS A **HOME**. BUT WITH THE **ULTIMATE ANNIHILATION** OF THE EVIL TECHNO-TYRANT **DOCTOR IVO ROBOTNIK**, THE REBELS HAVE RETURNED TO **MOBOTROPOLIS**--

--THE **CITY** FROM WHICH THEY WERE **CAST** OUT SO LONG AGO.

AND WHAT OF **KNOTHOLE?**

SINCE ITS JAUNT INTO ITS OWN TEMPORAL ZONE THREE HOURS INTO THE **FUTURE***, THE VILLAGERS ARE NO LONGER COMFORTABLE LIVING THERE. **WHY?**

* IT HAPPENED IN SONIC ARCHIVES VOL.13 -- ED

FOR ONE THING, AS YOU MOVE TOWARDS THE OUTSKIRTS OF THE VILLAGE, AN **INVISIBLE BARRIER** KEEPS YOU FROM THE REST OF MOBIUS ON ALL SIDES.

ANOTHER IS, THE **ONLY** WAY IN OR OUT OF KNOTHOLE'S TEMPORAL ZONE IS THROUGH THE GREAT OAK SLIDE. IT MAKES TRAVEL BACK AND FORTH, ESPECIALLY WITH SUPPLIES, THAT MUCH MORE DIFFICULT.

NOW, SOME SAY IT'S A **GHOST TOWN**, BUT THEY'RE **WRONG**.

THERE IS ONE **FORMER MEMBER** OF THE RESISTANCE WHO STILL **EMBRACES** ITS FAMILIAR FOREST **SURROUNDINGS**--

--ONE WHO HAS BECOME SO **ACCUSTOMED** TO THE WAY OF THE **WARRIOR**, THAT LEAVING HIS CITY BEHIND WAS THE ONLY REAL **ALTERNATIVE**. BUT--

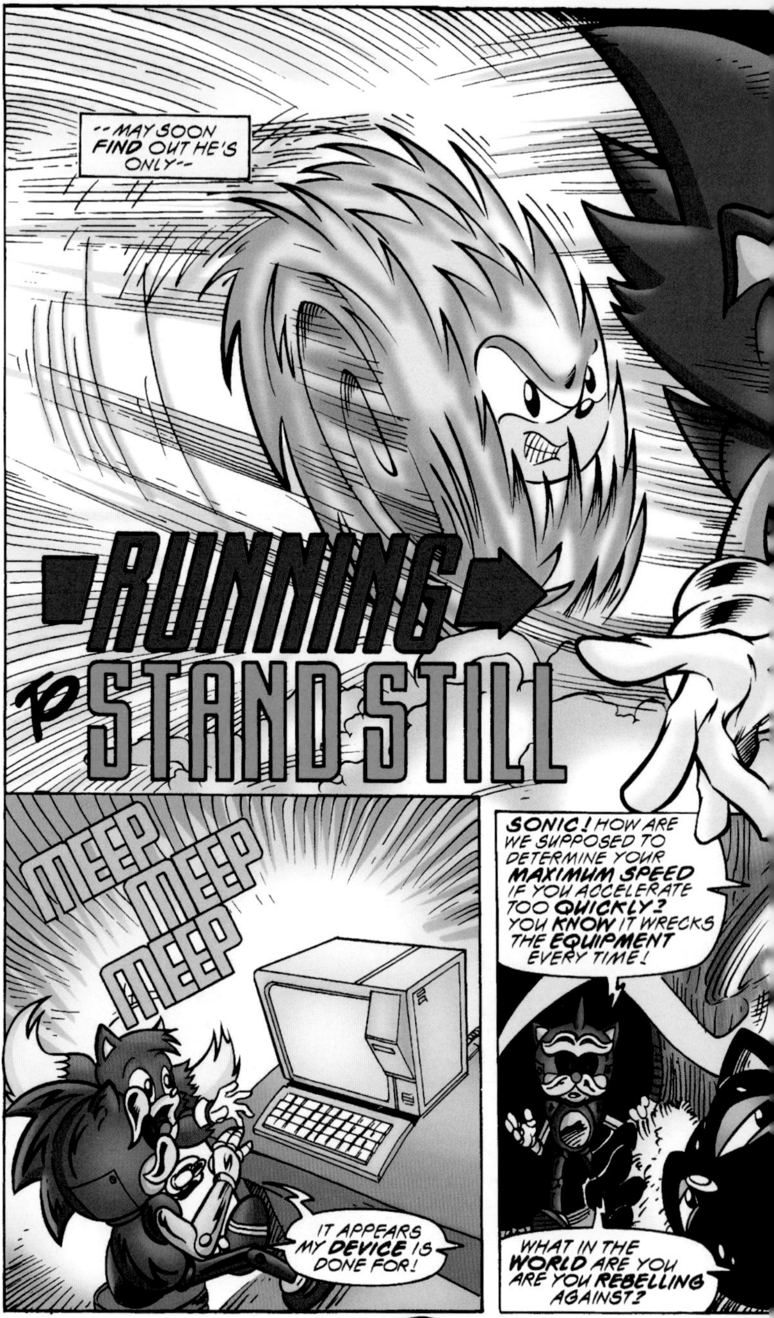
--MAY SOON FIND OUT HE'S ONLY--
RUNNING TO STAND STILL
MEEP MEEP MEEP
IT APPEARS MY DEVICE IS DONE FOR!
SONIC! HOW ARE WE SUPPOSED TO DETERMINE YOUR MAXIMUM SPEED IF YOU ACCELERATE TOO QUICKLY? YOU KNOW IT WRECKS THE EQUIPMENT EVERY TIME!
WHAT IN THE WORLD ARE YOU ARE YOU REBELLING AGAINST?

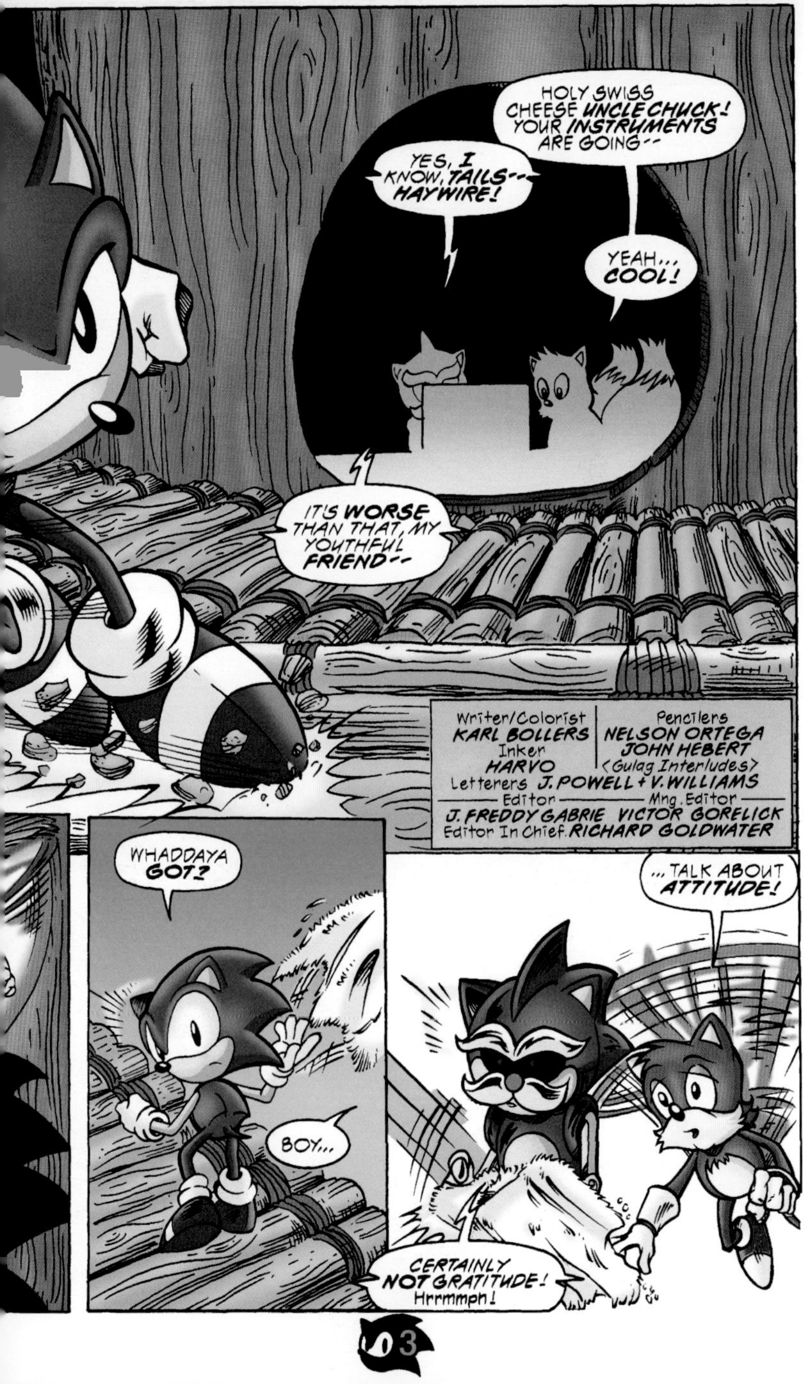
HOLY SWISS CHEESE UNCLE CHUCK! YOUR INSTRUMENTS ARE GOING--
YES, I KNOW, TAILS-- HAYWIRE!
YEAH... COOL!
IT'S WORSE THAN THAT, MY YOUTHFUL FRIEND--
Writer/Colorist KARL BOLLERS
Inker HARVO
Pencilers NELSON ORTEGA JOHN HEBERT <Gulag Interludes>
Letterers J. POWELL + V. WILLIAMS
Editor J. FREDDY GABRIE
Mng. Editor VICTOR GORELICK
Editor In Chief RICHARD GOLDWATER
WHADDAYA GOT?
BOY...
...TALK ABOUT ATTITUDE!
CERTAINLY NOT GRATITUDE! Hrrmmph!

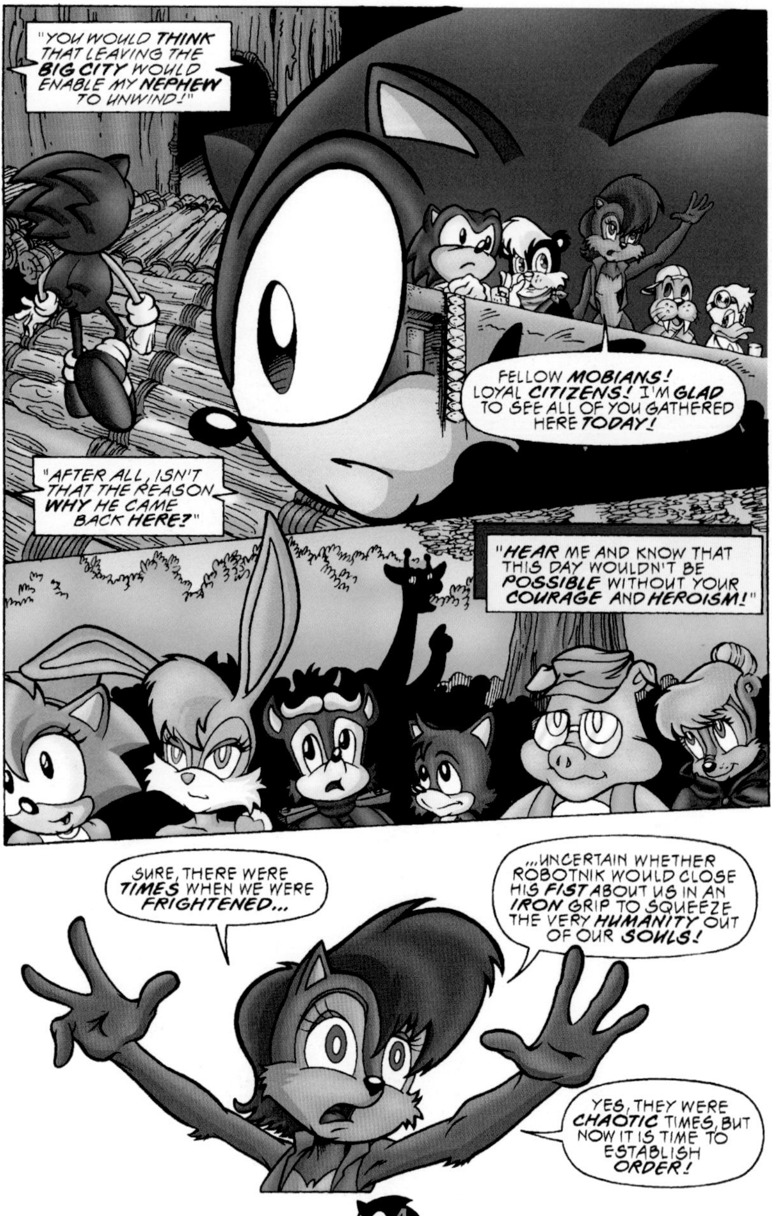
"YOU WOULD THINK THAT LEAVING THE BIG CITY WOULD ENABLE MY NEPHEW TO UNWIND!"
FELLOW MOBIANS! LOYAL CITIZENS! I'M GLAD TO SEE ALL OF YOU GATHERED HERE TODAY!
"AFTER ALL, ISN'T THAT THE REASON WHY HE CAME BACK HERE?"
"HEAR ME AND KNOW THAT THIS DAY WOULDN'T BE POSSIBLE WITHOUT YOUR COURAGE AND HEROISM!"
SURE, THERE WERE TIMES WHEN WE WERE FRIGHTENED...
...UNCERTAIN WHETHER ROBOTNIK WOULD CLOSE HIS FIST ABOUT US IN AN IRON GRIP TO SQUEEZE THE VERY HUMANITY OUT OF OUR SOULS!
YES, THEY WERE CHAOTIC TIMES, BUT NOW IT IS TIME TO ESTABLISH ORDER!

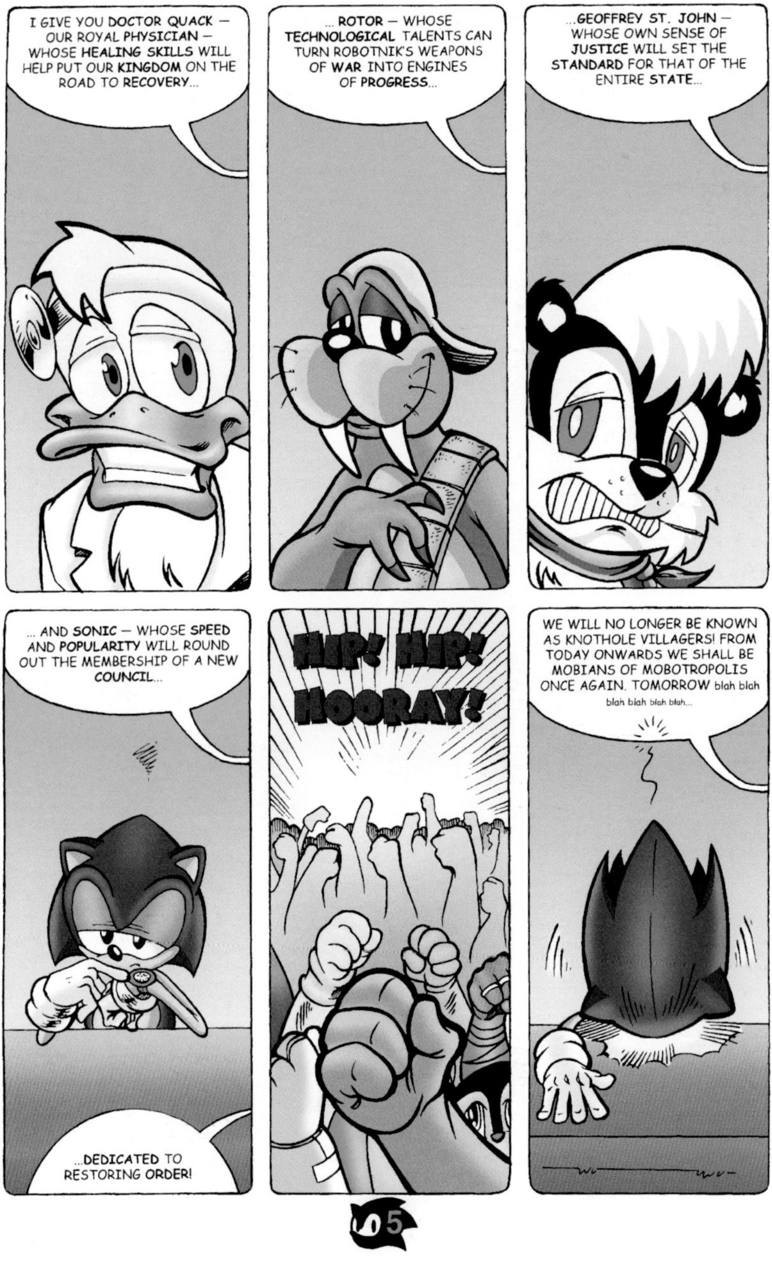
I GIVE YOU DOCTOR QUACK — OUR ROYAL PHYSICIAN — WHOSE HEALING SKILLS WILL HELP PUT OUR KINGDOM ON THE ROAD TO RECOVERY...
... ROTOR — WHOSE TECHNOLOGICAL TALENTS CAN TURN ROBOTNIK'S WEAPONS OF WAR INTO ENGINES OF PROGRESS...
...GEOFFREY ST. JOHN — WHOSE OWN SENSE OF JUSTICE WILL SET THE STANDARD FOR THAT OF THE ENTIRE STATE...
... AND SONIC — WHOSE SPEED AND POPULARITY WILL ROUND OUT THE MEMBERSHIP OF A NEW COUNCIL...
...DEDICATED TO RESTORING ORDER!
HIP! HIP! HOORAY!
WE WILL NO LONGER BE KNOWN AS KNOTHOLE VILLAGERS! FROM TODAY ONWARDS WE SHALL BE MOBIANS OF MOBOTROPOLIS ONCE AGAIN. TOMORROW blah blah blah blah blah blah...

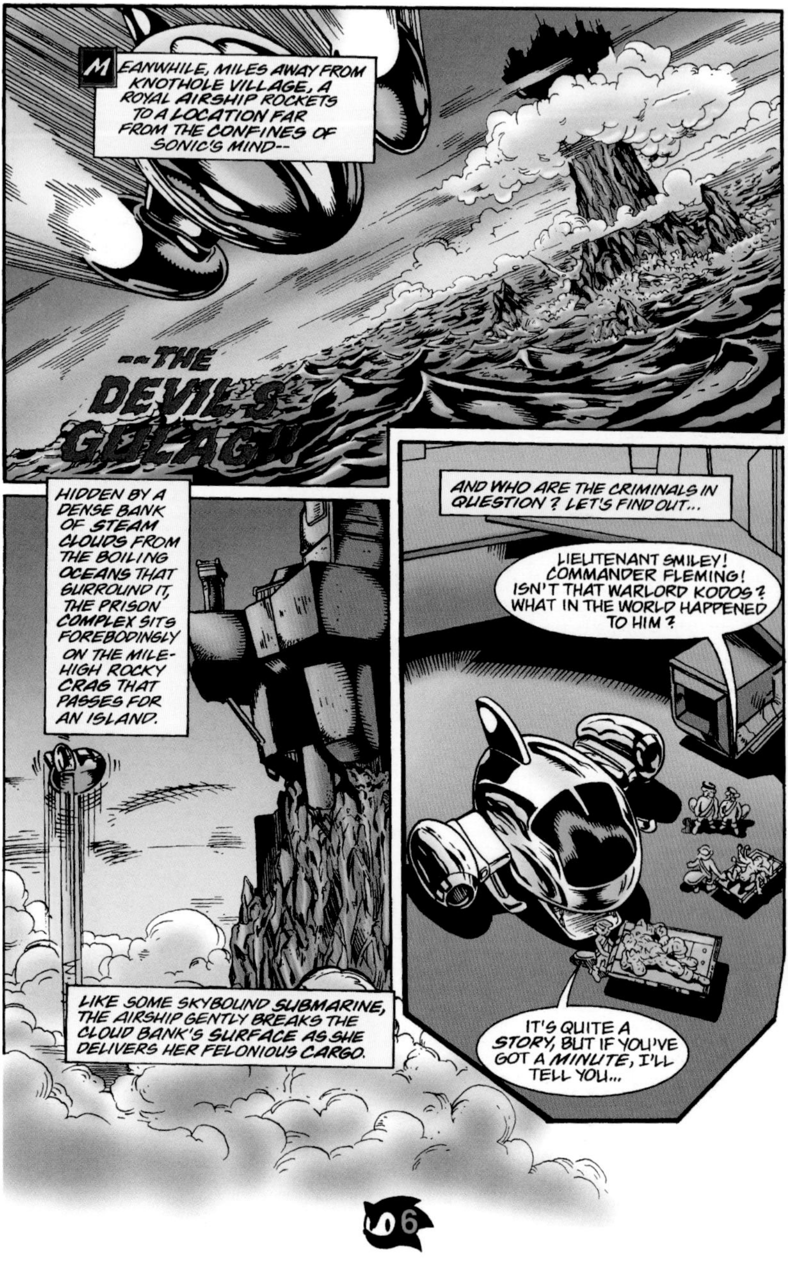
MEANWHILE, MILES AWAY FROM KNOTHOLE VILLAGE, A ROYAL AIRSHIP ROCKETS TO A LOCATION FAR FROM THE CONFINES OF SONIC'S MIND--
--THE DEVIL'S GULAG!!
HIDDEN BY A DENSE BANK OF STEAM CLOUDS FROM THE BOILING OCEANS THAT SURROUND IT, THE PRISON COMPLEX SITS FOREBODINGLY ON THE MILE-HIGH ROCKY CRAG THAT PASSES FOR AN ISLAND.
LIKE SOME SKYBOUND SUBMARINE, THE AIRSHIP GENTLY BREAKS THE CLOUD BANK'S SURFACE AS SHE DELIVERS HER FELONIOUS CARGO.
AND WHO ARE THE CRIMINALS IN QUESTION? LET'S FIND OUT...
LIEUTENANT SMILEY! COMMANDER FLEMING! ISN'T THAT WARLORD KODOS? WHAT IN THE WORLD HAPPENED TO HIM?
IT'S QUITE A STORY, BUT IF YOU'VE GOT A MINUTE, I'LL TELL YOU...

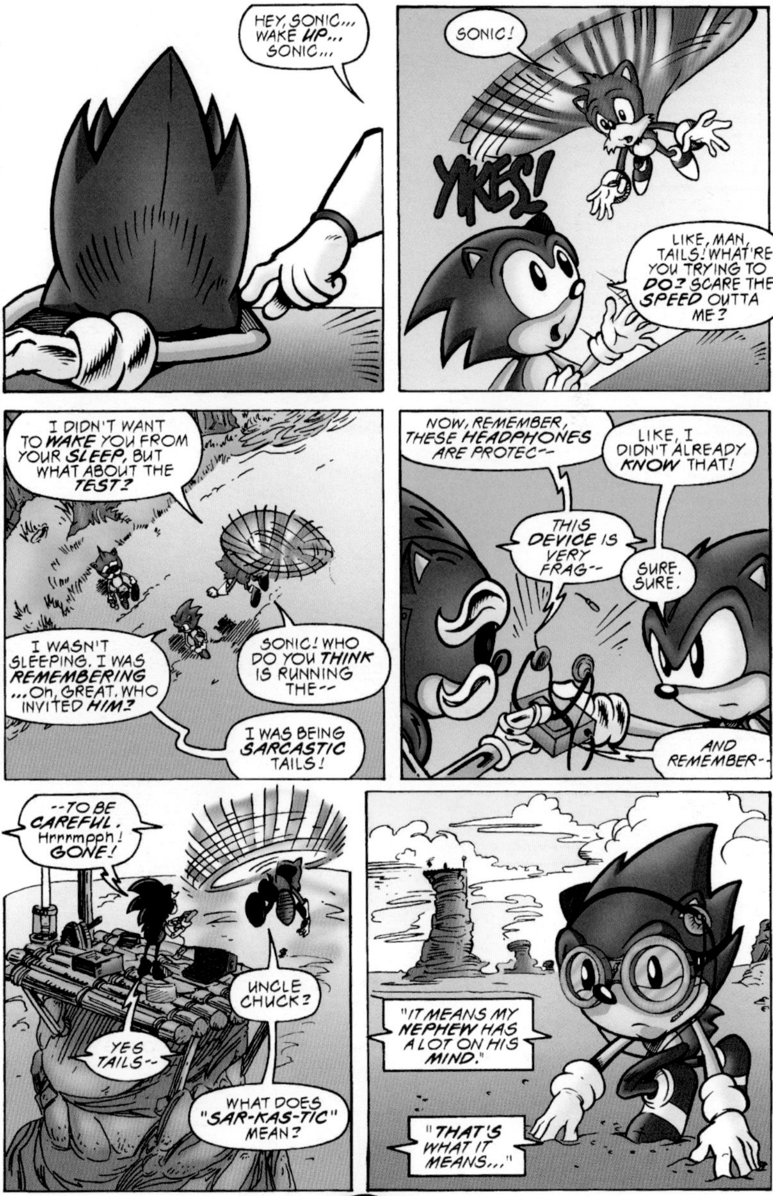
HEY, SONIC...
WAKE UP...
SONIC...
SONIC!
YIKES!
LIKE, MAN, TAILS! WHAT'RE YOU TRYING TO DO? SCARE THE SPEED OUTTA ME?
I DIDN'T WANT TO WAKE YOU FROM YOUR SLEEP, BUT WHAT ABOUT THE TEST?
I WASN'T SLEEPING. I WAS REMEMBERING ...Oh, GREAT. WHO INVITED HIM?
SONIC! WHO DO YOU THINK IS RUNNING THE--
I WAS BEING SARCASTIC TAILS!
NOW, REMEMBER, THESE HEADPHONES ARE PROTEC--
LIKE, I DIDN'T ALREADY KNOW THAT!
THIS DEVICE IS VERY FRAG--
SURE. SURE.
AND REMEMBER--
--TO BE CAREFUL. Hrrrmpph! GONE!
UNCLE CHUCK?
YES TAILS--
WHAT DOES "SAR-KAS-TIC" MEAN?
"IT MEANS MY NEPHEW HAS A LOT ON HIS MIND."
"THAT'S WHAT IT MEANS..."

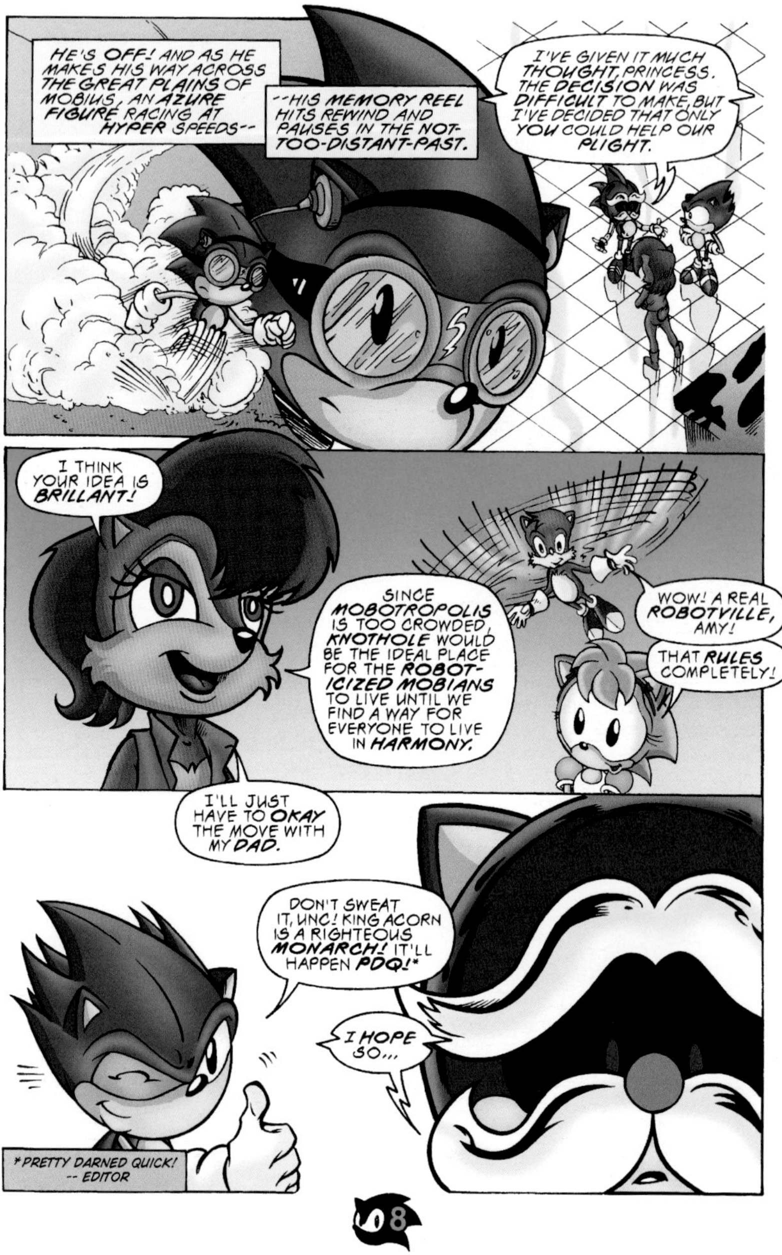
HE'S OFF! AND AS HE MAKES HIS WAY ACROSS THE GREAT PLAINS OF MOBIUS, AN AZURE FIGURE RACING AT HYPER SPEEDS--
--HIS MEMORY REEL HITS REWIND AND PAUSES IN THE NOT-TOO-DISTANT-PAST.
I'VE GIVEN IT MUCH THOUGHT, PRINCESS. THE DECISION WAS DIFFICULT TO MAKE, BUT I'VE DECIDED THAT ONLY YOU COULD HELP OUR PLIGHT.
I THINK YOUR IDEA IS BRILLANT!
SINCE MOBOTROPOLIS IS TOO CROWDED, KNOTHOLE WOULD BE THE IDEAL PLACE FOR THE ROBOTICIZED MOBIANS TO LIVE UNTIL WE FIND A WAY FOR EVERYONE TO LIVE IN HARMONY.
WOW! A REAL ROBOTVILLE, AMY!
THAT RULES COMPLETELY!
I'LL JUST HAVE TO OKAY THE MOVE WITH MY DAD.
DON'T SWEAT IT, UNC! KING ACORN IS A RIGHTEOUS MONARCH! IT'LL HAPPEN PDQ!*
I HOPE SO...
*PRETTY DARNED QUICK! -- EDITOR

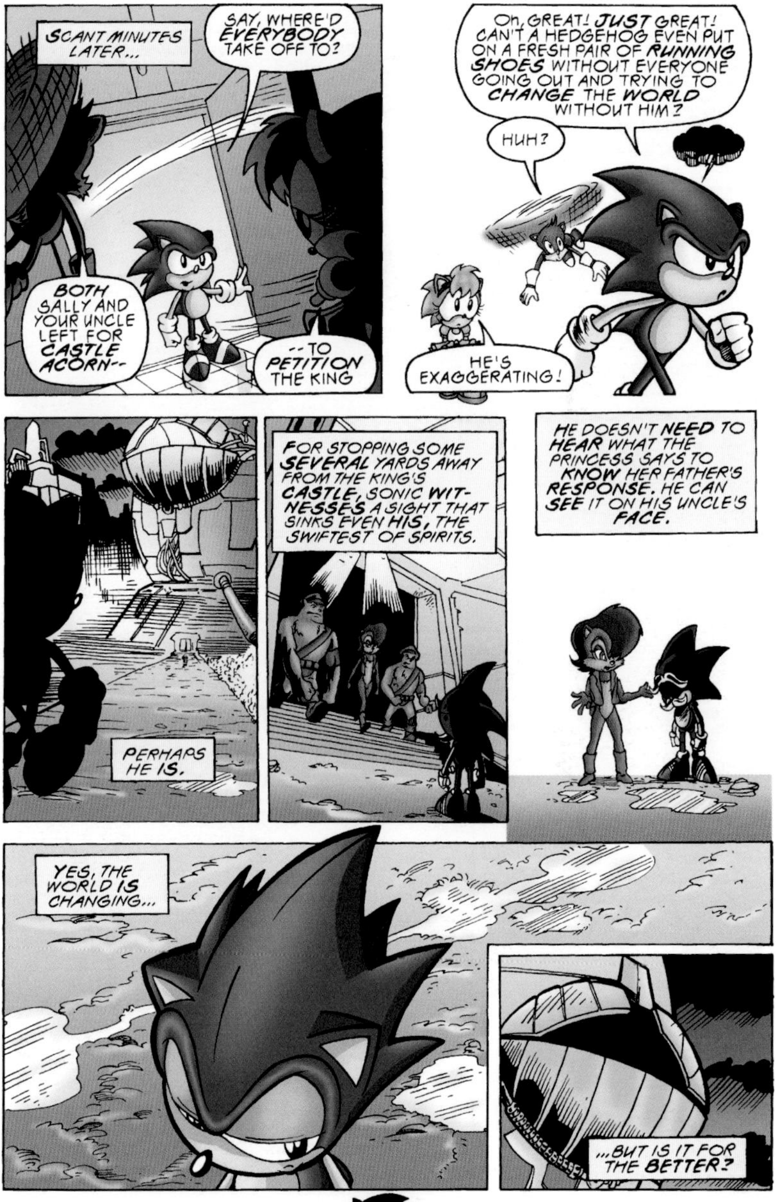
SCANT MINUTES LATER...
SAY, WHERE'D EVERYBODY TAKE OFF TO?
BOTH SALLY AND YOUR UNCLE LEFT FOR CASTLE ACORN--
--TO PETITION THE KING
Oh, GREAT! JUST GREAT! CAN'T A HEDGEHOG EVEN PUT ON A FRESH PAIR OF RUNNING SHOES WITHOUT EVERYONE GOING OUT AND TRYING TO CHANGE THE WORLD WITHOUT HIM?
HUH?
HE'S EXAGGERATING!
PERHAPS HE IS.
FOR STOPPING SOME SEVERAL YARDS AWAY FROM THE KING'S CASTLE, SONIC WITNESSES A SIGHT THAT SINKS EVEN HIS, THE SWIFTEST OF SPIRITS.
HE DOESN'T NEED TO HEAR WHAT THE PRINCESS SAYS TO KNOW HER FATHER'S RESPONSE. HE CAN SEE IT ON HIS UNCLE'S FACE.
YES, THE WORLD IS CHANGING...
...BUT IS IT FOR THE BETTER?

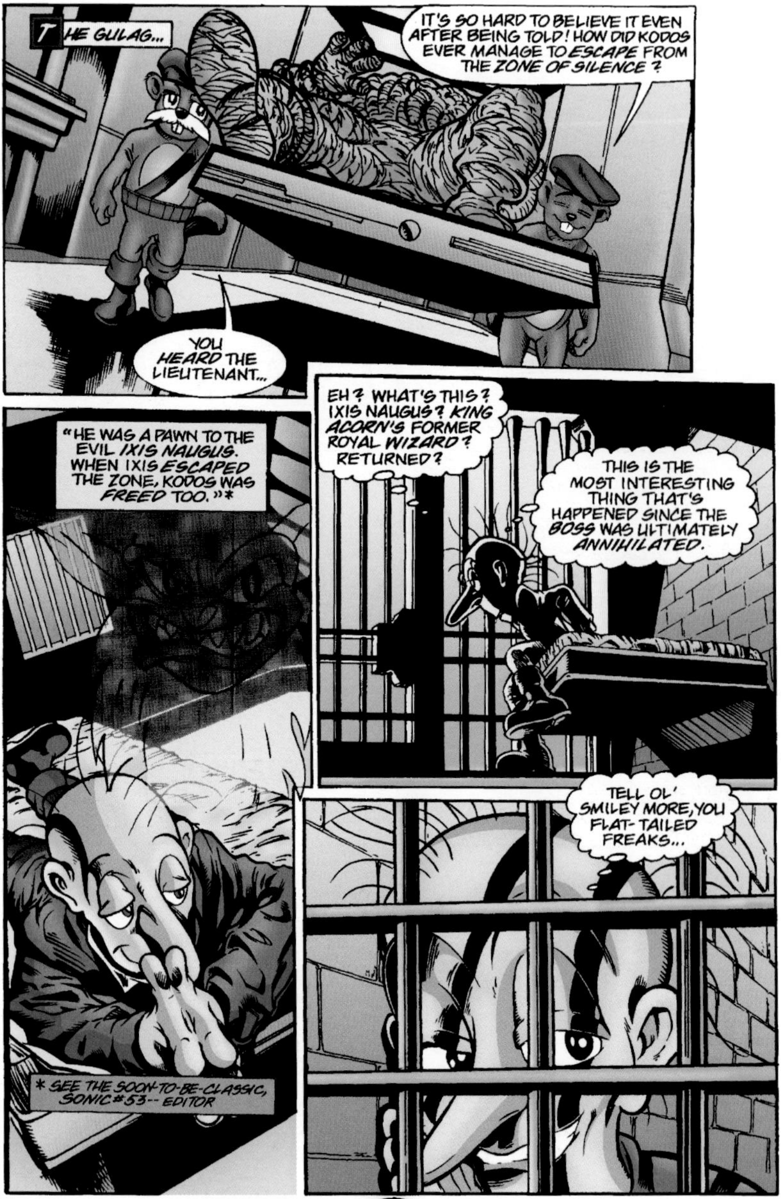
THE GULAG...
IT'S SO HARD TO BELIEVE IT EVEN AFTER BEING TOLD! HOW DID KODOS EVER MANAGE TO ESCAPE FROM THE ZONE OF SILENCE?
YOU HEARD THE LIEUTENANT...
"HE WAS A PAWN TO THE EVIL IXIS NAUGUS. WHEN IXIS ESCAPED THE ZONE, KODOS WAS FREED TOO."*
* SEE THE SOON-TO-BE-CLASSIC, SONIC #53-- EDITOR
EH? WHAT'S THIS? IXIS NAUGUS? KING ACORN'S FORMER ROYAL WIZARD? RETURNED?
THIS IS THE MOST INTERESTING THING THAT'S HAPPENED SINCE THE BOSS WAS ULTIMATELY ANNIHILATED.
TELL OL' SMILEY MORE, YOU FLAT-TAILED FREAKS...

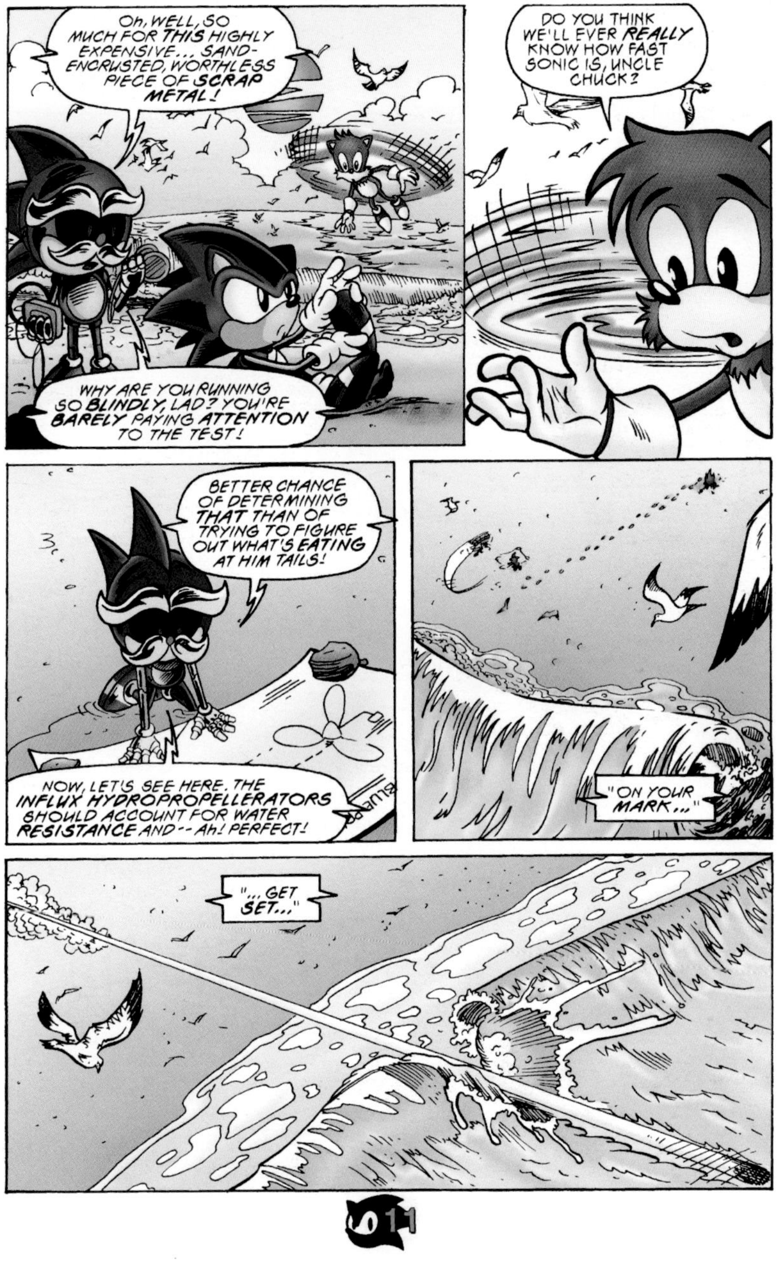
Oh, WELL, SO MUCH FOR THIS HIGHLY EXPENSIVE... SAND-ENCRUSTED, WORTHLESS PIECE OF SCRAP METAL!
WHY ARE YOU RUNNING SO BLINDLY, LAD? YOU'RE BARELY PAYING ATTENTION TO THE TEST!
DO YOU THINK WE'LL EVER REALLY KNOW HOW FAST SONIC IS, UNCLE CHUCK?
BETTER CHANCE OF DETERMINING THAT THAN OF TRYING TO FIGURE OUT WHAT'S EATING AT HIM TAILS!
NOW, LET'S SEE HERE. THE INFLUX HYDROPROPELLERATORS SHOULD ACCOUNT FOR WATER RESISTANCE AND -- Ah! PERFECT!
"ON YOUR MARK..."
"...GET SET..."

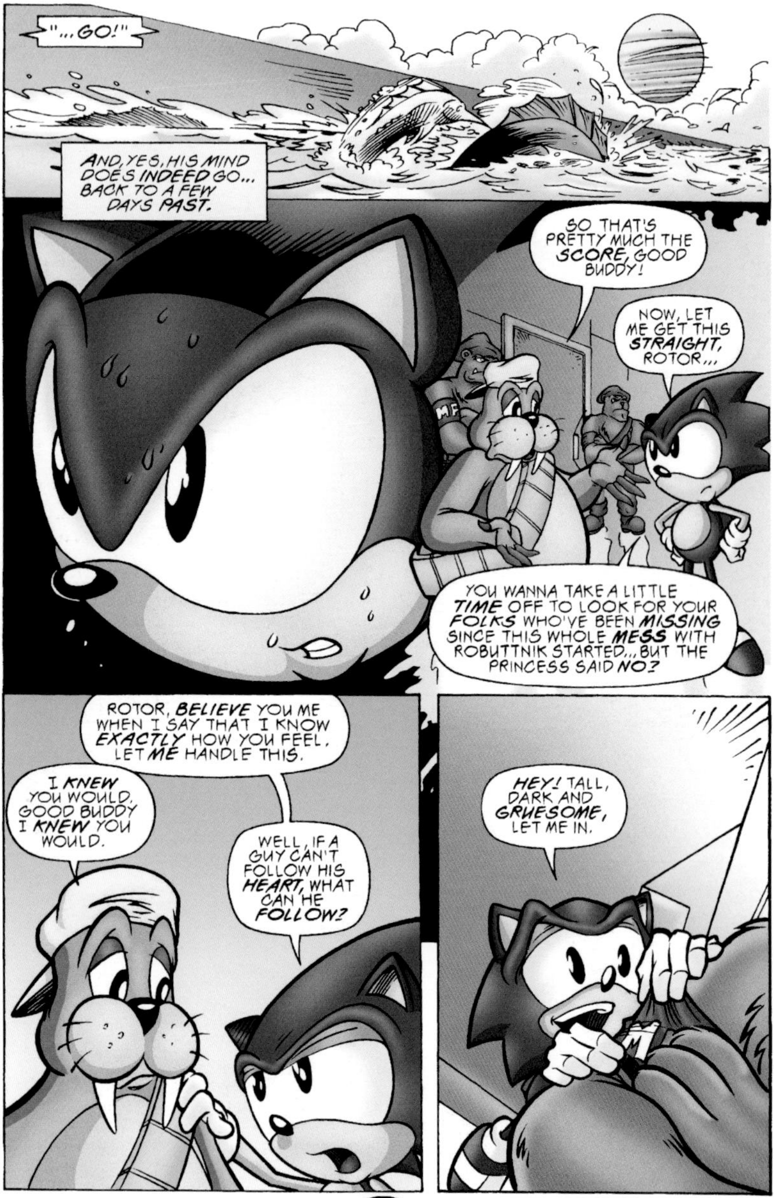
"...GO!"
AND, YES, HIS MIND DOES INDEED GO... BACK TO A FEW DAYS PAST.
SO THAT'S PRETTY MUCH THE SCORE, GOOD BUDDY!
NOW, LET ME GET THIS STRAIGHT, ROTOR...
YOU WANNA TAKE A LITTLE TIME OFF TO LOOK FOR YOUR FOLKS WHO'VE BEEN MISSING SINCE THIS WHOLE MESS WITH ROBUTTNIK STARTED... BUT THE PRINCESS SAID NO?
ROTOR, BELIEVE YOU ME WHEN I SAY THAT I KNOW EXACTLY HOW YOU FEEL. LET ME HANDLE THIS.
I KNEW YOU WOULD, GOOD BUDDY I KNEW YOU WOULD.
WELL, IF A GUY CAN'T FOLLOW HIS HEART, WHAT CAN HE FOLLOW?
HEY! TALL, DARK AND GRUESOME, LET ME IN.

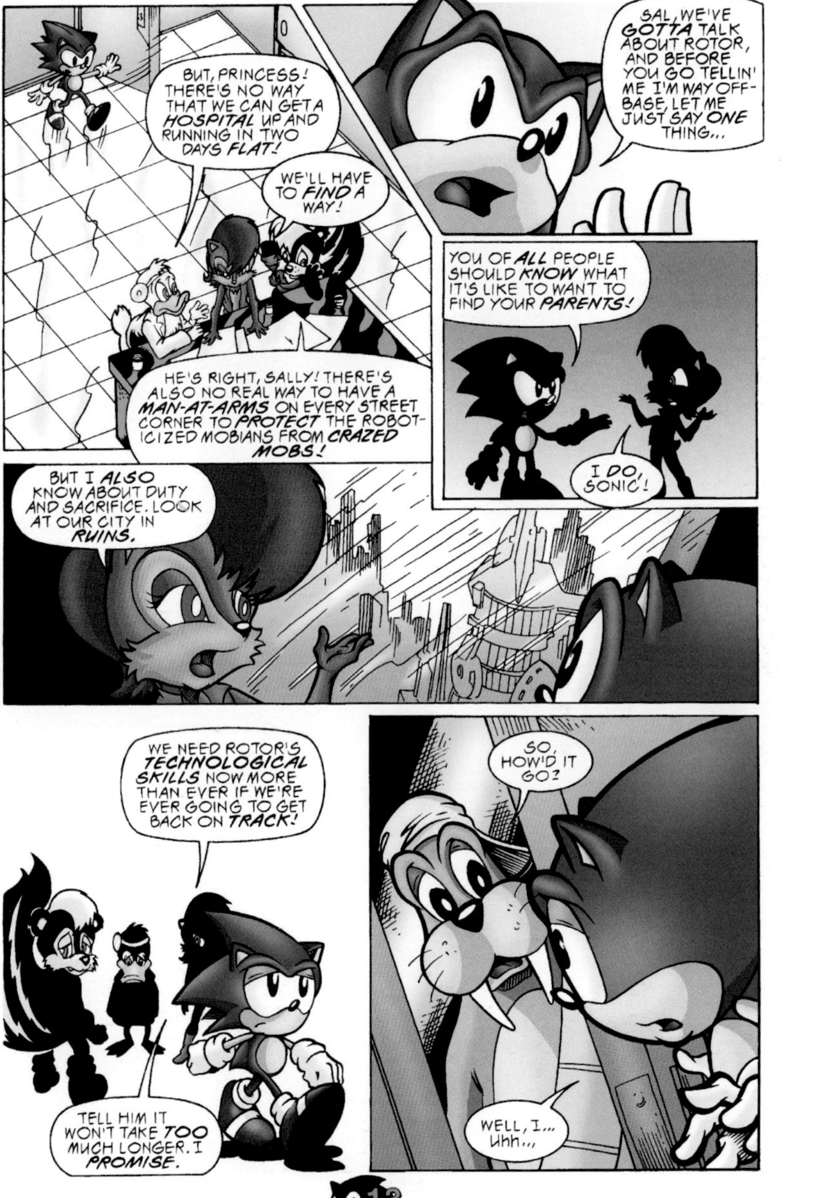
BUT, PRINCESS! THERE'S NO WAY THAT WE CAN GET A HOSPITAL UP AND RUNNING IN TWO DAYS FLAT!
WE'LL HAVE TO FIND A WAY!
HE'S RIGHT, SALLY! THERE'S ALSO NO REAL WAY TO HAVE A MAN-AT-ARMS ON EVERY STREET CORNER TO PROTECT THE ROBOTICIZED MOBIANS FROM CRAZED MOBS!
SAL, WE'VE GOTTA TALK ABOUT ROTOR, AND BEFORE YOU GO TELLIN' ME I'M WAY OFF-BASE, LET ME JUST SAY ONE THING...
YOU OF ALL PEOPLE SHOULD KNOW WHAT IT'S LIKE TO WANT TO FIND YOUR PARENTS!
I DO, SONIC!
BUT I ALSO KNOW ABOUT DUTY AND SACRIFICE. LOOK AT OUR CITY IN RUINS.
WE NEED ROTOR'S TECHNOLOGICAL SKILLS NOW MORE THAN EVER IF WE'RE EVER GOING TO GET BACK ON TRACK!
TELL HIM IT WON'T TAKE TOO MUCH LONGER. I PROMISE.
SO, HOW'D IT GO?
WELL, I... Uhh...

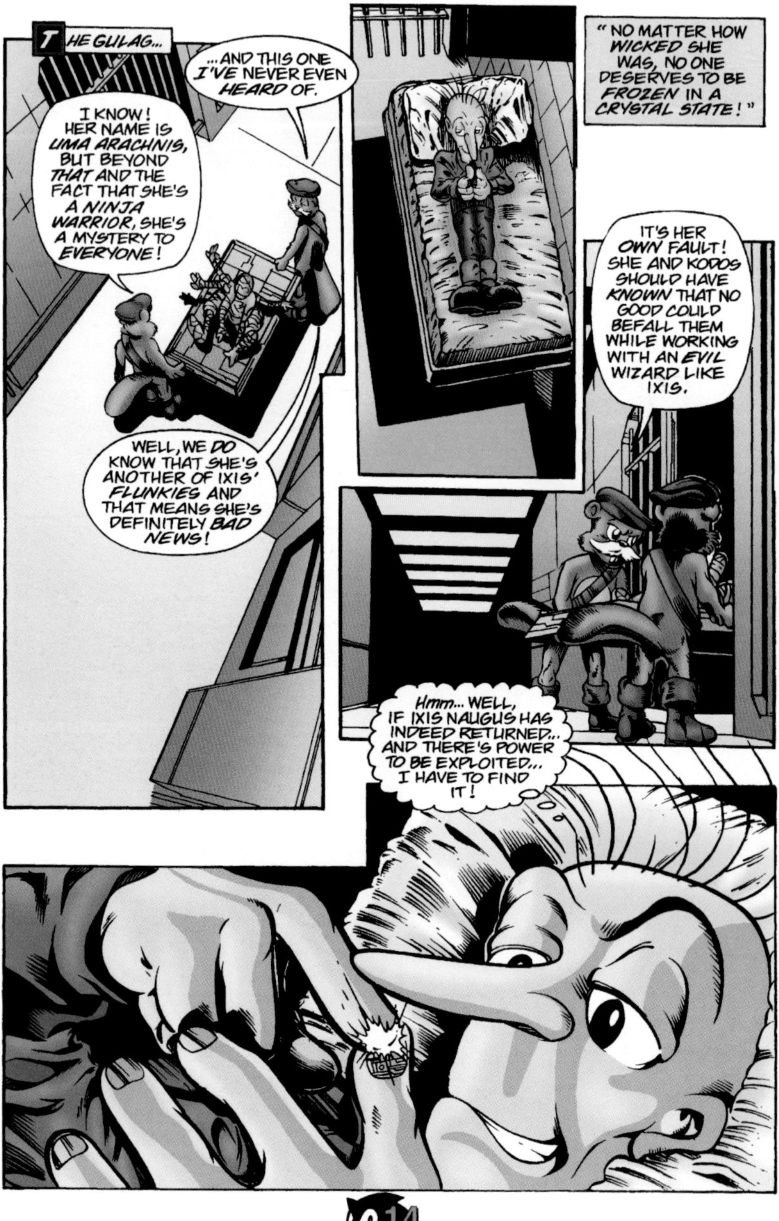
THE GULAG...
...AND THIS ONE I'VE NEVER EVEN HEARD OF.
I KNOW! HER NAME IS UMA ARACHNIS, BUT BEYOND THAT AND THE FACT THAT SHE'S A NINJA WARRIOR, SHE'S A MYSTERY TO EVERYONE!
WELL, WE DO KNOW THAT SHE'S ANOTHER OF IXIS' FLUNKIES AND THAT MEANS SHE'S DEFINITELY BAD NEWS!
"NO MATTER HOW WICKED SHE WAS, NO ONE DESERVES TO BE FROZEN IN A CRYSTAL STATE!"
IT'S HER OWN FAULT! SHE AND KODOS SHOULD HAVE KNOWN THAT NO GOOD COULD BEFALL THEM WHILE WORKING WITH AN EVIL WIZARD LIKE IXIS.
Hmm... WELL, IF IXIS NAUGUS HAS INDEED RETURNED... AND THERE'S POWER TO BE EXPLOITED... I HAVE TO FIND IT!

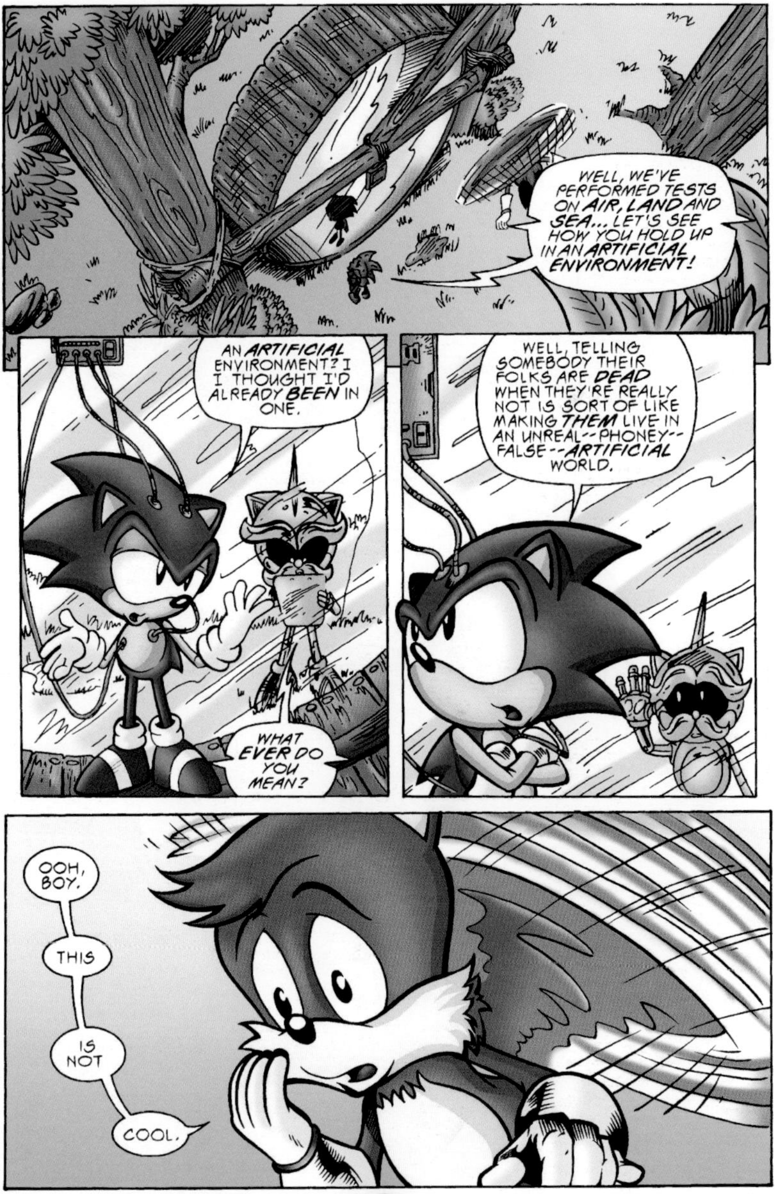
WELL, WE'VE PERFORMED TESTS ON AIR, LAND AND SEA... LET'S SEE HOW YOU HOLD UP IN AN ARTIFICIAL ENVIRONMENT!
AN ARTIFICIAL ENVIRONMENT? I I THOUGHT I'D ALREADY BEEN IN ONE.
WHAT EVER DO YOU MEAN?
WELL, TELLING SOMEBODY THEIR FOLKS ARE DEAD WHEN THEY'RE REALLY NOT IS SORT OF LIKE MAKING THEM LIVE IN AN UNREAL--PHONEY--FALSE--ARTIFICIAL WORLD.
OOH, BOY.
THIS
IS NOT
COOL.

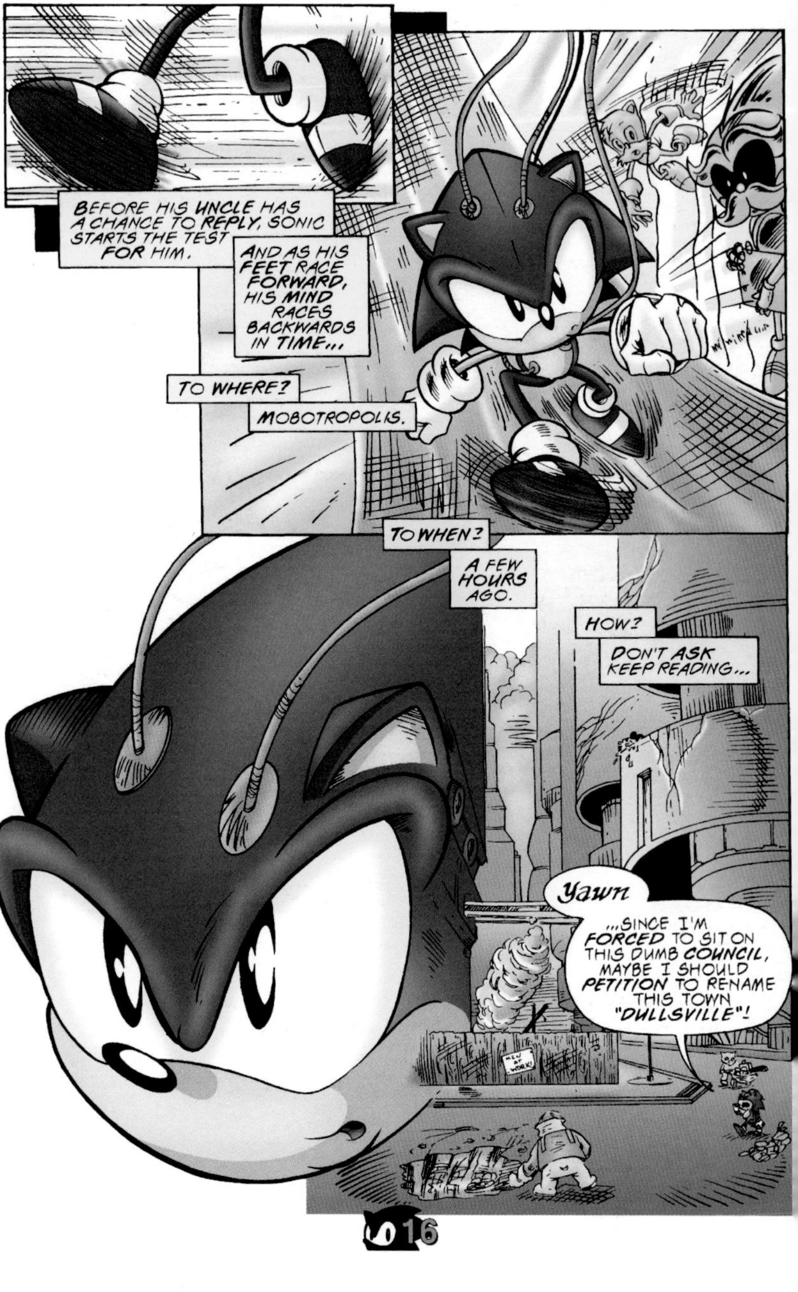
BEFORE HIS UNCLE HAS A CHANCE TO REPLY, SONIC STARTS THE TEST FOR HIM.
AND AS HIS FEET RACE FORWARD, HIS MIND RACES BACKWARDS IN TIME...
TO WHERE?
MOBOTROPOLIS.
TO WHEN?
A FEW HOURS AGO.
HOW?
DON'T ASK KEEP READING...
Yawn
...SINCE I'M FORCED TO SIT ON THIS DUMB COUNCIL, MAYBE I SHOULD PETITION TO RENAME THIS TOWN "DULLSVILLE"!

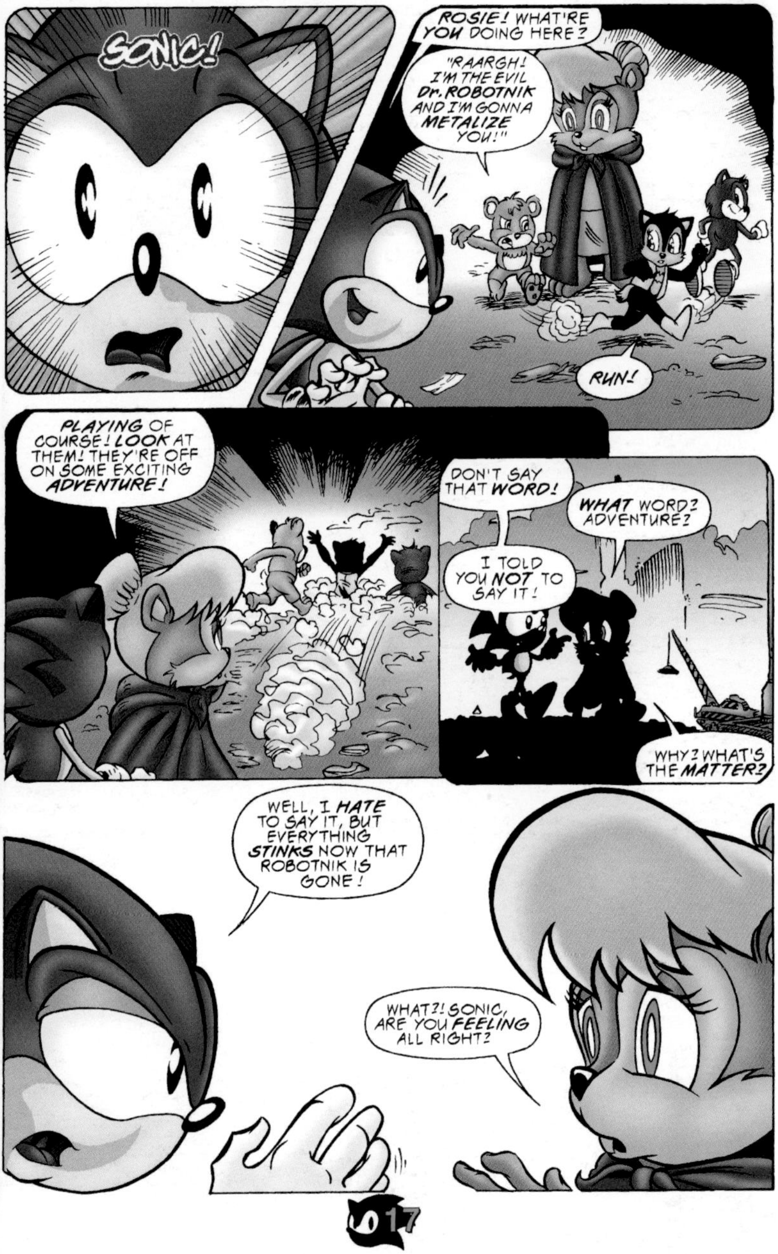

SONIC!
ROSIE! WHAT'RE YOU DOING HERE?
"RAARGH! I'M THE EVIL Dr. ROBOTNIK AND I'M GONNA METALIZE YOU!"
RUN!
PLAYING OF COURSE! LOOK AT THEM! THEY'RE OFF ON SOME EXCITING ADVENTURE!
DON'T SAY THAT WORD!
WHAT WORD? ADVENTURE?
I TOLD YOU NOT TO SAY IT!
WHY? WHAT'S THE MATTER?
WELL, I HATE TO SAY IT, BUT EVERYTHING STINKS NOW THAT ROBOTNIK IS GONE!
WHAT?! SONIC, ARE YOU FEELING ALL RIGHT?

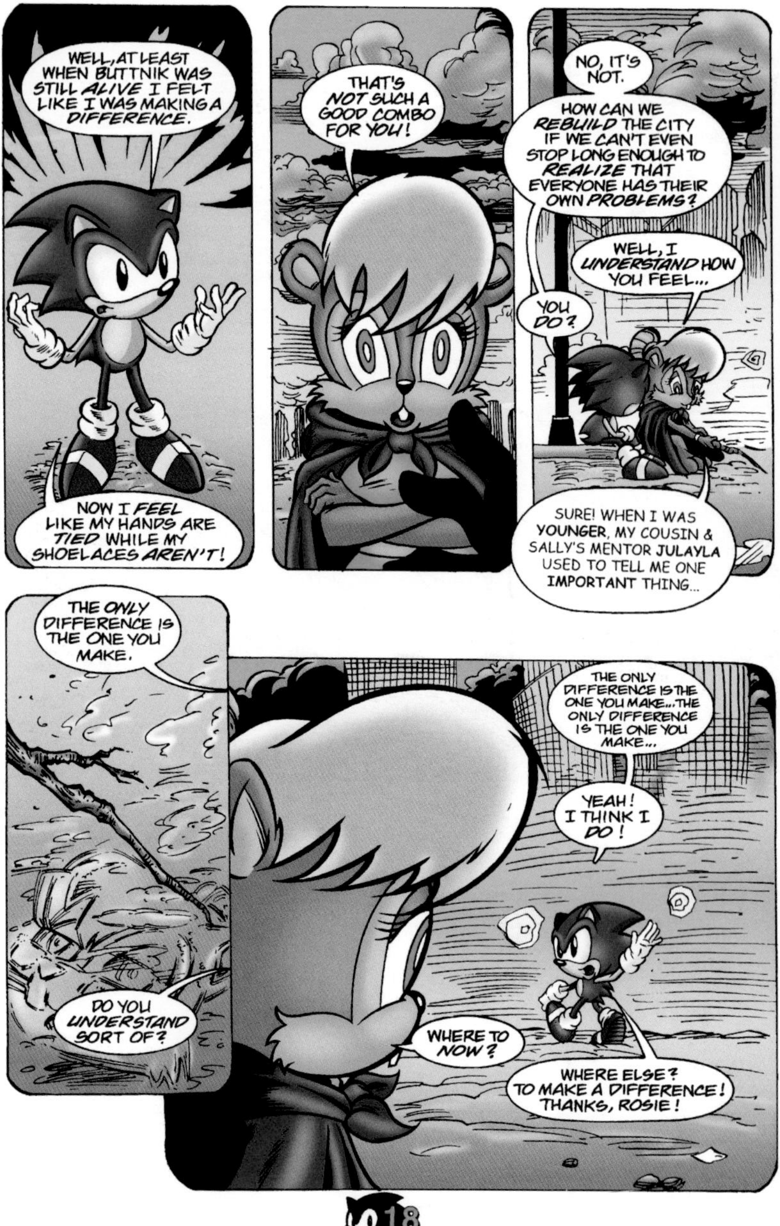
WELL, AT LEAST WHEN BUTTNIK WAS STILL ALIVE I FELT LIKE I WAS MAKING A DIFFERENCE.
NOW I FEEL LIKE MY HANDS ARE TIED WHILE MY SHOELACES AREN'T!
THAT'S NOT SUCH A GOOD COMBO FOR YOU!
NO, IT'S NOT.
HOW CAN WE REBUILD THE CITY IF WE CAN'T EVEN STOP LONG ENOUGH TO REALIZE THAT EVERYONE HAS THEIR OWN PROBLEMS?
WELL, I UNDERSTAND HOW YOU FEEL...
YOU DO?
SURE! WHEN I WAS YOUNGER, MY COUSIN & SALLY'S MENTOR JULAYLA USED TO TELL ME ONE IMPORTANT THING...
THE ONLY DIFFERENCE IS THE ONE YOU MAKE.
DO YOU UNDERSTAND SORT OF?
THE ONLY DIFFERENCE IS THE ONE YOU MAKE... THE ONLY DIFFERENCE IS THE ONE YOU MAKE...
YEAH! I THINK I DO!
WHERE TO NOW?
WHERE ELSE? TO MAKE A DIFFERENCE! THANKS, ROSIE!

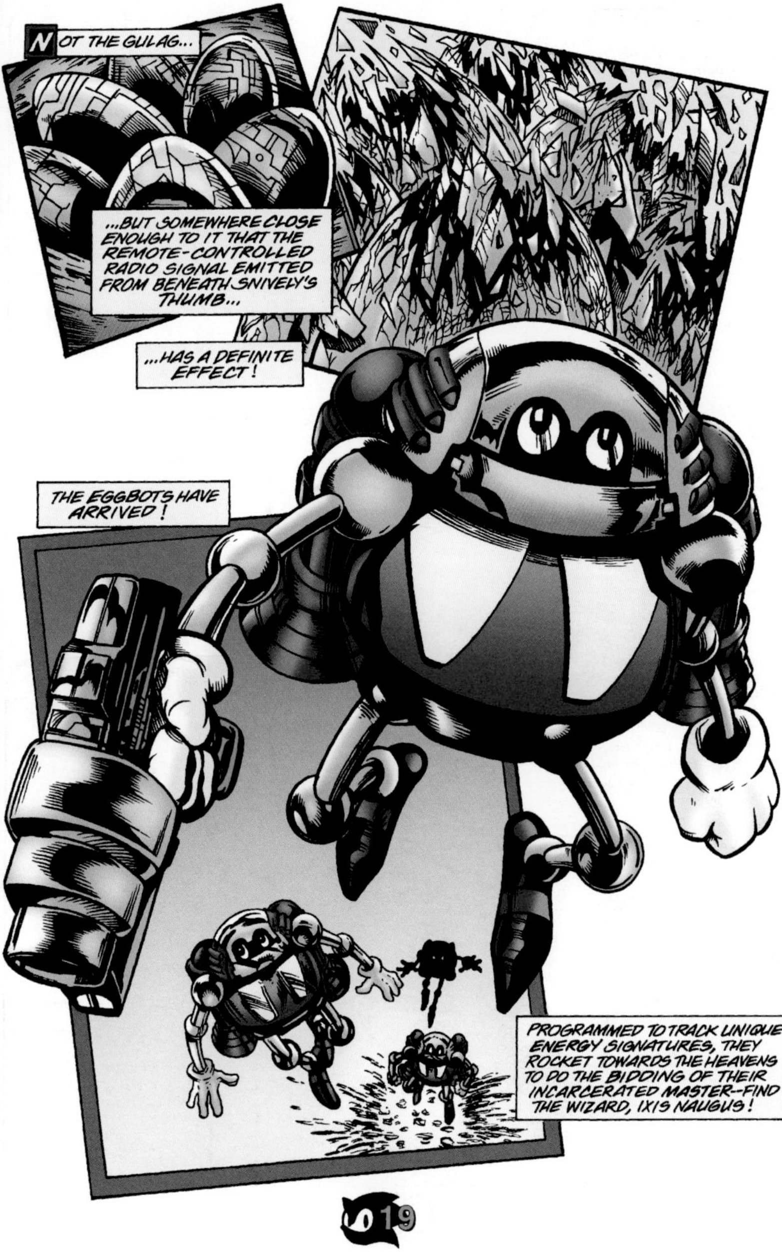
NOT THE GULAG...
...BUT SOMEWHERE CLOSE ENOUGH TO IT THAT THE REMOTE-CONTROLLED RADIO SIGNAL EMITTED FROM BENEATH SNIVELY'S THUMB...
...HAS A DEFINITE EFFECT!
THE EGGBOTS HAVE ARRIVED!
PROGRAMMED TO TRACK UNIQUE ENERGY SIGNATURES, THEY ROCKET TOWARDS THE HEAVENS TO DO THE BIDDING OF THEIR INCARCERATED MASTER--FIND THE WIZARD, IXIS NAUGUS!

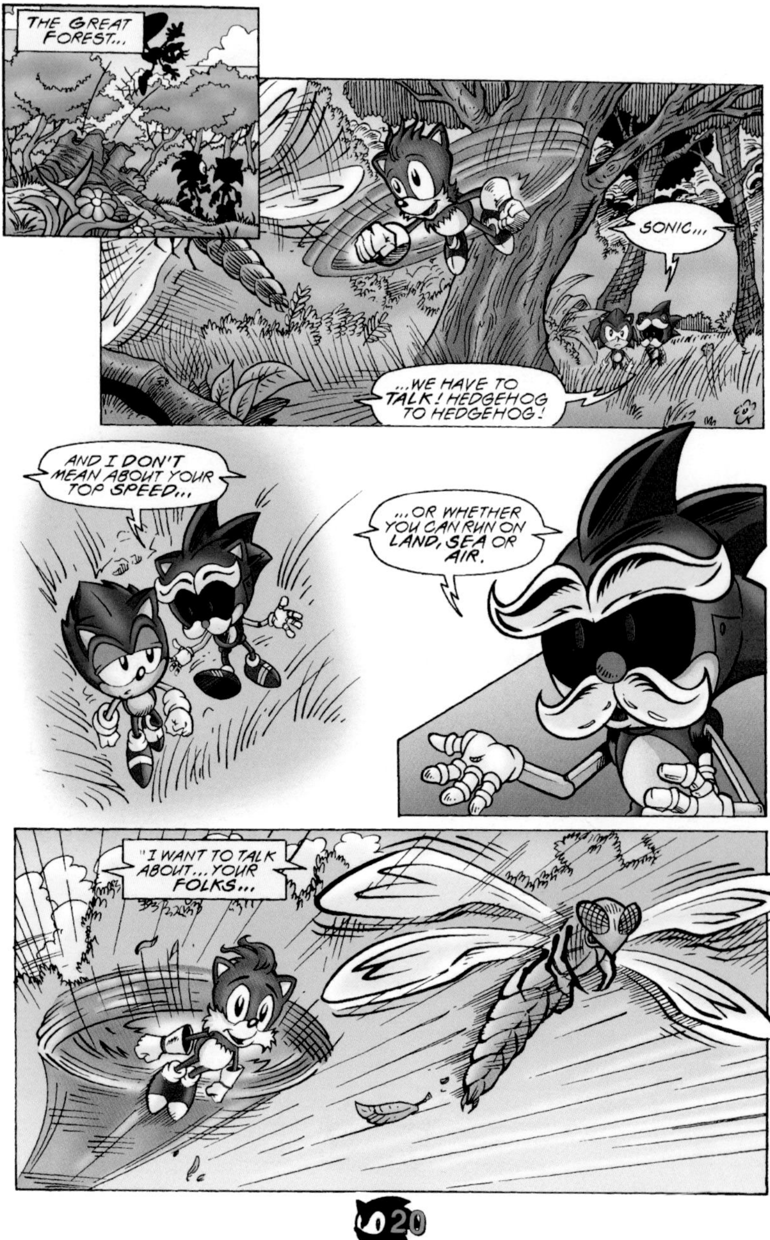

THE GREAT FOREST...
SONIC...
...WE HAVE TO TALK! HEDGEHOG TO HEDGEHOG!
AND I DON'T MEAN ABOUT YOUR TOP SPEED...
...OR WHETHER YOU CAN RUN ON LAND, SEA OR AIR.
"I WANT TO TALK ABOUT... YOUR FOLKS...

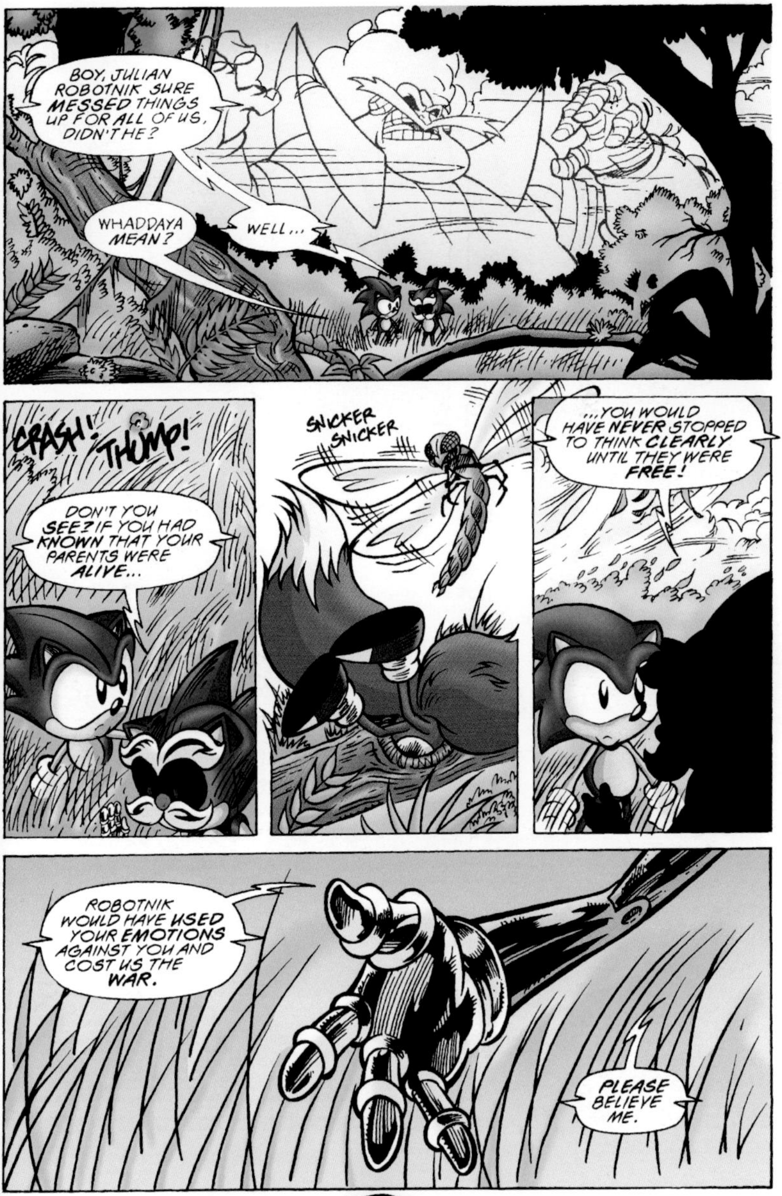
BOY, JULIAN ROBOTNIK SURE MESSED THINGS UP FOR ALL OF US, DIDN'T HE?
WHADDAYA MEAN?
WELL...
CRASH! THUMP!
DON'T YOU SEE? IF YOU HAD KNOWN THAT YOUR PARENTS WERE ALIVE...
SNICKER SNICKER
...YOU WOULD HAVE NEVER STOPPED TO THINK CLEARLY UNTIL THEY WERE FREE!
ROBOTNIK WOULD HAVE USED YOUR EMOTIONS AGAINST YOU AND COST US THE WAR.
PLEASE BELIEVE ME.

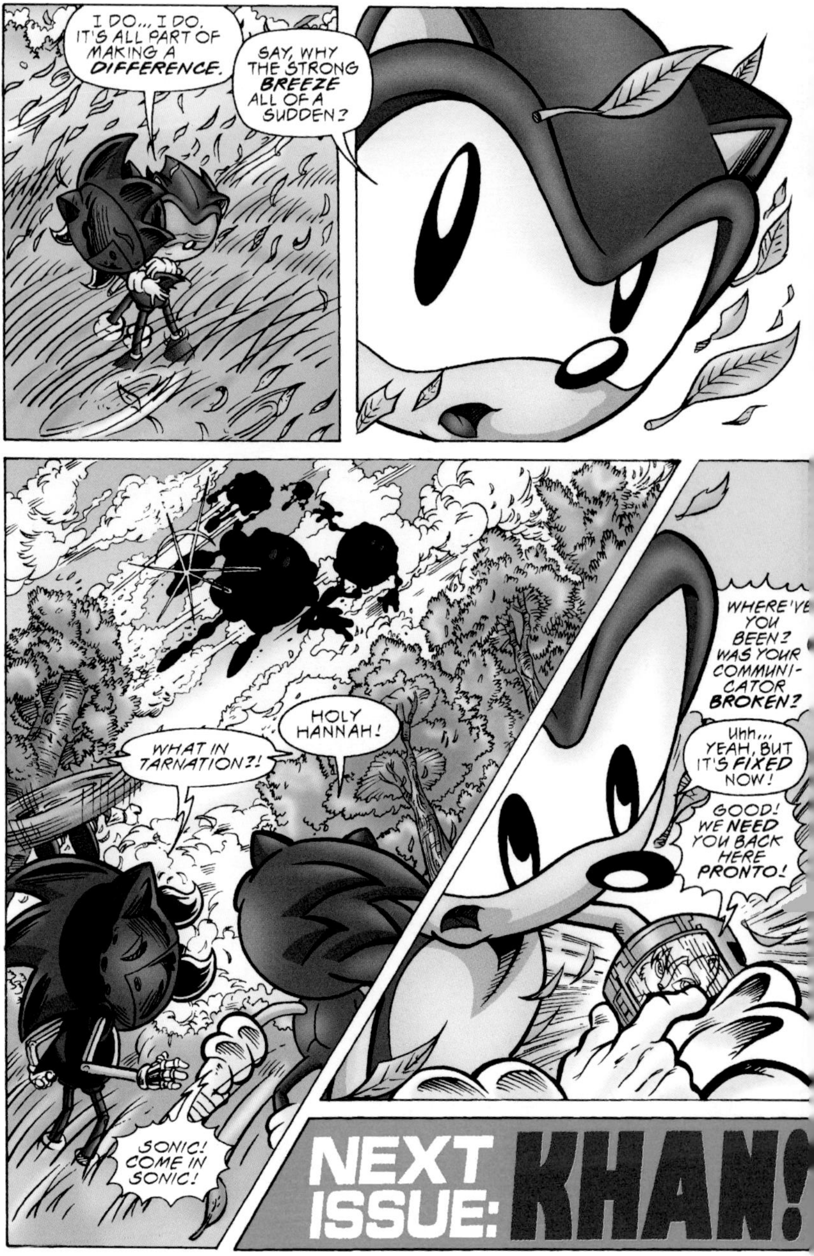
I DO... I DO. IT'S ALL PART OF MAKING A DIFFERENCE.
SAY, WHY THE STRONG BREEZE ALL OF A SUDDEN?
HOLY HANNAH!
WHAT IN TARNATION?!
SONIC! COME IN SONIC!
WHERE'VE YOU BEEN? WAS YOUR COMMUNI-CATOR BROKEN?
Uhh... YEAH, BUT IT'S FIXED NOW!
GOOD! WE NEED YOU BACK HERE PRONTO!
NEXT ISSUE: KHAN!

SONIC THE HEDGEHOG ™

Welcome to a brief who's who
of the Sonic universe.
You have just read some
of the earliest
and most loved stories from the
Sonic comic. We thought
you'd like to learn a little extra
about a few of your
favorite Sonic characters.

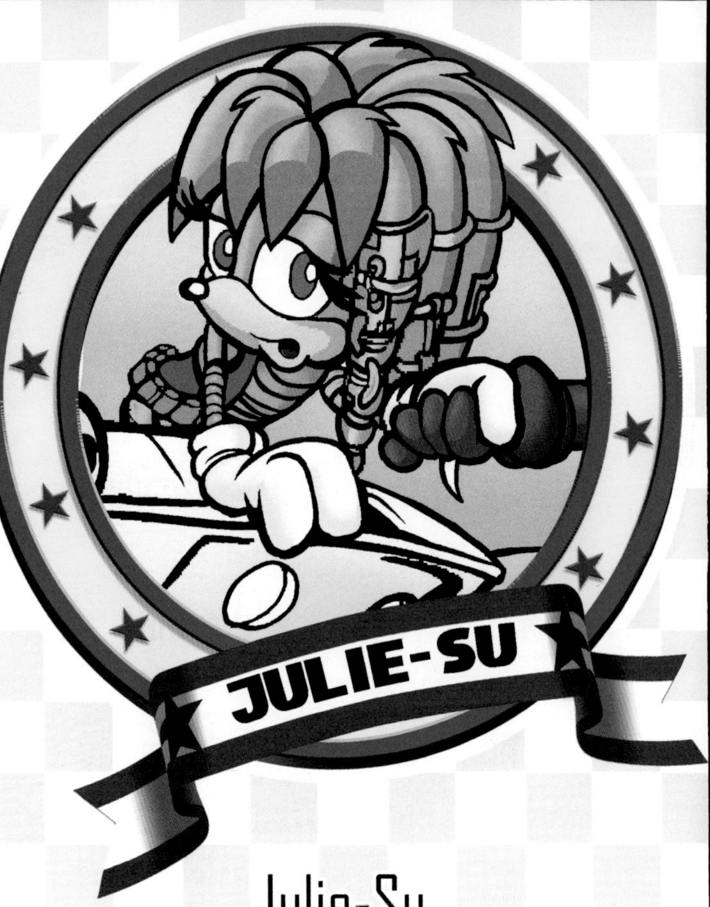
JULIE-SU

Julie-Su

Formerly a member of the sinister DARK LEGION, Julie-Su renounced her evil ways when mysteriously drawn to the Guardian of the Floating Island - KNUCKLES THE ECHIDNA! But will their friendship blossom into something more?

JULES & BERNIE

Jules & Bernie

Sonic's parents were once soldiers during the epic GREAT WAR! Sadly, they became two of the very first Mobians to be roboticized by WARLORD JULIAN, who would later become DR. ROBOTNIK!

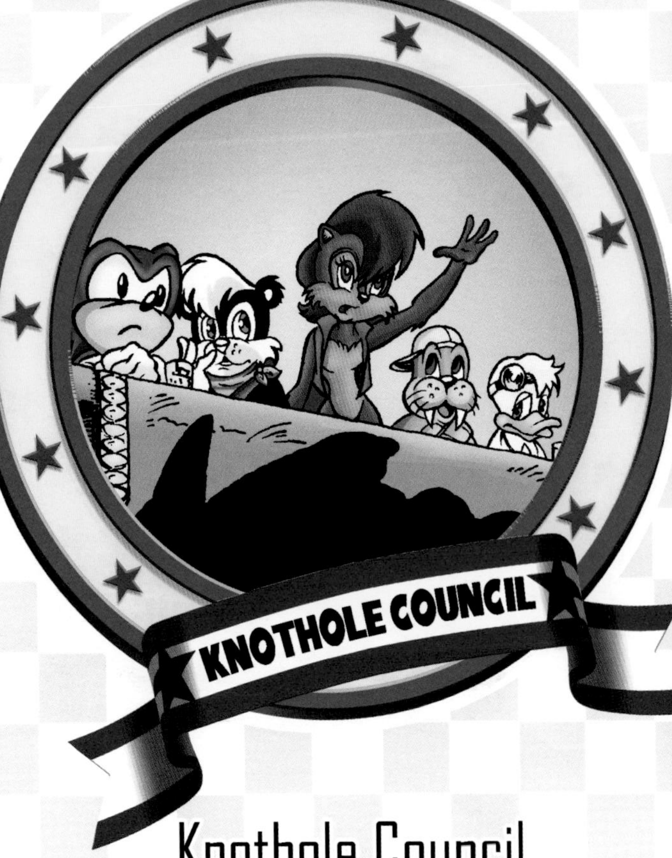
KNOTHOLE COUNCIL

Knothole Council

After the fall of Dr. Robotnik, Princess Sally recognized that a provisional government would be necessary to organize the people and begin to rebuild society. Sitting on the council: Sonic, Geoffrey St. John, Sally, Rotor Walrus and Dr. Quack.

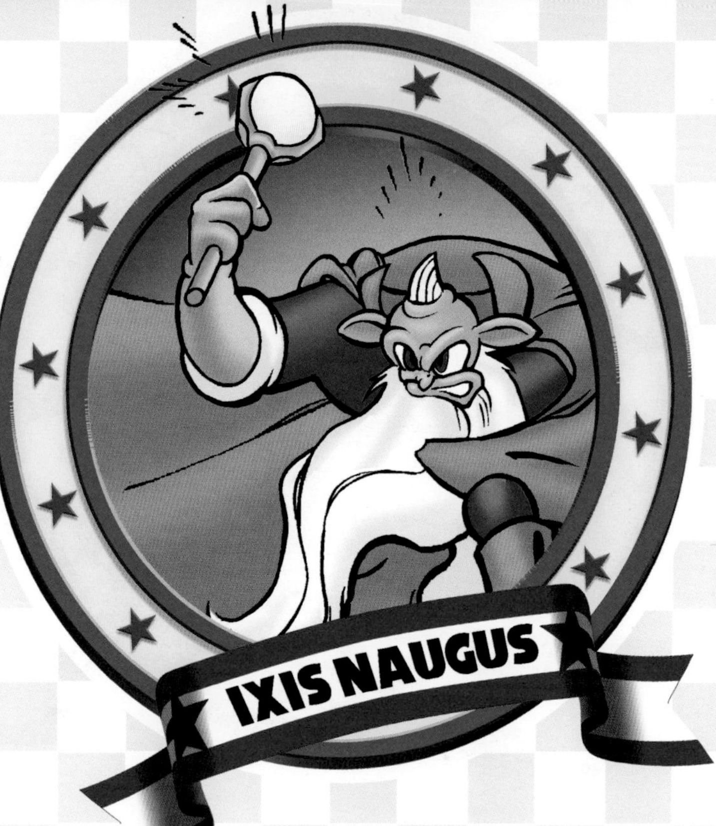
IXIS NAUGUS

Ixis Naugus

One of the most powerful villains to ever terrorize the planet Mobius, Naugus is a survivor of the ancient ORDER OF IXIS. A super-powered magician with command of the elements, this evil wizard is commited to commanding the throne of Acorn!

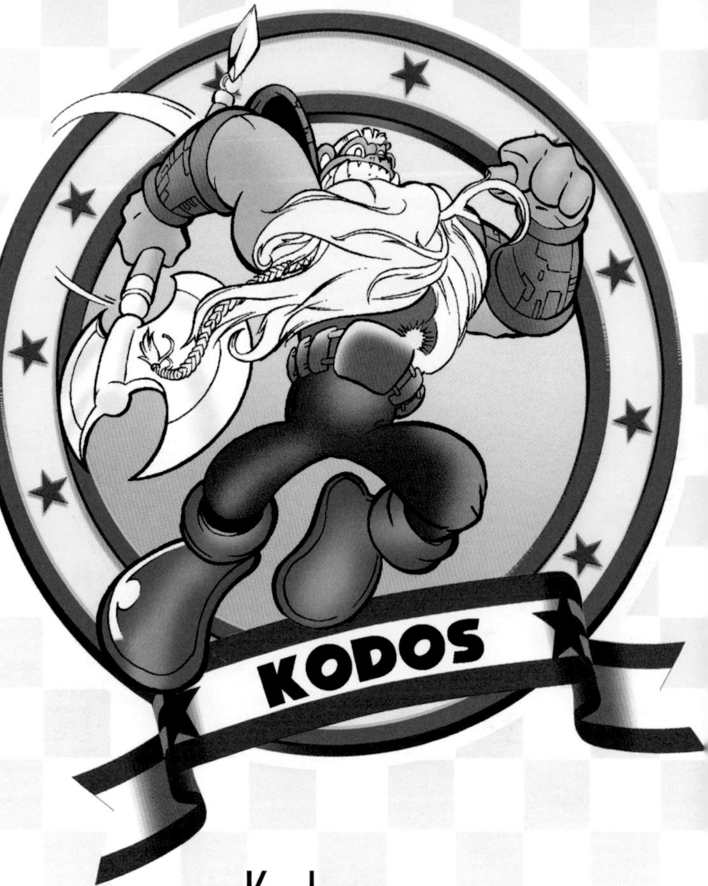
KODOS

Kodos

Once the commander of the Acorn Kingdom's military forces, Kodos was betryaed by Julian Kintobor (aka Dr. Robotnik) and imprisoned in the ZONE OF SILENCE. Escaping with Ixis Naugus and Uma Arachnis, Kodos' new reign of terror would appear to have just begun!

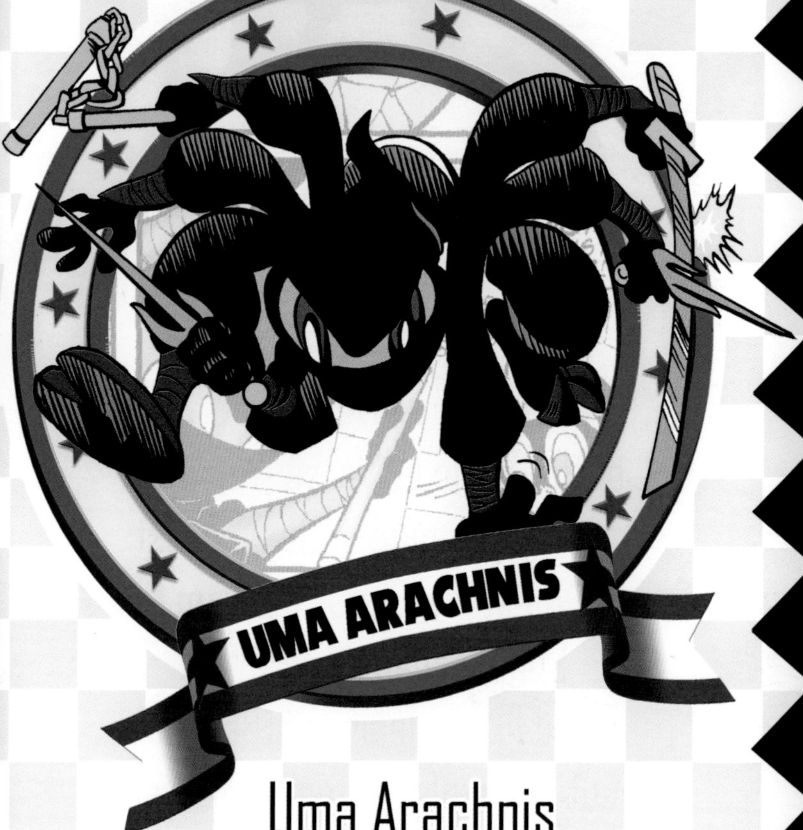
UMA ARACHNIS

Uma Arachnis

A gifted and powerful warrior, Uma was imprisoned in the Zone of Silence and has joined forces with the evil wizard Ixis Naugus! While Uma's intentions are unknown, she has already proven herself to be a force to be reckoned with!

SONIC THE HEDGEHOG™

Welcome to a brief what's what of the Sonic universe. You have just read some of the earliest and most loved stories from the Sonic comic. We thought you'd like to learn a little extra about a few of the items and places that make the Sonic universe so awesome!

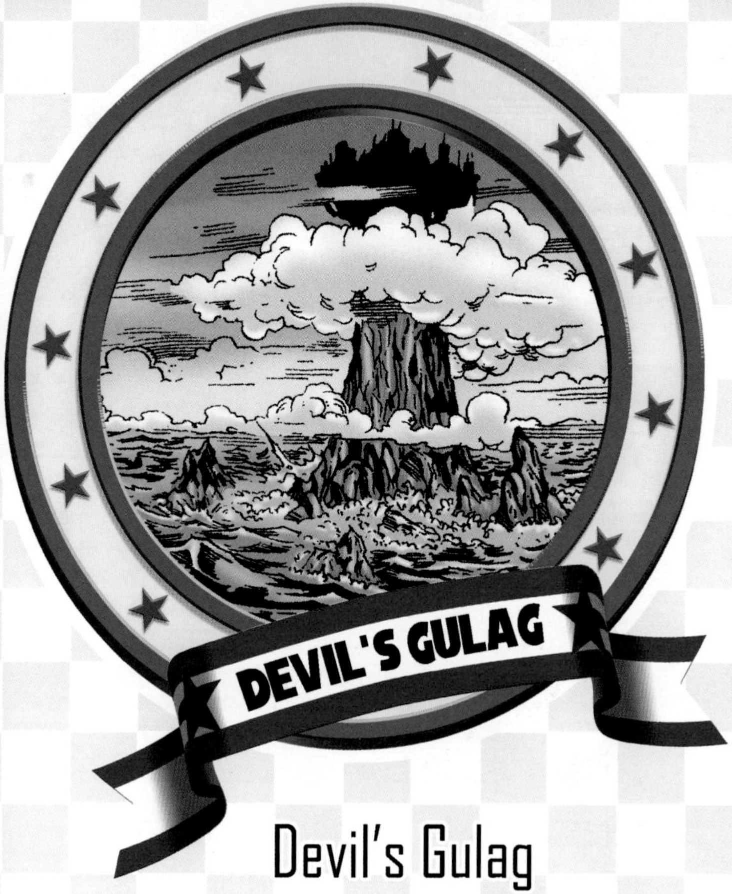
DEVIL'S GULAG

Devil's Gulag

Where do you hold the most vile, dangerous and powerful villains in all of Mobius captive? Look no further than the Devil's Gulag! Surrounded by boiling seas and a cloak of steam, this perilous, towering prison is home to the worst of the worst!